Emerald Secrets

Saltwater Romance
Book 2

Rhonda Forrest

Valeena Press

Enjoy - Saltwater Romance Series

Chapter One

Lachie wiggled his toes, enjoying the passive stretch of his legs against the plush end of the couch. At one hundred and seventy-two centimetres tall, he nestled comfortably amidst the soft embrace of the leather cushions, which had doubled as his makeshift bed for the night. He ran his tongue over his teeth and winced at the lingering aftertaste. Last night had spiralled into a wilder affair than he had expected. Rubbing his hand over his bare stomach, he lamented the consequences: one too many beers and, he inwardly groaned, a series of tequila shots, complete with salt and lemon to complete the revelry.

These days, partying and drinking too much were a rarity for him. The era of consuming copious amounts of alcohol had faded into the past, years ago. At thirty, he was drawn more to life's simple pleasures: a tasty meal, a glass of fine wine, and the company of good friends. He had come to believe that the zenith of happiness lay in the embrace of stability. For him, true contentment blossomed when the currents of life flowed seamlessly, devoid of any significant or unwanted change in his routine. He preferred the tranquillity of intimate gatherings, far removed from the pulsating beats of loud music, the frenetic energy of dance floors, or women seeking more than engaging conversation. Past relationships involved commotions, events, and complications that he felt were unnecessary and should not have arisen. Why complicate life when you could let the days ebb and flow without any interruptions?

However, his aversion to unnecessary commotion didn't equate to a lack of adventure; far from it. Amidst the calmness of his daily routine, which revolved around his work and the serene island life he cherished, he found avenues to let off steam. Whether casting his line into the depths for a fishing session, snorkelling over the nearby reefs, or engaging in any other outdoor activity that brought him closer to the ocean, he embraced adventure with open arms. For him, the essence of living was not in the chaos of a busy life, but in the simple experiences that connected him to nature.

As long as his travels and daily routines were planned well ahead of time, he coped.

As his father, Chris, often told him, 'Spontaneity is not your middle name, Lachie. More like, Deliberate Determination. He'd take that. It wasn't an insult, more a compliment in his eyes.

But he could be spontaneous. Look at last night. When he returned to his cabin and found that his brother Jasper had told a few of his mates they could bunk there for the night, he had acted 'spontaneously' and instead let himself into one of the resort's deluxe suites to sleep in comfort.

As he shifted onto his side, his gaze fell upon his discarded shirt, trousers, and shoes strewn haphazardly across the timber floor beside him. He couldn't help but chuckle at the sight of his dishevelled attire. The memory of Prue, his last girlfriend, flashed through his mind. She would have been appalled by his casual disregard for tidiness, especially sleeping in nothing but his jocks. It was one of the first things he had disposed of when she left: five pairs of men's pyjamas she had bought him, that oddly she found very sexy. Although he was a stickler for neatness and everything running to plan, Prue was on another level.

His mother, Evie, had been right. She had picked Prue's jealous, controlling streak right from the start. She tried to tell him subtly, dropping hints about the warning signs he seemed blind to and even persuading his father to have a serious man-to-man talk with him. He sighed. Her efforts were to no avail, and he had stubbornly forged ahead, learning his lesson the hard way. Pummelling the cushion into a more comfortable position under his head, he closed his eyes. He missed Prue sometimes. She had some special qualities. But never again. No women. He was happy by himself. As he told his parents, they would have to rely on his four younger siblings if they wanted grandkids.

Opening his eyes, he directed his gaze towards the vast area framed by the large glass sliding doors that dominated the wall before him. He had arrived back just a few days ago after three months down south, and had been looking forward to warmer weather. Today however, the sky wore a sombre hue of grey, with heavily bruised clouds looming over the nearby islands. The sky and sea colour differed from their usual vibrant blue. Lifting his head slightly, he surveyed the ocean's expanse. The surface was crowned with frothy white caps, stirred by a brisk southerly wind. A sailboat scuttled across the waves, using the power of the gusts to get to its destination.

Sinking back into the comfort of the couch, Lachie couldn't help but notice the subtle disruptions to the usually tranquil scene outside. Even the horizon pool, just beyond the glass doors, mirrored the restlessness of the sea, its surface rippling with small waves, occasionally splashing over the edge in miniature cascades.

It was a good day for not doing much, he thought. There was no hurry. He had nothing planned for the day. Closing his eyes, he moved to a more relaxing position, wishing he had a throw or cover to pull over himself. He would suggest some more light blankets for the lounge rooms the next time he spoke to his mother. She still liked to be involved in running the family's latest property acquisition and prided herself on the interior decorating of the rooms at *Vivre* – a luxurious resort on their private island in the Whitsundays. The property hadn't always been called that. When they first bought the fifteen-hectare island five years ago, it had been called *Island Paradise*. The grounds and buildings were run down and overgrown, exactly what his mum and dad were looking for. Much of the island had been left like that, apart from the resort, which over recent years had come to be known as one of the most luxurious and well-situated in the area.

With a smile playing on his lips, he couldn't help but admire his parents' unwavering commitment to running businesses and staying actively involved. Despite being in their early sixties and boasting a portfolio of properties and equity in other interests substantial enough to secure their place on Australia's rich list, they chose not to retire and sail off into the sunset. His father's original business, which involved building surfboards and producing surf gear, was called *Vivre*. The name included the letters in his mother's name, Evie. Today, the company boasted a range of business ventures, the most adventurous being the island and the resort.

He looked forward to letting them know he had made the most of the one vacant unit at the resort following his brother Jasper's party. They would be relieved he hadn't continued partying with the rest of the guests. Who knew where they had all ended up?

Lachie was thankful he hadn't attempted to keep pace with his party-loving younger brother. Jasper had always been, and likely always would be, the quintessential life of the party, known for his adventurous and risk-taking spirit. Let him have that way of life and the problems that sometimes came with it, Lachie mused. What could be better than resting on a cosy couch on an overcast, windy day? With his eyelids growing heavy, he cast one final glance at the ocean before surrendering to a deep and restful sleep.

Chapter Two

The jiggling of keys in the front door stirred him from his sleep. He lay still, his eyes shut while listening to someone talking on a phone as they opened the door and entered the room behind where he lay. Whoever it was obviously thought the unit was empty, which it should have been according to the booking schedule. He looked down at his clothes and for a moment, thought about sitting up and revealing he was there. But the phone conversation seemed interesting, and he listened as the girl, who sounded young, walked across the timber floor. Because of the positioning of the walls in the room, she would not know anyone was on the lounge unless she stepped in front of it. From the sound of her footsteps, she had gone in the other direction.

'I know, Grace. I'm looking after myself.' She giggled. 'No, I haven't found a husband. Sweet Jesus, I've only been out here a few months and if you could only see the fellas that come from these parts, you'd be horrified.' He listened closely as she stopped talking and placed some belongings on the kitchen bench. A tap running and the fridge door opening and shutting indicated she was still in the kitchen area. 'Oh my God. You've never seen anything like it. Lord almighty save us. I thought our lads were full of booze and bad manners, but they aren't a scratch on what these idiots are.' More water ran, perhaps into a bucket.

'Big and brawny and full of shite. All they're blatherin' about is fishing, surfing, and swigging back pints. I worked at a big party here last night. It took all my might to smile and keep my mouth closed. Dumber and dumber. That's how I'd describe them.'

There was silence for a while and Lachie listened hard but couldn't hear what was being said on the other end of the line. After a while the young girl started up again. 'Yes, Grace. Sure, they all look good and they're kind on the eye, but there's nothing between the ears. For them, it's all about their muscles and drinking. They get drunk and full of bullshit just the same as our lads. I'm not going to find a husband around these parts. I think that joke has worn thin.'

More silence. By now he had realised the girl in the kitchen must be one of the new resort staff hired while he was down south. 'Hang on. I've got to put the phone down for a tick to grab something off the top of the fridge.' He flinched when she laughed loudly and shouted across the room, obviously so the person on the phone could hear her. 'Last lot that stayed here has left a stash of drugs on top here. Idiots. More without a brain to share. It's thousands of dollars to stay here and they're stupid enough to leave their dope on top of the fridge. Probably worth more than my wage.'

He twisted his face, wishing he could hear whatever the person called Grace was saying. It was hard enough following the conversation from this end because the girl's thick accent was difficult to understand. Irish, he thought. Definitely Irish. He tilted his head a bit to hear better as she laughed loudly. 'Sure, I hear you loud and clear. They might be a good ride, but it's useless if they can't string a sentence together. Hang on, I'll put you on speaker. I need to scrub some stains off the kitchen bench. I'll stop in a moment and put my feet up. We're on an hourly rate, and this place is pretty clean. Owners are filthy rich anyway. Australia is full of capitalists with more money than they know what to do with.'

By now Lachie was starting to become annoyed. He thought about getting up and making his presence known, but the conversation wasn't bad entertainment on a Saturday morning. At least now he could hear Grace's voice on the other end, which sounded much like the girl in the kitchen. An Irish accent that, if the conversation hadn't been what it was, might have been appealing.

Grace spoke more quickly, and he concentrated hard to decipher her words. 'Oh, Kat. Maybe get in amongst it and enjoy yourself. You're only young once. Perhaps you'd have more luck in the outback. Go ride a cowboy, darlin'.' Finally, he had a name for the voice behind him. Kat.

'Please, spare me,' Kat continued. 'I've met some of them. Those fellas from out west come to the coast for a good time. Cars, shooting pigs, and raising cattle are the limits of their conversation. 'Chat's scarce with any of them. You all think I've journeyed all this way in search of a husband, but it seems I've taken a wrong turn. Not a chance of finding anything of the sort here. Hold on, I'll take a seat. You should see this place, Grace. Million-dollar views. Bloody amazing. I'll take you off speaker though. The reception is shite.'

Now there was only one end of the conversation again. Kat continued to talk. 'You said you rang for a reason.' There was a lengthy silence, and Lachie stared at the ocean, watching a seagull flying against the wind. The bird didn't make any progress and eventually dropped out of sight. 'No, Grace. They won't catch me with anything. There's no way I'm going to jail.'

Kat got up and he froze as he heard her walk behind the couch and enter one of the bedrooms. 'Are you there, Grace? Hang on, I'll put you on speaker again. I've just put my feet up. Oh my God, mercy me, if you could see this bed. It's bigger than our entire bedroom back home.'

Grace's voice sounded again. 'Aren't you supposed to be cleaning? Don't go getting the sack. You've hopped through enough jobs as it is.'

'Don't worry, there are plenty of jobs here. Aussies don't want to do cleaning jobs. I don't know why. Everything is spotless here today. I'll chat for a bit longer and then I'll buckle down,' she sighed. 'Everyone is so far away. I miss you all something fierce.'

'Well, it's just as well you're a long way away because two of those idiot O'Rourke cousins of ours, Kiaran and Seamus, are after your neck. They're saying they know you've got it. All the jewellery was supposed to be in the safe and only Aunty Doreen and Granny had access. I said how would you have it? You're in Australia, and to give up on looking, but they're bloody persistent. Everyone knows it's missing. Mum tried to tell them it was only an imitation, but they smelled a rat. If it weren't for that stupid woman on the antique show on the telly, they wouldn't even be worried about it. Everyone is looking for it. You know they've gone to the police and reported it stolen? They want you to go to jail for robbery. Please, Kat, be careful and remember what Mum says about the curse of lying. It'll bring you bad luck.'

'Are you kidding me? They've gone to the police? Idiots!'

'I hope you're in a safe place because everyone, apart from our family, is saying you've nicked it.'

'They can talk all they like, but they won't find me, or it. I can't believe they even remembered she had it. Granny couldn't stand either of those boys anyway. She said they were crooks. She wrote to me several times; the last letter arrived shortly before she passed. I've kept them all.'

'That one on the telly was worth near a million. Did you say Granny wrote to you? How did you get mail with no fixed address?'

'I was working at the Dingo Beach Pub back then. There's a post office agency at the store there. You can get mail sent to it.'

'Did Granny ever say anything about it in her letters?'

'No. What's done is done because now she's not here anyway, so what does it matter? Listen, Grace, I've got to go. I need to vacuum and clean the bathrooms. I suppose I'd better do something to earn my wage this morning.'

'Can you not talk a bit longer? I'll have to tell you next time about the excitement at the christening I went to last week. You know, Merleen from work? It was her baby. Holy Mother of God. You've never seen anything like it. The priest had a little microphone on, and when he was out the back after the ceremony was finished, we could hear him talking about how ugly the baby was. He said it took after the mother. Then there was a fight at the pub afterwards. The Brendan brothers against the O'Connors. Who'd invite all of them and then keep them topped up with Guinness? It was a right bust-up. Police, ambulance, and even the fire brigade were called in the end. And I need to tell you about the street singing on Friday night. A busker went off with a song and before he finished, there must have been a few hundred of us singing along with him in the street. It was grand. I wish you'd been there.'

'Sorry to miss that. Look I've got to go.'

'Well, my darlin' sister. Keep looking for a lad. Maybe you'll have to set sail to New Zealand to find one. What-ever happens, I hope you can lay low. There's nothing in the will to say it was left to you and even that idiot, Johnny, is getting in on the act. He's appeared out of nowhere and reckons if you have it, half of it is his. I know you well and I have my suspicions. Take care, I really don't want to visit you in jail.'

'Johnny O'Hara. Jesus, where did he spring from and fancy him thinking I owe him anything? What an idiot. He's got no right to anything from me.'

The rest of the conversation was lost, as the bathroom door closed and the toilet flushed, drowning out the words.

Only the last goodbyes between the two sisters were audible when the background noises stopped.

'Bye, Grace. I miss you and give my love to everyone. Thank you for sticking up for me and don't say too much about anything. The less said the better.'

'Bye, big sis.' Talk again soon.'

Chapter Three

Water running in the bathroom signalled that the cleaner, Kat, had actually started to do some work. Music sounded from where she was and he heard her singing along to Sinead O'Connor's, *Nothing Compares to You.* She didn't have a bad voice, he decided, although her attitude towards men, work, and her connection to whatever crime she had committed left him in doubt as to whether she should be employed by their family business.

He knew it was hard to get good staff sometimes, and the backpackers were a regular source of workers, but how thorough were the background checks? If someone was chasing her for theft or reporting her to the police, she was probably stealing or doing illegal things while in their employ. If there was one thing he hated, it was drama. Life was supposed to go nice and steady with no complications, or getting involved in intense episodes that didn't need to occur.

Just as he was about to sit up, a door slammed and he

caught a glimpse of her as she exited the bedroom, vacuum cleaner dragging behind, her voice loud and clear as she sang along to the chorus. She pushed the vacuum vigorously across the timber floor, and he had his first proper look at her. She looked Irish, he decided, with pale skin and reddish-brown hair that was tied back. Her waifish figure was covered with a white apron, a tiny pair of denim shorts and a white T-shirt underneath.

Her face wasn't visible at first because she was concentrating on the floor. It wasn't until she reached the area near the end of the couch that something made her look up. Perhaps she sensed his presence, or someone watching her. Her body froze as her eyes locked with his, and he quickly sat up, remembering that all he wore were his jocks. The vacuum cleaner continued to run, its noise not loud enough to cover her shriek. Holding the stick of the cleaner high in the air, she waved it around, dragging it closer and causing the electrical plug to come out of the socket. The relentless hum of the motor dwindled to a quiet murmur before its echo faded away. For a moment there was silence, and he reached down and grabbed his jeans from the floor.

Her voice was high-pitched. 'Don't you come near me. I'm warning you. I'll scream the place down and ... and ... there are cameras in here. They'll be able to track who you are and it won't take long to find you. You're on an island. Don't move.'

He held his arm out as she waved the stick closer. 'Whoa. Steady on.' He held his jeans over his jocks.

'I'm going to back away and if you even move a muscle, I'll ... well... I'm a black belt in karate, plus I have a gun in my back pocket and I won't hesitate to use it.' She put her hand around the back of her shorts. Her eyes were wide and strikingly blue, and for a moment, he was drawn by their intensity. As her hand remained in her back pocket though, he wondered if she really did have a gun. Surely not.

'Hold your horses,' he muttered, standing up and pulling on his jeans. At least if he was going to get shot, he wanted it to be with his pants on. 'I just slept on the couch for the night. No one had this unit booked. You've woken me up, and you're not in danger. My family owns this place.'

She flicked one eyebrow high. 'Sure. Sure. And my mother is the bloody Queen of England. Now, get out. Be off with you.'

He laughed and picked up his shirt, calmly putting it over his head. By now, he was sure she didn't have a gun. Otherwise, she would have pointed it at him. He rearranged his shirt and sat down to put his shoes and socks on. 'I'm not lying about who I am. Look on your phone. Google search, Lachie McIntosh, *Vivre*. HR manager and a list of other roles.'

Keeping one hand in her back pocket, she dropped the vacuum stick and pulled her phone out, which was still playing music. Glancing up and down, trying not to take her eyes off him, she googled his name, twisting her mouth when she came across some photos and information.

'Jesus Christ, Sweet Mother Mary. You are Lachie McIntosh.' She placed the phone back in her pocket, then used both hands to smooth over her apron. A few stray strands of hair were also pushed back into place as she straightened up and tried to look confident. 'Well, you shouldn't have just lain there and scared the bejeesus out of me. I thought you were a murderer and it was the end of my existence. I saw my entire life and all my family flash in front of me. Why would you lie there like that and not let your presence be known? For God's sake, I nearly wet my pants.'

He felt his eyebrows rise at the last part of her rant. 'No. You're safe. I'm your employer and I stayed here and didn't get up because I was in a deep sleep, until you started carrying on.'

'Well, I don't really have a gun. Don't worry. I just made that up because I thought you were going to murder me. I don't carry arms. I wouldn't do that. I don't want you to think I have a gun. That was pure bullshit. I don't even know how to shoot one. I mean I've never even held one. Believe me, I wouldn't bring a gun to work. I like my job. No guns for me.'

'I figured that.' Pulling his socks on slowly, he looked her up and down. 'Well, Kat is it? I'll get out of your way and let you finish your work. I've only used the lounge to sleep on so you'll find everything else as it was.'

She came to stand nearer, staring hard, her eyes scrutinising him. 'You were at the party last night. I served you drinks. I remember your face.'

He tried to think of who had been serving the drinks. 'I don't recall seeing you. There were quite a few people working though and a number of new staff.'

'I was in the kitchen cooking and cleaning, until right near the end.' She pulled a face and he could tell she was thinking that being tucked away from everyone had been a good thing. 'I only served for the last half hour.' Her last two words, 'thank God', were muttered but he was sure he heard them correctly.

'Jasper's party.' He ran his hand through his hair, thinking that it would be matted and that he probably looked a sight with his hangover and crushed shirt. 'Big night.'

She made another condescending face, and he went to say more but didn't. What was the use? He had been so drunk by the end of the night that he didn't even remember her serving drinks.

Suddenly it must have dawned on her that he may have heard her earlier phone conversation. Her voice changed, and she tried to sound more official, like she was posh and in control of the strange situation that was unfolding. She straightened up, pushing her hair back behind her ears. 'You didn't by any chance hear any of my conversation with my sister, Grace, did you? I was talking to her as I was cleaning. I mean, I didn't stop to talk. I can chat and work at the same time.'

He twisted his mouth as if he was trying to recall the last half hour or so. 'No. I never heard a thing—just the Sinead O'Connor song. I was in a deep sleep. Your singing woke me up. Not a bad voice.' He wanted to add, 'for a thief,' but held his tongue.

She wiggled her shoulders and sniffed. 'Are you sure you never heard anything?'

'Should I have? I'm hungover. Nothing much wakes me at the best of times.'

'Okay, then. I'll get on with my job. I don't like to waste time talking and there's plenty to be done.'

Straightening his clothes, he looked out through the window. He ran his hand across the glass doors. 'These need cleaning,' he said. 'It doesn't look like they've been done for a while.'

She glared at him before bending down and picking up the vacuum cleaner from where she had tossed it. He stood silently, watching as she retreated to the bedroom without another word. The sound of the vacuum started again, and he picked up his wallet from the nearby table and made his way out through the front door. He was halfway down the path that led away from the unit when she called out to him from the front doorway.

'Hold up. Wait a sec,' she called as she walked quickly towards him. Holding her hand out she passed him a brown paper bag. 'I found these drugs on top of the fridge. I'd say whoever stayed here last, left this packet behind.' She muttered, 'More idiots,' before turning away and making her way back to the unit.

Chapter Four

Kat leaned back on the closed front door and held her breath. What the hell had just happened? A morning that started looking like an easy gig had become something else. She shook her body, hoping to shake off the uneasy feeling that had settled in the pit of her stomach. But the agitation clung to her like a stubborn shadow, refusing to dissipate as she walked towards the glass doors. Peering at the view, she tried to put the conversation and chain of events into perspective. Had he heard her talking to Grace? If so, what parts did he hear? She couldn't recall when Grace had been on speaker and when she hadn't. What had she said herself? 'Jesus, Mary and Joseph,' she exclaimed out loud. 'How? Why?' She placed her palms on the glass, looking outwards. For some reason she always seemed to get herself in trouble. 'Your foot is always in your mouth,' her Granny had always told her.

Her heart ached when she thought of Granny. The old lady would have loved this view, even on a day like today. Grey, moody and windy, the weather was much like where they come from in Galway, minus the cold. She stood on tiptoes to look further to the north, the nearby islands visible across the water. Although it was an ocean view, it differed vastly from where she had grown up. Her granny's place, a hundred-year-old cottage in Clifden, situated on what was known as the Wild Atlantic Way, was just over an hour away from where Kat and her family lived in Galway, on the western coast of Ireland. As a child, and until she moved to Australia, Kat spent as much time with Granny as she had with her own family.

Granny Mae lived by herself; her husband of fifty years, Rory, lost in a fishing boat tragedy when Kat was twenty. Grandad should have retired long before, but he loved the sea and the thrill of the catch. He was fit and strong. Kat shivered. It had taken days for his body, and those of the other two trawlermen, to be found. There had been no distress calls made that night and it had been some comfort to the family to be told that the accident would have happened very quickly. The stormy conditions were extreme and had moved in rapidly. With the navigational equipment on board broken and communication cut, there wasn't anything anyone could do. When rocks tore apart the trawler, all three men on board perished at sea.

She tried not to replay Grandad's funeral in her mind. It had taken years to get the scenes out of her mind; her granny inconsolable, her mother's brother and sister, along with the group of cousins and friends, sobbing as the curtains drew across the coffin. A month later they had attached a little plaque to the rocks on the headland near Granny's cottage. The same afternoon, Kat had gone on a boat with the rest of her family for what promised to be an emotional and solemn occasion, scattering Grandad's ashes in his beloved bay. It was what he had always wanted.

Granny hadn't come out on the boat. She stood on the shoreline and at exactly five o'clock they were to throw the contents of the wooden box out into the ocean. The timing was imperative so that Granny would know exactly when the ashes had left their hands and Grandad had found his resting place. Of course, nothing had gone to plan. At first Kat's brother, Ronan, who had been made responsible for the actual tossing out bit, had trouble getting the sealed plastic bag that contained the ashes out of the box. 'I reckon it's glued to the bottom somehow,' he said as he leaned out over the rail. It had been on the tip of Kat's tongue to tell him to bring the box back over the rail so that they could help, but her mother had intervened before she could speak.

'Don't throw the plastic bag in the ocean,' her mum had said. 'I've heard of stupid people who just throw the sealed bag in completely. The entire lot just sinks to the bottom of the ocean. Those ashes need to come out of the bag. Give it to your father. He'll fix it.'

Her father had carefully taken the plastic bag containing the ashes out of the box, which he thought Ronan was holding tight. But the timber box that had been a family heirloom and had held every family member's ashes as far back as anyone could remember, slipped out of Ronan's hands and plonked straight down into the ocean. It quickly sank and Ronan swore loudly as it resurfaced briefly and started to bob up and down on the waves. For a moment there was silence and the thought crossed Kat's mind that it was the quietest her family had ever been when they were all together. As they watched helplessly, the box moved further away, an empty ashes container on its own journey. Soon a large wave carried it off and before long it disappeared.

'Lord be,' her mother exclaimed. 'That's the end of that.'

'At least the ashes are still here,' Ronan declared as he leaned out over the railing, trying to get a final glimpse of the box.'

'Careful, Dad,' her sister Grace added, closing her eyes. 'The wind is picking up. Oh Lordy, I feel seasick. There's too much bobbing going on for my liking. Hurry up and get it done.'

The wind was indeed getting stronger and by the time her dad finally held the plastic bag carefully over the railing, at thirty-five minutes past five, the boat was swaying from side to side. When Kat glared up at the captain, he gave her a cheesy grin and a wave, his hands firmly on the wheel. He's enjoying every minute of this, she thought. A bird's eye view of our antics down here on the deck.

Kat turned back to the task at hand, hanging onto Grace to steady herself. A sudden jolt as the boat came down the crest of another wave caused her to exclaim, 'Jesus Christ, we'll all end up at the bottom of the bloody Atlantic Ocean alongside Grandad and the timber box in a minute. Granny was smart staying on the shore.'

Eventually, the boat steadied, and with feet spread apart, her dad gestured for Ronan to hold the bag with him as they emptied it into the ocean. Her mum had a piece of paper in her pocket with some words written on it that Granny wanted read as the ashes went into the sea. 'Hang on,' she said.' I need to get the words out to read. Give me a minute.' Her dad and Ronan hesitated, both glaring at Mum as they held the bag over the ocean, their bodies lurching with each wave as they tried to remain steady on their feet.

'Okay,' her mum said, holding the piece of paper in one hand and struggling with her other hand to put her glasses on. 'Blind as a bat I am. Okay. Now I'm ready.'

Just as she said that, a strong gust of wind ripped the paper out of her hand and it flew off into the air. For the second time that day her mother was speechless as she stared at Dad, not knowing what to do or say.

Grace was beginning to look green and started to make retching noises. 'Just tip the bloody ashes in,' Grace shrieked. 'It's getting rougher. I'm feeling mighty sick.'

Ronan looked at his dad, who gazed around at them all. 'Let's do it, son.'

As they held the bottom of the plastic bag and the ashes started to fall out, Kat breathed out slowly. But the respite from calamities was short-lived when a sudden burst of wind swept over the boat and picked up the ashes. She wasn't sure what happened next, because suddenly her face and everyone else's was covered in Grandad's ashes.

'Holy feck,' her mother said, adding to the blasphemous words that everyone else was yelling out. Grace ran to the side of the boat, the sound of her vomiting loud and clear, even over the babble of everyone blaming each other for Grandad's ashes now being attached to their clothes and faces.

* * *

By the time they returned to shore, everyone had calmed down, cleaned up and scraped what they could off each other and the floor of the boat. 'Grandad's ashes are in the sea,' her mother said. 'Just remember that.'

When they returned to Granny the first question she asked was, 'And everything went well? You read my words, Orla? Did you like the poem I wrote called *Five O'Clock?*'

'Yes, Mum,' Orla replied. 'It was beautiful and everything went splendidly.'

Granny looped her arm through Kat's, glancing quizzically at Grace, whose face was as white as a ghost's. 'Heavens above, Grace. You look like you've seen a banshee. Perhaps a stiff drink is in order. You know, I sensed your Grandad's ashes mingling with the water precisely at five. I felt his presence beside me. Well done, everyone. I had every bit of confidence in all of you to give him the grand send-off he deserved.'

* * *

Not long after Grandad died, Kat had decided to do some extra study. She could do most of the classes online, so she moved in with Granny for the next two years. Those years forged special memories and she smiled as she now pressed her face up against the glass, watching the white-caps cresting across the ocean surrounding the Whit-sunday Islands. She pulled her thoughts back to the present. Now Kiaran and Seamus were prying where they shouldn't. Trying to look for something they wanted that was worth a lot of money. Well, they could rot in hell for all she cared. They wouldn't find it. More important were Grace's words while she was cleaning the bathroom, before they said goodbye on the phone this morning. They echoed in her ears. 'You and Granny were tight, Kat, and none of us believe you would have taken it without her giving it to you. Just watch yourself, though; those two cousins of ours are up to no good.'

Chapter Five

By the time she finished cleaning, she had convinced herself that the man she encountered this morning had not overheard her conversation with Grace. She had only been working at the resort for two weeks and had already decided it would be a good place to live and work for a few months, so she didn't want to get the sack before she had even settled in. It was clear he had not been lying when he said he was hungover. If her memory served her, he had seemed as drunk as the rest of them at the party, downing shots of tequila as though there was no tomorrow.

The men from last night blended in her memory: scruffy hair, bronzed skin, and the same laid-back attire of jeans and untucked shirts. The party's host, Jasper, resembled this Lachie character, prompting her to connect the dots. Someone had mentioned that Jasper was from the family who owned the resort. They were brothers, she realised. The party, orchestrated by Jasper, was a gathering of his friends, with plenty of food and alcohol involved. She had watched through the kitchen servery as women wearing skimpy dresses, tiny shorts, and even smaller tops danced in amongst the men, who mainly stood around talking and drinking.

Some of the girls were backpackers she knew from Airlie Beach, many working in the shops and restaurants that lined the town's main street. It hadn't worried her that she wasn't amongst the crowd, having fun. Although she enjoyed dancing and partying, tonight's crowd and drunken conversations were not what she would choose. It had been annoying enough to serve them drinks for the final hour and have to listen to their baloney.

At the night's end, Jasper and a couple of his pals tried to coax her into joining them for a boat excursion. There had been some ill-mannered comments about her red hair and Irish heritage, which put her in no mood for any more of their jokes, so she swiftly veered in the opposite direction. Thank goodness for the seclusion and quiet of the worker's cabin she had been assigned as part of her agreement to work on the island.

As she packed up her cleaning equipment and took one last look around the rooms, she reminded herself that this wasn't a permanent position. It was just a fill-in job. Until she found what she was really looking for. What that was, she didn't know. Her university degree was in fine arts, but now she wasn't sure how she was going to get a job in that field. There weren't many jobs in regional areas where she could use her qualifications. If she wanted to work at an art gallery or make money from her art, she would need to head to one of the cities on the coast.

This working holiday to Australia was supposed to bring adventure and time to sort out what she wanted in life, but there hadn't been any light bulb moments so far. Deep down she knew that even though the Whitsundays, and now the *Vivre* resort and island, were beautiful spots to live and work, she wouldn't find her dream job here. Where to next? Having grown up in a small town, spending her days nestled in the cosy embrace of her Granny's village, she had grown accustomed to a simpler pace of life. Bustling crowds, hectic streets, and the chaos of city living held no allure.

She had tried another place before she came here. For the two months before *Vivre*, she had served beers at the Dingo Beach Pub. The pub was located in a remote village to the north of Airlie, but the scenic spot had been a bit too small and isolated for her liking. She adored the region, relishing its beauty and charm, yet once again a restlessness had stirred within her. Despite the friends she had met and the memories made during her time at Dingo Beach, it had been time to move on to something different. When she spotted the vacancies at *Vivre* she quickly applied online and immediately won a job. The area was desperate for workers and jobs were easy to get.

Chapter Six

Making his way back to the office, Lachie tried to process the whirlwind of events and conversations that had unfolded this morning. His mind was muddled and he cursed himself for drinking so much last night. Thank God he stopped when he did. No doubt Jasper would be sleeping off a hangover, probably in his cabin or on one of his mates' boats anchored just off the beach. When he reached the office, he grabbed a cold bottle of water from the fridge, the cool liquid offering some relief to his parched throat. He threw the parcel that Kat had given him in the lost property box and picked up a local newspaper that had recently been delivered. Something to read while he rested today.

With water in hand, he started to make his way towards his cabin, situated further down the beach. Tucked away in a cluster of five, these cabins were reserved for the family's use, nestled amidst the bushland for added privacy from the holidaymakers.

A long, cool shower and a strong cup of coffee helped restore his vitality, and with some leftover pasta and meatballs, along with copious amounts of cold water, he started to come to life. The glass front doors of the cabin opened up onto a grassy area that reached down to the beach. He shaded his eyes against the sun that had pushed its way through the clouds. Jasper's boat was anchored not far offshore, and he could see a group of people on its decks. A couple of girls in bikinis sat with their legs dangling over the side and there was Jasper, lying down with his head resting in one of their laps. Typical, he thought. His brother always had plenty of women around him. He never settled with any of them though. He was a drifter, moving with the surf and the waves. He loved his brother who was the closest to him in age, but they were chalk and cheese. Where Lachie was punctual and driven by routine, Jasper threw caution to the wind and, for that matter, seemed to go wherever the wind blew, although lately he did seem to have settled down a bit, committing to working full-time at the resort. No doubt, Lachie thought, because he wanted to save some money for his next trip.

His thoughts drifted to the girl called Kat. From the look of her pale skin, it wouldn't appear she had much experience with water sports or outdoor activities. Interesting, he thought. Why would she want to come and work on an island if she didn't at least swim, snorkel or want to go out in the sun? Maybe it was an excellent place to hide out. Remote, where no one would find her, or ask too many questions.

Turning back inside, he reached for his laptop and signed in to the resort's intranet. It was time to find out who this Kat really was, and whether she should continue to be employed.

* * *

There was a reason Lachie had been put in charge of administration here on the island. Record keeping and business were his forte. As much as he loved being outside, he knew his business skills and what he had learned during his university studies were invaluable, ensuring everything kept ticking as it should.

His parents had given Jasper the same opportunity when he asked. 'Sure, you can give the office a go. But Lachie is in charge and you have six months to prove yourself. I'm not sure why you think it will suit you, but let's see how this works.' His father had been fair in encouraging Jasper to try what he thought he might like to do, despite predicting it wouldn't work.

He lasted six weeks before deciding office work wasn't for him. Instead, Lachie talked him into designing new furniture for the family cabins and a timber bench for the foyer of the resort. 'Jas, you're a master in design and timberwork. Just go with it. I don't know why you don't stick to that. We could do with some heavy timber recliners for on the beach as well.'

'I don't feel like making timber furniture is real work. I don't want to bludge off Mum and Dad. I need to contribute, like you are.'

In the end they had compromised and now Jasper was in charge of the workers who did the landscaping, gardenwork and maintenance of the resort's grounds, as well as doing any odd job that needed doing. 'Jack of all trades,' Lachie said. It worked well and still gave Jasper time for diving, fishing and socialising. All of which he loved.

Lachie and Jasper's younger three siblings all lived down south, not far from where his parents lived on Stradbroke Island. Millie ran the main office for *Vivre* on Stradbroke Island, while Rusty and Hazel were both still at university in Brisbane. Lachie was looking forward to heading south to see them, hopefully in the not too distant future. For now though, he needed to have a closer look at their employee, Kat. Last year, they had unfortunately employed someone who had forged a working visa and also had a criminal record. He thought he had been more vigilant with background checks since then, but workers were often sneaky and lied to gain a job at the resort. Most were honest and worked hard. However, there had been instances over the years where theft and illegal activities had needed to be investigated by the police. The last thing he needed was to employ a thief. He would run a mile to avoid being involved in anything shifty.

It didn't take him long to locate a folder that contained the resumes and details of everyone who had applied for the job of cleaner and waitress. He read Kat's letter and resume aloud, pressing the cold bottle of water to his forehead and swallowing a couple of Panadol as he went.

'*Kat MacCullagh, born September 24, 1994, County Galway, Ireland. Educated at Galway University, Bachelor of Fine Arts, Master in Fine Arts.*'

He took another sip of water before reading further. Scanning over the list of skills and achievements, he tried to remember if he had looked over her resume before. Georgia, an older lady who helped in the office, was usually given the job of hiring overseas workers when he wasn't there. She was known for being thorough and not putting up with any nonsense. He did notice however, that she had not ticked the box that showed Kat had provided a police check.

He scanned the paperwork again. No police check was attached, as per the requirements. Only last week, the till at the bar was short three hundred dollars. It was unusual for that to be the case and he wondered ... Surely not. There were quite a few new staff at the resort. There had been an influx after the borders had opened and the Covid restrictions were lifted. Thank goodness that was in the past. The effects on their business ventures had been disastrous and like so many others, they had held their breath, tightened the budgets where they could and hung on while everything remained closed.

Now the tourists were back in droves and, thank goodness, so were the overseas workers who were essential for running a resort. It wasn't much help if they were stealing though. He googled her name, trying to locate a social media account or anything that would give him some more information. The only connection that came up was on someone else's page, where her name had been printed below a photo of six young women who had won a singing competition at the local pub. She looked younger in the photo which had been taken several years ago. Cute he thought. Too cute.

Chapter Seven

He slept for a couple of hours after his detective research. Not that he had come up with much, apart from the fact that they had employed someone without a police check. He would need to follow it up tomorrow. When he woke, he could hear Jasper and some of his mates talking out on the lawn at the front of the cabin. The others were leaving. Returning to Airlie Beach probably to get ready for another night out in one of the pubs there.

He stretched out on the couch where he had been asleep. He seemed to have spent most of his time horizontal today. Jasper came through the open sliding doors and threw himself into one of the single lounge chairs. 'What a night. What a day. Where have you been? We've had a great day out on the boat.'

Lachie sat up. 'I know. I could see you from here. My head is just starting to clear. I've had a thumping headache all day from those tequilas.'

'You're out of practice.' Jasper said, his hand running through his dark hair. 'Where's your stamina?'

'I lost it years ago when it comes to drinking. Can't stand feeling sick. No more for me.'

They talked about the night, laughing and going over the crazy antics of some of Jasper's mates. 'Did you see the blonde Swedish girl I ended up with? Gorgeous,' Jasper said, closing his eyes. 'Loved my boat she did. Nice. Real nice.'

'You know, Jasper, those girls come and go. Do you think you'll ever settle down?'

'No way. I'd rather be playing the field than not getting any at all like you.'

They bantered back and forth. Lachie looked at the clock on the wall. 'I'm going to go to the restaurant tonight. Just to keep an eye on everything.'

'You do that. I'm going to catch up on some sleep. It'll be an early night for me.'

'By the way, have you come across the Irish waitress called Kat? She has red hair, sort of a brownie-red colour. She would have been employed while I was down south.'

'Yeah, yeah. I know the one. Skinny legs, and blue eyes. I tried to get her to come out to the boat last night but she disappeared. Not very social. Keeps to herself, although I think she's made friends with some of the girls and she talks to Jock, the gardener, quite a bit.'

'What do you think about her?'

'Aloof, judgy, but what a looker. Eyes and lips to die for and those legs. Even her ...'

Lachie butted in. 'Workwise I meant.'

'Oh. Workwise? She seems okay. Head down and

hasn't complained about anything. Worked at Dingo Beach Pub for a while. Why? Are you keen on her?'

'Jesus, no. I mean, no. I just had an encounter with her this morning and discovered she hasn't done a police check. I wondered about her honesty, especially considering money went missing from the till last week.'

'I reckon it's that fella we put on who's from Melbourne. The new barman. He's shifty as anything. Not sure why Georgia thought he would be okay. I don't think it would be that girl stealing, although, as we've learnt before, appearances can be misleading. She might look cute and appear to be honest, but you just can't tell sometimes. I'll watch out for her.'

Chapter Eight

When Kat entered the restaurant, the first person she saw was Lachie McIntosh. She had only been here for two weeks, but before last night and then this morning's encounter, she had not come across him before. Maybe he came and went, like a lot of the other workers here. She put her head down and looked the other way, pleased that she had taken the hem up on her black trousers so they didn't drag across the floor. She only had one pair of black pants and she had put the hem down to wear them out in Airlie Beach last weekend. For work, wearing flat closed-in shoes instead of high heels meant the black pants had been taken up and down a few times.

A couple of the Swedish girls had convinced her to go to a nightclub in Airlie, and it had been fun for a while. The night dragged on though, and with no way to get back to the island and her cosy bed in her cabin, she had endured the girls laughing and drinking until the sun came up in the morning. At least the ride back on the small boat that plied back and forth between the islands had been smooth and she had even seen some dolphins on the way. She had become good friends with the Scottish lad, Jock. He was twenty-four and they got on like a house on fire. He filled the role of taxi driver for the resort's small boat and she sat up behind the steering wheel with him, laughing and joking when the spray from the waves wet them. 'In your Scotland and my Ireland, we'd be freezing if we got wet from the ocean,' she yelled to him over the sound of the boat motor.

'Aye, not here though,' Jock said. 'The water is warmer than our baths back home.'

The other girls were sprawled out on bench seats that ran along the side of the boat. 'Look at them, frying their skin in the sun,' Jock said. 'Trying to cure their hangovers with Vitamin D. Hang on to your hat Kat. Let's wake them up.'

Kat squealed as he made the boat go faster and they bounced over some bigger waves that had been made by the wake of another boat going in the other direction.

Water splashed over the bow and one of the girls half fell off the seat, her legs flying in the air, her glare directed towards Jock. When he slowed down, the boat steadied and the girls went back to trying to sleep. What a life, Kat thought. Who would want to go back to the winters of Europe or Ireland? The Whitsundays was really a grand place to be.

* * *

It wasn't all about play though, and now as she started her shift, she donned her black apron and started preparing the bar. The resort boasted twenty luxurious units, as well as a row of dongas and five small cabins that were used for staff accommodation. She had been lucky enough to score one of the cabins to live in and was enjoying having a private and cosy space to call her own. There was also the McIntosh family's private area, which had five larger cabins and an outdoor kitchen.

The resort guests usually came to the restaurant for their meals. After all, she thought, if you had the money to stay at *Vivre* you certainly didn't need to cook. The resort, which was in a breathtaking position amongst the islands of the Whitsundays, was where the rich and famous came for their vacations. The week before she started work, a group of famous American actors and actresses who were making a film in the area, stayed in the most lavish units at the resort. She scrubbed the counter and repositioned some glasses, making sure everything was in order. Standards were high and that suited her fine. Moving further along, she polished the taps on the beer tower dispenser, the surfaces shiny and spotless by the time she finished. There was no way she was going to rely on any one else to clean. Not everyone took as much care as she did. The other bar worker tonight was the fella, Mal, from Melbourne. He didn't talk much, which suited her. She liked to get on with her job and hoped the night would go smoothly and quickly.

She noticed Lachie sitting at a small table to the side, a cold beer in front of him. He stared out the window beside him and she followed his gaze. Lights from boats tied up near the jetty flickered in the growing darkness, and bamboo flares positioned on the foreshore lit up the beach as well as the backdrop of coconut palms and other trees that lined the shore. She sighed. The island really was paradise.

* * *

Before long the guests started to file in. Orders, including cocktails and other fancy drinks, kept her busy and she spent the night behind the bar serving drinks to those enjoying their meals. She liked not being in the kitchen or serving meals. Drinks were an easier option for her, and she kept up easily with the orders. Mal didn't seem to rush too much, taking ages to methodically mix a cocktail. He had an uncanny skill of making sure he was behind her when someone neared the bar, or was cleaning something when drinks needed to be served. A work avoider, she thought. She didn't care though. As long as she was kept busy and did her job well, she was happy.

When she noticed that Lachie's beer was finished, she approached him to see what he would like. 'Would you like another drink?' she asked, using her most polite voice.

'Thank you. I'll have a house shiraz with my dinner.'

She was about to turn when he spoke again. 'You seem to know what you're doing behind the bar?'

'I've done a bit of pub work in my life. I worked at Dingo Beach before I came here, so that gave me an insight into Australian pub life.'

He chuckled. 'Would you say this place is a bit

different to there? Not that I'm dissing Dingo or anything.'

'Sorry? Dissing? I'm not sure what you mean?'

'Oh, I'm not knocking it. It's just a bit different to here.'

'Were you thinking it was going to get knocked down? I didn't hear that.'

This time he laughed. 'I mean, I'm not criticising the place. Knocking. Dissing. It all means the same.'

She frowned. 'The bar and restaurant are different here, but I've found people much the same wherever I go in Australia. I'll get your drink.'

* * *

Tipping up his glass and finishing the last of his beer, Lachie watched Kat as she strode back to the bar. He realised he hadn't seen her smile. Such beautiful blue eyes, yet not a smile or spark to match. Not this morning and not now. Her face was set in a calm demeanour, her expression serious yet inviting. He watched her go back and forth, quickly noting that she was doing three times as much work as the other bar worker, Mal. It appeared that Mal was letting her do all the serving while he cleaned and took orders from the tables.

Lachie kept an eye on the workings of the restaurant. When the two Swedish girls came out of the kitchen, they stopped to talk to Kat. Blonde, gorgeous and their English spoken with a pleasurable clipped accent. No wonder Jasper was keen on socialising with them. When they served his meal, he thought how vibrant and chatty they were, and he thanked them for doing a great job. They were having a great time, travelling the world and working wherever they wanted.

Not long after he finished his meal, three middle-aged men came to join him at his table. Two of them dragged a couple of other chairs over, and he greeted them warmly. They were good friends of his parents and also owned property in the Whitsundays. Staying a night at *Vivre* would allow them to check out the recently built horizon pool and the extra cyclone-proofing that had been added to all the cabins.

They talked for an hour or so, until the men stood up to leave. 'Game of cards back at the room if you want, Lachie. Poker.'

He grinned. 'No way. You guys are experts at that game. I remember Dad's stories. I don't want to lose my hard-earned money to you three. I have my night planned and, unfortunately, I don't have a card game on the agenda. I'll save my money, thanks.'

'You got plenty of cash. Just a couple of hands.'

He declined and waved them off. They were nice blokes, but he remembered well the stories his father had told him about their all-night card games and the amount of money that flowed across the table. The rest of the guests had left the restaurant, most of the kitchen staff had also finished, and there were only a few workers left cleaning in the kitchen, as well as Kat behind the bar. She looked up from wiping the bench when he approached. 'Good night,' he said. 'You do a good job. Thank you.'

'All good. It's not hard. The guests are always pleasant here.'

She moved over to the till, took the drawer out and started to count the night's takings. Not many used cash these days, but it was surprising how many wealthy people seemed to carry money and liked to splash it around. No doubt she had probably taken a few tips tonight. It was what bulked up the backpackers' pay and, although it wasn't as much as they might get in Europe or Britain, it added to their pay packets.

He spoke to her about closing the cold rooms as she divided the money and counted. It needed to be balanced against the EFTPOS machine and receipts. She looked like she knew what she was doing and the thought crossed his mind that maybe she was more than just a good waitress and cleaner. Sometimes they needed workers in the office and after watching her work, perhaps he'd keep her in mind for any jobs that came up in that area. Maybe he'd been a bit harsh in his judgement of her after their first interaction. He turned to leave but then turned back again. 'Oh, I forgot. I happened to look at your job application and we don't have a police check for you. You'll need to supply me with one as soon as you can.'

Her eyes sparked and her head tilted to one side. 'I beg your pardon? Did you just ask me for a police check? Like an official one. Are my ears hearing right?' Her eyebrows lifted high. 'Might I ask why?'

Her change in tone and the abrupt way she spoke took him back a little. 'It's not an issue. It should have been done when you were employed. I was away and it was missed by Georgia, who employed you. No big deal. Just get it to me as soon as you can. Thanks.'

'Did Georgia miss anyone else? I think there were two other workers put on the same week. Do they have one? I'm not sure it's regular practice to have a police check unless you're working with children, and I don't see too many of them here.'

She was starting to annoy him. 'What other workers provide isn't any of your business. We pride ourselves here on high standards and I need a police check to complete your paperwork.'

Now it seemed as though fire was coming out of her eyes. 'I'll take that as a no, that others didn't have to provide one.' She straightened up, her face set like stone, her eyes boring into his. 'You overheard my conversation this morning. You got wind of what I said. You said you didn't, but now I think you did. Is that the reason for wanting a police check? They didn't ask for one at Dingo Beach Pub. They were happy to take me on my word and work ethic.'

He noticed her Irish accent became stronger when she was annoyed and he needed to listen hard when she spoke. His words were paced and clear. 'Look, it's standard procedure. I need the paperwork. End of story.'

'And, what if I don't.'

He shrugged and turned around, feeling the brunt of her anger against his back. 'I'm not going to repeat what I've already said. Goodnight, Miss MacCullagh.'

Chapter Nine

Slamming the money down on the counter, Kat slumped back onto a barstool. Her cheeks blushed crimson, and a fiery ache gnawed at her chest. She was done for. Her Irish police record would not look good in his eyes. The problem was that there were a couple of little, might she even say, tiny, misdemeanours that would be noted.

A year before she had left for Australia, along with her sister, Grace, she had stolen her cousin Seamus's ride-on mower. They had been drunk and her younger brother, Ronan, had dared them to go on an adventure. Over hill and over dale, they had ridden the mower together, hanging onto each other like two wild girls riding to the end of the world. A full moon had hung over them, lighting the country roads which fortunately had no other traffic. Grace had been very drunk though, more so than Kat, and she had been responsible for the steering. The end of the story was they landed up in the bog and, as much as they tried, they could not get the mower out. To add further chaos to the situation, neither of them had been able to find their mobile phone. This only added further merriment to their situation and Kat's side had ached from laughing so much.

'I'm sure I put my phone in the little glovebox here,' Grace said. 'But it's gone. Someone has stolen it.'

Kat had tried to check her pockets, but her coat was twisted and had become stuck between her and Grace. 'For God's sake. Look around us,' Kat said. 'There's no one for miles. No one stole it. I can't find mine either though.' Grace jigged up and down and then they had laughed so much that both of them ended up falling off the mower and landing in the mud. The bog was a dark mass of decomposed organic matter and Kat wrinkled her nose at the smell. She couldn't resist though and, picking a clump of mud, rubbed the cold damp matter into Grace's hair. Kat put on her voice of wisdom. 'This ancient shampoo has been centuries in the making. It comes with its own hint of moss and peat. Guaranteed to give you that natural, earthy glow.'

Grace, in her desire for retaliation, wasted no time. As Kat lounged with her legs stretched out before her, her sister gleefully smeared her face with the thick, soupy bog, all the while reciting her own version of a whimsical charm. 'This bog,' Grace proclaimed with a mischievous glint in her eye, her fingers moving deftly over Kat's forehead, 'enshrouds the hidden lore of Ireland's ancient past, and henceforth, your skin shall rival the silkiness of a newborn babe.'

The girls collapsed into further fits of laughter, their mirth echoing louder as they gazed upon Seamus's mower, now seemingly swallowed even deeper by the mud.

'We can't linger here all night,' Kat finally proclaimed, though reluctant to rise for fear of sinking further. Grace, undeterred, rose to her knees in mock appeal, her hands clasped as if she was praying. With a chuckle, Kat reminded her of their non-religious inclinations.

'Never mind, young Kat,' Grace responded, her voice echoing across the emptiness of the paddock. 'We're knee-deep in the holy land now, among the mischief-makers and muck-dwellers! Surely, someone will heed our call.'

It took considerable effort to extricate themselves from the bog, their boots squelching and sinking with each step as they trudged arm in arm, singing a tune while making their way to firmer ground.

'Jesus, Mary and Joseph,' Kat exclaimed upon finally reaching stable land. Fumbling in her coat pocket, she triumphantly retrieved her phone and raised it high. 'Behold, your prayers have been answered! My phone is here.'

Their younger brother, Ronan, picked them up and they returned for the mower the next day, towing it out with his car.

Seamus had not seen the humour in their prank and threatened to take action against them. He had always been a thorn in their side and they'd brushed his ranting off, thinking they had placated him with their promise to get it fixed and serviced. The mower was ancient and the repair man said that it was really only useful as a mode of transport, not to cut grass. He'd fixed it though and said it was like brand new and would now work better than it ever had. Even though they paid for the damages— which thankfully had not been too much—and bought him some beer, he still reported it to the police. The policeman was a friend of Seamus's and had made sure charges were laid. The fines had been small, but enough to irritate the two girls and make them hate Seamus even more. After that, Kat had also incurred a string of fines. She always seemed to be running behind schedule whenever she stayed at her Granny's. Balancing work and study led to frantic schedules, resulting in a heap of speeding fines. This also meant she lost her licence for a while.

Thank God Granny still drove and the two of them had a grand time together, rollicking all over the countryside with Granny behind the wheel. Granny had even come with her to university and sat in on a couple of the lectures. As she sat in the lecture hall in her green coat and matching hat, stockings and black shoes, Kat held her arm firmly, making sure she didn't raise her hand and ask any questions. It was one thing for an eighty-five-year-old lady to sneak in, but another if she started interrupting the lecturer.

If Granny had been alive today, she might have helped Kat forge a police check form. She'd always been good at writing, and was up for that sort of thing. Reference letters, school notes and even a false age identification card to get into a rock concert had been an easy project for someone who loved to copy other people's writing. Signatures and letters were her speciality. 'Full of shite I am,' Granny said. 'Tell me what you want, and I'll make it up for you. You just remember where you got your artistic ability from.'

But Granny wasn't here and this Lachie may not be so easily fooled. 'Ah, feck it,' she muttered, her voice carrying a hint of resignation. Pushing herself up from her seat, she strode over to the till, ready to tackle the night's takings. With a practised hand, she counted the notes and checked the receipts. She checked it again and again, but there was no escaping the truth. The till came up short, by a cool three hundred dollars. Same as last week.

Casting a glance around the deserted bar, she sighed. Only the distant clatter and banter from the kitchen hinted at any other presence. She reached for her phone, dialling reception, but received no answer. Her gaze fell upon a board at the back of the bar, adorned with a few scattered contact numbers. Among them, she spotted Lachie McIntosh's name and mobile number. Letting out a quiet groan, she punched in the digits, steeling herself for the conversation ahead.

It sounded like he hadn't even got back to his cabin when she rang and it only took him five minutes to return. 'I'm sorry to call you but there's only the kitchen staff left and this is not good.'

'How much.'

'Three hundred dollars. Same as last week.'

Her stomach lurched at the way he looked at her and then back at the money. It was clear to her that he thought she had taken it. He wore a pious look on his face, his lips pursed as he recounted the takings. She stood patiently next to him. 'You can search my bag if you like. I haven't stolen any money. I know it doesn't look good, but I'm no thief.'

He went to say something and then stopped. 'Look. Let's go right back over everything. Maybe it's an error in the receipts. For over an hour they checked the night's takings and the paperwork. He shook his head and turned to her. 'It's not as if the cash takings are huge. We only leave five hundred in the float in case we get a crowd who only pays cash.'

She stood with her arms crossed, with nothing more to say.

'Let's call it a night,' he finally said. 'Pack all this up and I'll go through it again in the morning.'

She said nothing again, only picked up her bag and took off her apron. 'Do you want to check my bag?' she offered. His face was stern and she felt as though she was kid at school again.

'No. Let's talk in the morning.'

When she followed him out and turned and walked towards her cabin, she felt like she was a million miles from anywhere. Miles from the mainland, miles from Galway and miles from her family. A sky covered in stars and a full moon lit her way and she stopped and looked up. Gazing at the heavens reminded her of the nights she had seen the northern lights in Galway. It was a rarity to see them there, but with the right conditions — no cloud and little light pollution — she had been lucky enough to witness the spectacular sight. Homesickness tugged at her and she took one last look, a shooting star that she made a wish on making her feel happier for a moment. Maybe she wasn't cut out for this travelling gig. Perhaps there was something easier to do other than working in bars and traipsing around the countryside. Perhaps she should find another job, or location.

The thought of seeing her family again was tempting, but the idea of having to avoid Seamus and Kiaran, or any of the other O'Rourkes, quickly brought her back to her senses. At least out here, at a ten thousand miles distance, she was far away from them. A bird made a noise in the bushes and she jumped, remembering to use her phone as a torch. Too often she had encountered snakes on the path. Ugh, Australia, she thought. A beautiful sunburnt land. As the poem said that Jock had given her, the written copy now stuck on her fridge by a purple thistle magnet he had also gifted her; it was a land of sweeping plains. She tried to remember the rest. Something about ragged mountain ranges, floods and rains and how could she forget, a sea of jewels.

Sounds bloody lovely, she thought, but it was also a land where everything was deadly. 'Don't swim in the ocean in summer,' her workmates at the Dingo Pub told her. 'There are stingers, some so small you can't see them and you don't know you're stung until you have a heart attack and die. Other jellyfish are so long and huge that they'll wrap around your body a hundred times and strangle you and then sting you until the pain kills you.

Watch out for the crocodiles that lay in wait to death roll you and hold your body under the water before they munch you into little pieces and then spit bits out for the huge crabs to feast on. Keep away from the sharks that are so big they'll swallow you whole, and stingrays with a tail that will stab you and then leave you to die in agony. Not to mention the lethal spiders, some as big as dinner plates, as well as gigantic cockroaches and centipedes longer than a ruler, that... well one bite and you're a goner.'

She had eventually found out that the cockroaches that were so big you could put a saddle on them, weren't deadly at all. That didn't make their presence any less frightening though and she had needed to get Jock to get rid of them when they were in her room. Jock was always sympathetic to her aversion to bugs and the other reptiles that seemed to be everywhere. He was Scottish and had the same dislike for anything that crawled along the ground. He was only twenty-four but he had travelled to more places than anyone she knew. 'Aye, me mammy wants me home, but I keep roamin'. I promised I'd come back for her birthday next year, but we'll see.'

A huge toad that stood in front of her, daring her to pass, made her jump again. She stepped sideways, then the other way, but the fat bulbous creature didn't budge. 'Shoo,' she said. 'Off with you.' Still no movement. The path she was on was the only way back to her cabin, so she picked up a stick and standing well back, threw it at the toad. The enormous ugly amphibian stared at her with black bulging eyes before jumping off into the bush. She shivered and took a deep breath, continuing on and praying she didn't encounter anything else on the path.

When she reached her cabin, she threw her bag down and locked the door behind her. Thank the stars for her own sanctuary. She resolved to rid herself of the lingering scent of the bar with a long, hot shower before retiring to bed. But first, there was another task she needed to do. She fired up her laptop, intent on submitting her application to get a police check. By tomorrow she could be looking for a new job, and having the paperwork in order would undoubtedly work in her favour. Even if her past held a few indiscretions, possessing the check would provide some semblance of reassurance. She could already hear Lachie's voice in her mind, querying whether she'd followed through. That's if he didn't sack her straight away.

Chapter Ten

Jasper was sitting having a drink at the front of the cabins when Lachie returned. He poured himself a wine and joined his brother. A few timber recliner chairs were scattered on the front lawn, which was the perfect place to sit and take in the view. Today the wind had all but gone and only a slight breeze filtered through the palm fronds above them. Bats called out as they flew from one tree to the other and a lonely curlew sounded from further down the beach.

Above them the sky was full of stars, the Milky Way stretching from one side to the other. 'Satellites,' he said to Jasper, pointing to a string of four bright lights tracking across the sky. 'Elon Musk's satellites.'

'Smart Bastard,' Jasper replied. 'Why didn't we think of that? He'll be the richest man on the planet.'

'I'm quite happy with surfboards, fishing gear and resorts. None of us are into the tech world. We're more in tune with nature and the ocean.'

Jasper crossed his feet and put his hands behind his

head. 'Bloody lucky we are. Lucky that Mum and Dad had their heads screwed on right with their businesses over the years. They said they had their ups and downs, but look at the result. From one surfboard to what we have now.'

'Yeah, lucky for them we're all interested in the business and have found our specialised niches. No one is really settled though,' Lachie mused. 'Well not you or I. The other three are still young. I often think I'd like to settle down. Sometimes I feel as though something is missing. I haven't really hit where I want to be.'

'Back with Prue?'

'What, where I want to be? Bloody hell, no. Definitely not. If anything, she made me run in the opposite direction from being in a relationship.'

Jasper sat up and looked at the night sky. 'You stick to your routine a bit too much for my liking. You need to let your hair down more often. Maybe you need to join me at the nightclubs and parties a bit more. There are always plenty of women there.'

Lachie leaned back in his chair. 'I'm over those nights. Anyway, I'm happy, just not one hundred percent though. Sometimes I think it would be nice to have someone to share everything with.'

'I get like that when I see Mum and Dad together,' Jasper said. 'They're still in love. Over thirty years and they still cuddle and act like they're teenagers having their first romance. How do you find that, Lachie? Where do you find it?'

'I'm not sure, but it's something special. Maybe one

day. Who knows. I'm surprised to hear you say that. I thought you loved the single life and playing the field.'

'Oh, believe me I do. It's just every so often, you know, you sort of wonder what it would be like to have a family of your own. Jees, listen to me. It's the moonlight that's making me crazy. What am I saying? No one will tie me down. I've got a lot I want to do and places I want to see. How did you get on at the restaurant tonight? What was the meal like?'

'Bloody delicious. I had a dozen oysters and then the chilli mud crab.' Lachie patted his stomach. 'That Italian chef is the best. I might pay him more to make sure he hangs around. He's worth his weight in gold. Sings opera as he cooks and seems to be in a world of his own, but his meals are delicious and there's nothing he can't cook. Someone will try and poach him for sure.'

'Make sure you do pay him more then. Always the problem with these workers. They all move on. How are those new ones going?'

'Well, I have a story. I watched the new girl Kat and the fella from Melbourne who we put on at the same time. Both were employed when I wasn't here. The Irish girl works really well, is super organised and has a good manner with the guests. I had thought once she settles in, she might be a candidate for some of the office jobs. The other bloke seems a bit lazy and is slow, but overall the place ran well. The trouble was, the till was out three hundred dollars again. She rang me just after I left and I went back and double checked, but it's definitely down three hundred.'

'What! How can that be? We don't take a large

amount of cash. You'll have to start leaving a smaller float. Do you think she rang you to make it look like she hadn't taken the money?'

'I'm not sure. She worked the till nearly all night. I hardly saw him near it. The other point is, that for some reason, Georgia didn't get a police check from her. I'm a bit suspicious. On the surface she seems good but ...'

'You didn't sack her, did you?'

'I didn't. I remained calm and made sure there was not even any hint of an accusation. It's hard to believe she would steal, because she doesn't look like the type of girl who would do that. But we've been caught before.'

'I'm really glad you didn't sack her.'

'Why?'

'The Swedish girls rang me this afternoon. Two of them are leaving on the boat tomorrow. Travelling up to Cairns to work on the islands up there for a bit.'

Lachie sat upright. 'Jees, we'll be down two workers. I know they love to travel, but I wish they'd work for longer. Maybe we could employ some local people.'

'I'm not sure. We tried that before and didn't get much of a response. They can earn way more out at the mines. You can't really blame them. But if you do decide to sack Kat, maybe wait until we get some others in. Otherwise, you and I'll be serving drinks and waiting on tables!'

Chapter Eleven

The front door of the office was wide open and Kat walked in with confidence, ready to face whatever was to come. She had slept solidly last night. Being on her feet all night, together with the constant flow of work and the stress of the till being out, had sent her into a deep sleep. Sometimes she coped better when things were disordered. Chaos was her family's middle name and when everything ran smoothly it almost felt like something was going to go wrong.

Now she had to worry about a police check, and a boss who may or may not, have overheard her private conversation; and to add to it all, money missing from the till. Again. Never a dull moment.

This morning she had time off and it was a grand change not to be donning the typical black and white garb mandated for tending the bar and restaurant. The resort provided polo shirts emblazoned with their company's crest, or you could also choose a white collared shirt, complete with the emblem of the resort embroidered on the pocket. However, today she wore a short floral frock, her feet relaxed in a pair of thongs. When she first arrived in Australia, she adamantly swore she wouldn't be caught dead in either crocs or thongs. They looked disgusting and hardly met her standards for proper footwear. However, it didn't take long for the allure of comfort and practicality to outweigh her initial reservations. Working in locations near the beach, she quickly found them to be indispensable staples in her wardrobe.

This morning she decided to go to Lachie, rather than wait for him to come to her. He was sitting behind a desk, typing on the computer when she came to stand in front of him.

She didn't wait for him to look up, instead getting straight into what she had come for. 'Good morning. I wondered if you found where the shortfall in the till was?'

He looked up, a hint of surprise on his face. 'Good morning. No. I haven't found it. Don't worry about it. I'll talk to Mal today and see if he has any ideas how the two of you managed to be out.'

'Mal's off on two days leave. He left for Airlie on the boat this morning.'

'I'll ring him then. It's highly unusual to be out that much, and for two weeks in a row. Don't worry about it though, just continue on with your job.'

She raised her eyebrows. No mention of the police check. 'Righto. Thank you.'

* * *

Lachie finished up what he was doing and leaned back in his chair. This Kat girl was an enigma. On the one hand she appeared honest and professional, but on the other to hear her talk on the phone to her sister was a different story. Someone else came in through the door and he looked up to see the three men who had sat with him last night.

'Morning Lachie. Good to see you working,' one of them called Ted said.

'Hope you had a good night and didn't lose too much money,' Lachie quipped.

One of the others, Pete, added. 'Sorry to come and bother you, but there's been a theft. Ted's wallet and mine were stolen from our rooms while we were in Scott's room playing cards last night. Just the wallets and some loose cash that was lying on the dresser. On a better note, your young gardener, Jock, joined us for our card game. Crafty Scotsman, he cleaned us all up. Bloody good card player.'

Lachie jumped up. 'What? Nothing ever gets stolen around here.'

'Well, we've spent all morning on the phone cancelling cards and reporting the theft. Seems like someone has already used Ted's card in Airlie Beach this morning. Bought themselves breakfast and went to the pub as soon as it opened. No doubt they're long gone, but the police are onto it anyway.'

The men talked and Lachie apologised further. 'Our till has been short two weeks in a row. While I was away, they hired a fella called Mal who's from Melbourne. No police checks were done. He also left for a couple of days break this morning. You can bet your life it's him. No doubt he won't return.'

'Sounds like it. Don't worry, we've had similar problems at our places and the police usually locate them. Good workers are hard to find.'

'I've got two Swedish girls leaving today. They only came in early this morning to let me know. They cleaned in the kitchen until late last night so it can't have been them, plus they're not leaving until later this afternoon. As far as I know, this Mal bloke is the only one who left this morning. He would have got a lift over with one of the local boys. They were tied up at the jetty early this morning and looking for a fare over. They make a bit of extra cash with some of our staff and holidaymakers.'

* * *

Lachie remained by the window, long after the men had left, his gaze fixed on the vast expanse of the ocean. Gratitude flooded his thoughts. Thank the heavens he hadn't jumped straight to accusing the Irish girl. There had been a moment, a fleeting temptation, but his years of managing staff had taught him the value of prudence. It was important to gather all the facts before any accusations are made. A sigh of relief escaped him; she was not a thief, at least not in his establishment. She lacked the telltale signs of deception or dishonesty. Whatever her history, she had not been responsible for the thefts here at the resort.

* * *

Over the next month, Lachie was kept busy catching up on office work that was left over from when he had been away. Georgia usually kept things up to date in his absence, but she was going through some health problems and now that he was back to manage everything, he had given her a couple of months off to recover. That meant he needed to be in the office most days, however there was still time for fishing and going out in the boat.

Finding new staff to cover the two who had left had also taken time and, as suspected, Mal had not returned. By the end of November everything seemed to be ticking along as it should be and with the wet season approaching, the resort was quieter than it had been during the previous months. Being in the office most of the time he had not run into Kat much. Today however, she walked in with a document in her hand. 'Could I please see you for a moment?' she asked. Once again, he noticed that she never smiled. What he would give to even see just a flicker of one on her face.

'Sure, sure. Take a seat. I'm just about to finish up for the day. It's a good day for snorkelling. I thought I'd go out on the small reef out the front here. Have you been out there much?'

She sat down, her back straight and the usual nonchalant look on her face. 'I try not to go out in the sun. I've read about the melanomas you get from living here. I don't want to add another fatal thing to my list from living in Australia.'

'We do have the highest rate of skin cancer in the world. But that's the beauty of the place, the outdoors. You need to learn to live with it.'

She didn't reply, and he shuffled uncomfortably in his seat. She had been so talkative and energetic when he first heard her on the phone to her sister. Did he make her feel awkward? He tried to engage her in conversation. 'You should go out to the reef one day. It's like nothing you've ever seen before. The colours of the fish, the coral and the clarity of the water on a good day. Have you ever snorkelled?'

'No. They tell me there are plenty of sharks out there.'

He laughed, hoping for some sort of joyful response in return. 'The sharks leave you alone. All the years I've been out there, I haven't been eaten yet. Snorkelling around the islands and on the reefs is like nothing else. It's not much good coming to these places if you don't try some of the activities.'

She pulled a face, a condescending look that made him stop talking about what she should get out and do. 'I've got my police check for you,' she said.

'Right. That's good. I can add your form to my files.' He held out his hand but she didn't offer the report to him.'

'Before I hand this over, I'd like to talk to you about a couple of instances that are listed on here that happened over the previous years back home. You may be used to workers with a clean slate but not everyone is perfect.'

Finally, he thought, he would find out her background and maybe get to the bottom of the conversation he had overheard. 'Okay. Tell me. You have my full attention.'

She twisted her mouth and he couldn't help but look

at her lips. There was something about her that he liked. A lot. Damn, she was attractive. From her red hair and vivid eyes, down to her tiny waist and slender legs. Her personality however, didn't draw him in as much as how she looked, which he knew was not a good sign. If only she would loosen up a bit and smile, or even make a joke. She needed to have fun. He was a fun guy. Why was she so serious?'

Ignoring his scrutiny, she lay the piece of paper on the table so that it faced him. Her hands were small and he noticed she bit her nails. When she pointed to what she wanted him to see though, she was confident and assured. 'There are a couple of misdemeanours on here that really, well, really they're nothing. They might look bad, but in the big scheme of things they're hardly worth talking about. I could probably get them wiped off my record but I can't be bothered.'

'Okay, maybe just let me read it.'

'I'd like to tell you first what happened. It's a bit hard to tell from what's written on here. Like I said it's a big fuss over nothing. This one here,' she pointed to the writing, 'well, my sister and I may have stolen my cousin's ride-on mower one night and got it stuck in the bog. He hates my family, especially me, and he made sure we were both charged. I'm not sure about here, but in our country, this sort of thing sticks on your police record. These other offences are all speeding charges. I have a habit of driving fast on country roads, especially when I'm running late. It looks like a long list, but really it's not that bad. I'm not a criminal. I'm honest and you won't find a better worker.'

Picking up the document he looked over it, trying to keep from laughing. 'Is that it?'

Her eyebrows lowered. 'Yes. I can't change the past. It is what it is.'

Now he laughed aloud. 'You know you should loosen up a bit. How old are you? Twenty-eight? I'm sure I read that in your file. For someone so young you seem to carry the weight of the world on your shoulders. Be happy. Go out and have some fun. Go diving and live on the edge a bit. Otherwise, those frown lines on your forehead will become permanent. All work and no play are not a good way to live.'

When she stood up and glared at him, he held out his hand for her to shake. 'Friends. Please. If you're going to work for me, we need to be amicable.'

She did not offer her hand back. 'I could say so much, Mr McIntosh. But I choose not to because I want to keep my job. Good day.'

Chapter Twelve

The sight of her cabin was a welcome relief and she barged through the front door with a mixture of frustration and defiance before slamming it shut behind her. How dare he! How dare he presume to tell her how to live and to be happy. He couldn't possibly comprehend the struggle of scraping by on meagre wages while yearning for the comfort of home and family. Did he know the ache of grieving for a granny who was not even cold in the ground and who had been more than just family and a guiding light in her life? Could he understand the longing for the familiar sights, sounds, and scents of a quaint Irish village perched upon the rugged cliffs of the wild Atlantic? What right did he have to pass judgment? Him, with his wealth and good looks, had likely never known a day of hardship or longing. No doubt everything had been handed to him on a silver platter, nor would he have had to fight for what he desired. She seethed with indignation at the thought of his privileged existence, contrasting sharply with her own struggles and aspirations.

Throwing herself on her bed she buried her face in her pillow, the tears wetting the fabric. How she yearned for home, her heart heavy with longing. The ache of homesickness consumed her, a relentless desire for the familiar comforts. She yearned for loved ones, the warmth of her mother's cooking, and the laughter of old friends. What she would give to have been in the streets of Galway, singing along with Grace and hundreds of others. How she would love to see the typical brawl or chaotic calamity that usually happened at the pub or some other significant event like a wedding, birthday or christening.

Sighing, she thought how she could just ring up and book a plane ticket home. It was simple. Book, pay and fly. That exit plan was not going to happen though. She had not counted on being homesick, but to leave now would be to admit defeat in the face of her talk of wanting to be independent and adventurous. To return would also throw her into the path of Seamus and Kiaran and that was the last thing she wanted.

In her mind she listed all the things, other than work, that she had done since she arrived. Maybe Lachie McIntosh was right. She ran her hand across her forehead. Did she have wrinkles on her skin? Her mother always told her she frowned too much. Working and just sitting around in her cabin gave her too much time to think and miss everything and everyone. Perhaps she should throw caution to the wind and forget about the dangers of the sun and the million hazards that could kill you here in

Australia. Maybe she did need to get out and do something just for fun.

* * *

For the next week Lachie couldn't concentrate on his work. The searing eyes of Kat MacCullagh filled his thoughts and by the middle of the following week, he found himself walking towards her cabin. He knew from the roster that it was her day off. He also was taking a break today and, although he had plenty to keep him occupied, he was tired of pushing thoughts of her from his mind.

When he approached the cabin he noticed the front door was open. He called out, 'Hello. Is anyone home?'

Her voice sounded from out the back. 'Yes, come through.'

He had forgotten how small the workers' cabins were, although the space was probably comfortable for one person. The lounge and kitchen were all in one, with a bedroom and bathroom off to one side. A small courtyard out the back was surrounded by rainforest, the coolest place to sit on a summer's day.

Her back was to him and she continued with what she was doing. Positioned before an easel, she exuded an air of purpose, the canvas sitting neatly on the sturdy wooden frame. It was obviously a work in progress and he stood silently, watching her movements.

'Just a sec,' she said, 'I just want to finish this part.' Her brush danced across the surface, breathing life into the scene unfolding before her and he watched in awe as the colours on her brush brought life to the image.

The painting depicted the rainforest backdrop behind the workers' cabins, their courtyards serving as sanctuaries from the sweltering summer heat. Beyond the paved areas lay a lush embrace of towering trees and ferns, their presence casting a welcome shade and a noticeable drop in temperature. Thick foliage enveloped the perimeter, with only a few winding tracks daring to venture towards the mountains beyond. The contrast of tropical forest against the island's coastal beauty was a rare sight, and she had only seen it in a few select pockets of the Whitsundays.

With each stroke of her brush, she masterfully captured the essence of the canopy's rich shades of green, and the colours intertwined on her canvas, echoing the freshness that infused the air. She leaned back and tilted her head to the side, perusing her work. Suddenly she must have remembered that someone had called out and she turned around. Their eyes locked and he watched as her eyes widened.

'Oh, it's you. I thought it was one of the other workers,' she said. 'They said they would drop in my new work shirts.'

'No, it's only me,' he replied as he walked towards her. His eyes moved to the painting. 'That's good. Really good,' he remarked, drawing nearer to examine the intricacies that made up the picture. 'The colours, the mood, the coolness of the rainforest, you've captured it perfectly. Is this what you do in your spare time?'

She turned back to the painting and swept her brush

across the sky, her hand moving with practised ease to infuse the clouds with texture. 'I've got a degree in fine arts, as you might have gathered from your thorough examination of my resume.'

He ignored her subtle jab as he continued to watch her paint. 'Do you sell your work?'

'No. this is the first one I've done since I've been in Australia. The canvas and paints are expensive, therefore this one is small. Usually, I like to do much larger pieces.' She looked up at him as she placed her brush down and wiped her hands with a cloth. 'What can I do for you? Did you have something to ask me? My shifts are full so I'm not sure I can fit any more in.'

Clearing his throat, he was taken aback by an unexpected surge of nervousness. Despite his attempts to remain composed, he found himself captivated. She sat before him in a simple, loose cotton dress, barefoot and entirely at ease. Today her hair was out and cascaded freely around her face in long untamed strands. It was her eyes though that intrigued him. Blue and like the colour of the ocean, they held his as he stared at her. Although her gaze was intense there was a hint of vulnerability that tugged at his heartstrings. He couldn't work out if she was uneasy in his presence, or simply wasn't interested in talking to him. A tangible tension hung in the air, enhanced by the fact that her face seemed to lack the provision to smile.

With nothing to lose, except perhaps an employee, he decided to dive in and take the risk. 'I wanted to see if you'd like to come to the reef with me today. I'm taking the boat out in half an hour or so, while it's not too hot. I know it's short notice but you don't need to bring anything. Maybe just togs and a towel and make sure you have a hat. I have food and drinks on the boat. It's a magical day and the water is calm. You really should see what's out there.'

He could tell she was taken aback and it took her a while to answer. 'I wasn't expecting that.' Her eyes flitted around and he realised she was at a loss for what to say. Eventually she cleared her throat and looked back at him. 'What about the sharks?'

Smiling at her, he tried to ease her fears. 'You don't have to go in the water if you don't want. You can sit in the shade of the canopy and just look from the boat. It'll be a great day out on the water today. The weather is perfect. You really shouldn't miss seeing out there while it's at its best.'

She wiped her hands again, and thought for a while. 'Do you know what? I will. I will come with you. Yes okay. Give me a few minutes and I'll get some stuff together.'

* * *

As she hurried about the cabin, gathering bits and bobs and pondering what to take along, she found herself muttering under her breath, wondering what in the name of all that's holy had possessed her. 'Sharks, sunburn, and stuck with the boss. What on earth am I at?' Yet, casting a glance at the blue sky outside, she couldn't shake the feeling of his sincerity, as if he truly wanted her company, to show her what he obviously loved. 'Sure, maybe it's not as bad as I'm making it out to be,' she mused aloud. 'I might as well go.'

Lachie waited out in front of her cabin. She had changed into shorts and a singlet top, lathered herself with sunscreen and smothered her face in zinc. Holding tight to her long-sleeved shirt and a white hat decorated with blue stitching that had been her granny's, she shut the cabin door behind her. A rush of excitement coursed through her, her gaze lifting to the sky that was a canvas of the bluest hue she had ever seen.

'We don't get skies like that in Ireland,' she said to Lachie as she came up behind him. 'Not quite that blue.'

'From memory, the skies are more grey than blue.'

'Oh, so you've been there?'

'Yes, a couple of times. I spent five years overseas, backpacking and working at different places, much like you are. I know what it's like to live from day to day and be in low-paid jobs. Mind you I wouldn't swap those experiences for anything. My brother, Jasper and I went together sometimes, but other times I travelled alone. We were both determined to stand on our own two feet and not rely on any help from home. Best thing we ever did. Now we're both happy to stay in Australia and work in the family business.'

Neither talked as they walked towards the jetty where Lachie's boat was tied up. When he held out his hand to help her onto the boat, she took it, holding tight as she stepped onto the deck. It wasn't a huge boat but she could tell it was fairly new and probably very expensive going by the polished timbers, controls and glossy sides. It was called, *Evie*. 'That's my mum's name,' he told her. 'The boat belongs to the business, but when Mum's up here she uses it for fishing and going back and forth to Airlie.'

'Your mum fishes?'

'Yes. She always has. We own a bait and tackle shop, down south on Stradbroke Island. That shop is her baby. She's run it for over thirty years.'

'You have an interesting family.'

'Don't you? I thought Irish families were known for their banter and arguing, but deep down, as close-knit as any could be.'

'That's a fair assumption,' she said. 'I have two younger sisters, Grace and Eileen, and a baby brother, Ronan. He's a fisherman in between his studies. He'd love it out here.'

'We all love the ocean. Your family sounds similar to mine.'

For a split second he thought he saw the glimmer of a smile, but it was quickly gone. 'Oh, believe me, my family would be nothing like yours. We live in a house in Galway with only just enough room for all of us. Dad works on the railways, and Mum's a cleaner at the post office. Nothing has come easy, but we don't complain. It's been a grand life so far and we've managed for three of us to go to university. We live in chaos most of the time; we bitch, we fight and we love, but we stick together.'

'And now you're seeing the world.'

'I am.'

Chapter Thirteen

As they cruised away from the island Lachie thought about where he would go. There was a small reef not too far out that would be perfect, considering it was Kat's first time snorkelling. Before long he brought the boat to a halt. Now that he had Kat in the boat, he wanted to make sure she got to see the amazing sights the Whitsundays could offer. And what a day for it, he thought as he looked out across the ocean. Small waves lapped languidly on the side of the boat and a gentle swell rippled from the east, causing very little movement. The water was glassy and out further, bait fish flicked on the surface, their splashing easily visible in the calm expanse.

Gazing towards the north, larger islands emerged, their slopes covered in dark foliage that today appeared tinted in shades of blue mirroring the clear sky. The sun's glow shimmered on the water, blurring the line where the horizon embraced the sea. 'We couldn't have asked for better weather,' he said as he steered towards where he wanted to go.

After a brief pause to make sure he was on the spot, he dropped anchor, the metallic clatter echoing briefly before settling into the seabed. With the push of another button, he erected the canopy, providing welcome shade against the already intense morning sun. Despite the early hour, the sun's rays were beginning to assert their warmth, casting the promise of a scorching day ahead in the cloudless sky.

Kat wore a long-sleeved shirt over her shorts and top and although her legs were bare, he could see they had been lathered with sunscreen. Her hat was floppy and she had to hold it with her hands to keep it from flying away. 'You need a good hat, or a cap for coming out on a boat. That one will end up in the drink.' He held out his hand and took it from her, placing it safely on a shelf under the seats. 'You won't need it now anyway. I thought we could snorkel first and then have something to eat.'

She stared at him without speaking.

'C'mon,' he said. 'I promise you're safe with me. The water is so clear today you can see anything coming from a mile away.'

'I'll get sunburnt.'

He pulled out a wetsuit from a box that held a variety of diving gear. 'This should fit you. That way you don't have to worry about sunburn or stingers.' She thought for a while before standing up. 'Okay. Let's do this. If this is my last day on earth, then so be it.'

Laughing loudly, he held the wetsuit out to her.

'Don't be so dramatic. The water is three feet deep out here. Nothing is going to happen. Best to wear wetsuits at this time of the year though.'

He went to the back of the boat to get some of the gear they needed. When he returned, she was trying to pull her wetsuit up over her bikinis. 'Ready?' he asked.

She scowled and wiggled her body to manoeuvre into the neoprene suit. 'Sure. Sure,' she replied. 'Give me a minute.'

* * *

Finally, she was ready, and Lachie jumped into the water first, giving her instructions and a demonstration on how to breathe through the snorkel and what to do once she got in the water. When she put her legs over the side of the boat, he helped her put on her flippers, laughing at the worried look on her face. 'You only live once, young Kat. Now jump in.'

Easing slowly into the water, she relaxed a little when he held out his hand and stood with her on the white sand underfoot. He showed her again how to breathe slowly and deeply through the snorkel and then pointed to where they would go. 'We'll take it slow and I promise I won't let go of you. Don't stand on any structures. When we stand up, it will be on the sandy areas only because we don't want to damage the coral. There are a few sandy patches along here in shallow water. We'll go into slightly deeper water along the edge of the reef and then when you're moving okay, we'll swim over the top of the reef.

She nodded and he sensed her nervousness. Giving her a reassuring grin, he pulled her into the water and they started swimming towards the reef. It didn't take her long to settle in with her breathing and she swam alongside him, quickly pointing out fish and some coral below. It was a mesmerising underwater world that was teeming with life and he hoped once she was immersed in the sights around them, she would forget her nerves.

She squeezed his hand when a school of tropical fish darted past, their neon colours bright in the clear water. He nodded and steered her towards the larger structures that lay not far below the surface.

As they glided over the myriad structures that rose up from the sea floor, they were surrounded by a kaleidoscope of colours; a mosaic of coral gardens, patterned with intricate designs and filled with a multitude of brightly coloured fish. He pointed out a large maori wrasse not too far in front of them. The fish's body was covered in vibrant colours, a mixture of green, blue and purple hues, with an elaborate maze-like pattern on its head. Kat's eyes widened beneath her goggles as she stared at the fish now swimming straight towards them. Lachie reassuringly squeezed her hand and gave her the thumbs up. They stayed stationary as the fish swam near them, its thick fleshy lip and prominent bump on its forehead making it an interesting sight in amongst the smaller fish that swam in schools around them.

Before long they reached a sandy seabed and they both stood and removed their snorkels for a moment. He pointed to a large turtle that paddled beside them, its huge shell just above the surface of the water, its flippers pushing the water back in a swirl behind its body. It looked at them and made a swooshing noise, before diving a little lower and skimming over the sandy bottom.

Kat watched the turtle until it swam out of sight. The look on her face was one of wonder and he knew that feeling; the amazement of the first time you saw an underwater garden, the moving feast of colour and marine life pushing everything else in your life to the side.

After a while they put their snorkelling gear back on and headed towards the boat. On the way back they swam beside bright clusters of coral with sea plants growing in between that moved with the currents that ebbed back and forth. A rocky section covered in bright anemones gave them another spectacular sight and they stopped to watch the soft-bodied sea animals that looked like massive flowers, swaying in the current. Kat squeezed his hand and shook her head in excitement when two small fish emerged from within the strands of the anemone. The fish were the popular clown fish made famous by the movie, *Finding Nemo*. A smile stretched across her face and he was over the moon that she was obviously having a great time.

He pulled on her hand as the small fish disappeared back within the anemones. They had stayed in the water for a lot longer than he had anticipated and his stomach was growling for food.

* * *

The wetsuit was too uncomfortable to leave on and she was keen to get back into her shorts and singlet. As she struggled to remove the wet rubber outfit which clung to her body like a suction cap, her mind whirled, and she knew she hadn't stopped talking since they got out of the water. She couldn't help it though. Her adrenaline was pumping and her skin tingled from the cool of the water as well as the aftermath of the experience. 'That turtle. It came so close. I swear to God, it looked me in the eye and said, you're a long way from Galway Bay. What are you doing here? And the colours of the fish, the coral, the plant-like growth sprouting in and around the reef. It's incredible. Wait until I tell them back home. It's like nothing I've ever seen before. I felt as though I was in a David Attenborough documentary.'

He came towards her, his hair wet and hanging on his shoulders. She noticed his chest, broad, toned, and tanned like the rest of his body. He'd quickly got his wetsuit off. Now he offered to help her. 'They're tricky sometimes. Do you need a hand to get that off?' he asked.

Pulling hard on the sleeves she tried to pull the suit off. 'And to see two Nemo fish. So close. And that huge fish with the lump on its head. Lordy be, the colours. I wish I could paint them. What a day. My life is complete.' She struggled, trying to wriggle out of the suit. 'Thank you. I'm stuck. Some help would be grand.'

She shivered a little and calmed down, her chatter silent when she felt his hands on her back. The zipper ran down the back of the suit and he unzipped it to just above her bottom. Now as he helped her push the thick material away from her shoulders and roll it down her body, her stomach flipped. He had strong hands and the fact that she only had bikinis on underneath was not helping. When there was only the part left on her ankles to go, she sat down on the seat and put her legs up while he pulled the remaining parts of the wetsuit from her body.

'That was fun,' he said, a cheeky grin on his face. 'It's not every day I get to rip a wetsuit from a beautiful red-haired young lady.'

'My hair isn't red. The colour is called cinnamon. My sister Grace has red hair. Flaming red to match her temper which is just a tad worse than mine.'

She could feel his eyes on her body. 'You better put that shirt on,' he said. 'The sun's hot. I would normally have come out to this reef earlier in the day, but it took me a while to work up the courage to come and ask you to join me. I was worried you would say no.'

She pulled her shirt over her head and slipped her shorts back on. 'I nearly did.'

'What made you change your mind?'

Thinking for a while, she looked up at him and smiled. 'It was the way you asked. I felt as if a friend was asking me to go somewhere.'

Lachie didn't speak for a while. He wanted to make sure his voice didn't betray how he was feeling. Her smile, a little crooked, but so inviting was hard to drag his eyes away from. She had white teeth, not perfect, but with eye teeth that jutted out ever so slightly giving her a mischievous look. Had she fallen from heaven? He looked again but she had turned to look out further. Suddenly she jumped up and down and grabbed his arm. 'Look over there. Something just came out of the water. It's a big dark shape.'

He looked out towards where she was pointing. 'It's a manta ray. A big one by the looks of it. He might come over here.'

The massive fish swam towards them, diving under the boat's hull when it neared. They both darted to the other side of the boat, peering at its expansive wings that glided through the clear water. A sleek body glistened under the dappled sunlight filtering through the water's surface and its huge form cast a shadow that danced playfully along the seabed below. They watched it until it dove down into the deeper water further out, its body now hidden beneath the waves.

She looked at him and shook her head as if she didn't believe what she had seen. 'Saints preserve us! Did you see the size of that? It was like something out of a fairy tale. I've never seen anything like it!'

He didn't say what he wanted and that was, that her smile was like something out of a fairy tale. Instead, he just stared, enjoying the excitement written on her face.

* * *

A picnic lunch that Lachie had the kitchen staff prepare, was a perfect way to complete the trip. They had worked up an appetite and the sandwiches and soft drinks quickly disappeared as they sat and talked about what they'd experienced on and around the reef. Kat finished eating and lay back in the shade, looking up at the sky. 'I don't want to go back in. This is the most beautiful place in the world.'

'Sorry, it was time to call it a day. There's work for both of us tomorrow. You know I'm surprised you haven't applied for the front desk job that's going. Leanna is leaving and we haven't had much interest. I thought you might prefer that job. Instead of bar work and cleaning.'

She sat up quickly. 'Are you serious? Really. Do you think I could do that job? I never applied because I didn't think you would consider me. I don't have experience in that type of work and I've only done bar and kitchen work, both in Australia and before I came here. Leanna is so, you know, well-groomed and efficient looking.'

'I've seen you work. You'd pick the job up easily. Are you interested?'

'Yes, sure I'm interested! I would love to do that job. It would be good to do something different. Do you get a uniform though, because I have hardly any good clothes?'

Laughing, he steered around a cluster of rocks that were jutting out of the water. 'Of course, you get supplied with a uniform. I wouldn't worry that you haven't experience in that type of work. Most of the girls who did that job previously hadn't knowledge of that sort of work either. As long as you have good people skills, which you do, you'll be fine. The others soon worked out what to do and I'll be around to help if needed. Jasper also knows how everything works. We've never had problems with anyone in that role. It's just that they keep travelling and moving on. You're a quick learner. Trial the role this week if you like. Leanna is there for another four days so she can train you and see if you're going to like it. If you do, you can slot straight into the position. I'm interviewing some other people for bar work and cleaning this week, so that will fill the gap when you swap over.'

'Are you kidding me? You're just going to give me the job?'

'Sure. Why not. I'll have a look, but I know the wage is more than what you you'd be getting at the moment.'

'You're joking. More money. New uniforms. You've made my day. A Nemo fish and a new job!'

Lachie had thought of Kat for the job a couple of days before. A notice had been put up and staff made aware of the vacancy, but no one had applied. She hadn't shown any interest which had surprised him. Thank goodness he'd asked her today. She'd be perfect for the role.

He slowed the boat. 'Look out there. Dolphins. Lots of them.'

Turning the motor off he let the boat drift, the silence adding to the surreal sight of a dozen or so dolphins diving in and out of the placid waters quite close to where they were. 'They're feeding on a school of fish. See the water frothing and splashing around them?'

When she didn't answer, he turned to look at her. Her eyes were full of tears and she held her hand over her mouth. When she put her hand down, he once again got a look at the world's best smile. 'I'm speechless,' she uttered. 'Wait until I tell them back home. Dolphins! And so close.'

'At different times of the year, when you come out here, you'll also see whales. I never tire of watching them, or the dolphins. Where I come from down south, Stradbroke Island, is also renowned for dolphins and whales. I've grown up watching them. But each time I see them is like the first time.'

'We do get dolphins and sometimes Minke Whales in Galway Bay. I've been out on the water with my brother, and a dozen or so dolphins swam alongside the boat. They were so quick and kept pace with us. Some of them leapt up in the air and others rode the bow waves. Like today. I won't ever forget it.'

* * *

By the time they tied up to the jetty and cleaned the boat, it was well after two o'clock. 'I really didn't think we'd be out there for that long,' Lachie said, 'I hope you didn't get too much sun.'

She held her hand out for him to help her out. 'I don't care. I don't care if I'm red as a lobster tomorrow or if I get covered in sunspots. The sunburn would be worth it. Thank you. Thank you so much, Lachie.' She smiled at him again.

'Thank you for smiling. I was starting to wonder if you did. It was my pleasure to show you the reef. It's our front and back yard and you should make the most of it. We can go out snorkelling again if you want. Now, don't forget about the reception job. I'll see you tomorrow afternoon around three at the front desk for a trial run with the afternoon shift. We'll see how you go and, if you think you'll like it, the job's yours.'

Chapter Fourteen

Of course, she loved the reception job. Who wouldn't? She got to dress up, wear a smart uniform with the name of the resort emblazoned on the front and sit in an air-conditioned area, acting all fancy and as if she had worked on the island forever. It would be her job to not only book the guests in and out, to cater to any needs or questions, but also to ensure the foyer and front desk area were tidy and organised. A brochure stand that told guests what to see and do in the area needed to be well-stacked, and a water bubbler had to be kept filled. There was a list of other admin type jobs, as well as replying to emails and phone calls. There was plenty to keep her busy.

On her days off, Lachie took her snorkelling. Each time they went to a different spot and each time she saw something different. She was becoming more and more relaxed in the water and now couldn't imagine not spending some time each week under or in the water. A couple of times they had seen small reef sharks, but

Lachie had shooed them away and assured her they were harmless.

Working in the reception role meant she no longer needed to work late at night. That left more time for herself, so she bought new paints and brushes the next time she was in Airlie Beach. She also bought herself some new clothes, the extra money with the new position coming in handy. Each Saturday morning she rang home and spoke to her mum and dad. They were going well but missed her terribly. She was also missing all of them, but it was winter for them and the short days and cold nights, along with the incessant rain they'd had in Galway over the last month, did not lure her into wanting to return home. Her mother, reminded her that she wasn't staying in Australia forever. 'Don't forget this is just a holiday. Don't you get any ideas of staying. You said you'd work for a year or maybe just a bit longer than a year.'

'I might stay for a bit longer than I thought, Mum. The government has changed the rules and I can work here for longer than what you used to be able to. They lost a lot of international workers with Covid, and the young people who fill all the roles that nobody else here seems to want, haven't come back in the numbers that are needed. Everywhere is screaming out for workers and I do love the weather here also. I'll just take each month as it comes.'

Now that she had found herself a good role at work, with a bit more coin in her pocket, she'd well and truly settled into island life. And to top it off, Lachie had taken her out in the boat every week. Some of the barriers she had put up at the start, slid a little, and now she wasn't afraid to let her true personality show. Back home she was known for her temper, an obstinate nature, and often way too much partying. She had declared when she came to Australia that she would try and conceal those traits. It would be an opportunity to reinvent herself and try not to be so impulsive or spontaneous. Those behaviours had sometimes got her into trouble in the past.

However, her ideas of keeping to herself and not socialising too much were starting to slip. Island life was slow, relaxing and without any worries. Everyone was friendly and mainly just out for a good time. Now that she had settled into a bit of a routine, there was plenty of time for fun and adventurous activities.

One night she even found herself agreeing to attend a small gathering that Jasper had organised. It was a gathering on the lawn out the front of his cabin and the theme was Hawaiian. She tagged along with the other girls from work, surprising herself that she had even agreed to dress up in a hula skirt and bikini top. As she lathered herself with a cream that Jock had kindly provided to ward off the pesky midges and mosquitoes, she couldn't help but notice the hint of a tan gracing her once-pale complexion. Bejesus, she mused. Who would have ever reckoned she'd be sporting a tan?

* * *

At least she was dressed for the conditions because the weather was downright sultry. With only a week to go until Christmas, she was informed that such conditions were par for the course. Before long, she encountered yet another unfamiliar term and sensation: humidity. Every hour, day and night alike, the air hung heavy and thick with moisture. Sweat became an unwelcome companion unless she sought refuge in air conditioning. The weather showed no mercy, and tonight, despite a gentle breeze wafting across the lawn, the oppressive air bore down upon her. She tipped back a cold beer, starting to comprehend why folks in the tropics took to the drink so readily.

'First time I've seen you have a beer,' Lachie said as he came up and stood beside her.

'I've never been so hot in my life. Nice shirt,' she said, eyeing him up and down.

'Jasper made me wear it. I think it's an old one of Dad's; an authentic bright pink Hawaiian shirt from the eighties.'

'It suits you. You look as though you could fit into that era.'

'I'm not sure if that's a compliment or not. But I'll take it as one.'

Jasper came up behind them and grabbed them both around the waist. He was tipsy and she giggled as he tickled her. Over the past couple of months, she had come to know Lachie and Jasper well, and now considered them to be good friends. Jasper reminded her of her sister Grace. Full of charm and life, but he drank too much and would party until the sun came up. Jock soon joined them and she hugged him, both of them laughing at each other's getup. He had become like a younger brother and if anyone understood what it was to be so far from home, it was Jock. Today he wore a hula skirt over his shorts, his skinny legs poking out from underneath. He had made a bikini out of coconuts and when she looked him up and down he wiggled his hips and moved his arms in the air. 'Wait until me mammy sees the photos. She'll have kittens. Her only son in a skirt and bikini.'

Soon, everyone was either sprawled out on the grass, or dancing under the palm trees to the music Jasper had playing. It was eighties music and the tunes reminded Kat of her mum and dad. 'You look like you're a million miles away,' Lachie quipped as he sat on the grass next to her. 'Jasper loves his music.'

'He has a good collection of songs,' she replied. 'You're right. I was a long way away. I'm thinking about when I was a teenager. Music was always playing in our house and, along with my brothers and sisters, we'd while away hours spinning our parents' collection of records. The music was always blaring, perfect for a lively jig on the timber floors.'

She thought about how their eager hands often skipped tracks or replayed tunes, adding more scratches to the well-loved vinyl. 'Does your family like music?' she asked.

'Yes. It was much the same. The record player and all the old records Mum and Dad kept for years. Cat Stevens, and Simon and Garfunkel. Bluesy music and lots of rock'n'roll.'

She laughed.

'What's funny?' he asked.

'Oh, I was just remembering times we had. I miss home something fierce, you know. We live in a small house so we do everything together. I was thinking about a night when my sister Grace and I were up on the kitchen table doing a little jig. My mum would have a fit if she found us up there dancing and singing. We were wearing clothes like we were going out somewhere really special. I remember Ronan throwing us the salt and pepper shakers to use as makeshift microphones. God behold, we belted out tunes like true Irish darlin's. *Mustang Sally,*' she reminisced. 'For many a moon, Grace and I harboured dreams of becoming just like the girls in the Commitments, or if fate didn't smile upon us, we were going to be the next Fleetwood Mac. There were squabbles aplenty over who'd don the mantle of Stevie Nicks. I won and Grace gifted me a sweeping black chiffon dress and a black felt top hat so that I could truly embody the part.'

Her memories were pushed aside as Lachie's arm brushed against hers and for a moment their eyes met. Every week she grew closer to him and the feelings she was starting to have scared her. She berated herself. They were friends. Nothing more. As her boss, he had never shown any other sign that their friendship was anything else.

She drank another beer, the amber liquid going down a bit too quickly. You would think with the night closing in, the air would cool. But obviously that was not what happened during summer in Australia. A few other staff members gathered around, a new girl who had taken

Mal's job telling crude jokes and getting plenty of laughs. Her name was Morag, and she was also Irish. She came from Dublin, on the opposite side of Ireland, which Morag reminded her was only a hundred and twenty-nine miles from Galway.

Before Kat set foot in Australia, she had thought of Dublin as quite a long way away. But now, after seeing the long distances between Brisbane to the Whitsundays, it seemed like it would only be a hop, skip, and a jump the next time she travelled it. Morag and Kat had a lot in common, united by their shared experience of the quirks and quibbles of Irish life. It was a blessing to have someone who could commiserate over the intricacies of missing the way of things back home.

As she giggled at one of Morag's quips, the music playing in the background wrapped around her, filling her soul with warmth. Jasper had a playlist that included her favourite U2 songs and she was struggling to keep her feet still when one of her preferred tunes came on. Jasper turned the music up, and when Morag grabbed her hand and led her over to the grassy area where a few of the other girls were dancing, she went with her. *Pride, In the Name of Love,* belted out from the small speakers that were placed on a stump nearby. It had been a long time since she had danced and now she instinctively moved with the music, seamlessly intertwining her steps with Morag's as the chorus swept in.

With their arms around each other, the two girls swayed to the rhythm, their movements fluid and grace-ful. As the music enveloped them, they intertwined, spinning each other around in a mesmerising dance. Their steps were in time with the beat, a blend of waltz and sway as they twirled in perfect harmony. Kat dipped under Morag's arm when she spun her under and they grinned at each other as the music became louder.

Their infectious energy soon spread, drawing others to join them on the front lawn, spinning around dancing, a blend of voices belting out tunes with unabashed gusto. When the tune, *It's a Beautiful Day* filled the air, a chorus of voices lifted in unison and the two girls harmonised with the melody. Kat felt the warmth of Lachie's arm around her waist, and she raised her voice to blend with his, adding her own joyful melody to the mix. A number of other songs followed and everyone joined in the singing and dancing. When the last song played, they all sat down on the grass, Jasper coming around with an esky full of cold beers.

He gestured at Morag and Kat. 'Surely you two girls could put on a show for us,' he said as he stood above them handing them a beer. 'You know, can you do that Irish dance stuff.' He stood straight and put his hands by his side, tilting his head from side to side and jumping up and down on the spot. 'You know, like Riverdance.'

Morag glanced at Kat with a mischievous twinkle in her eye, then with a grin turned back to Jasper. 'Ah, sure, we could give it a go,' she said with a playful lilt. 'But first, we need to ask – do you always dance like a duck with two left feet at a party, or is that just for special occasions?'

Jock called out, 'You look like a drunken emu trying to tango, or is that your signature move?'

Kat stifled a laugh, nodding in agreement. 'What do

we get in return? Because we're not dancing for just any old lad who thinks he's Michael Flatley reincarnated.'

Morag leaned in closer, squinting at him. 'Could we see that again? What sort of dance did you think that was… a kangaroo trying to salsa?' She winked playfully, unable to contain her merriment.

They both burst into laughter. 'Don't worry, Jasper,' Morag reassured him, patting his arm. 'We'll show you a proper Irish dance. Come on Kat.'

Kat stood up and grabbed Morag's arm, dragging her to a standing position also. They both took long sips of their beers before passing the empty tins to Jasper. 'Can you really Irish dance?' he asked them again.

Morag's face was one of shock. 'Did he just enquire if we could Irish dance? Did you actually ask that?' She looked at Jasper and then back to Kat.

Kat took another beer from Jasper and holding it high took a long drink from it. It was a long time since she had drunk so much, but it was stinking hot and this was going to be fun. Lachie looked at her, waiting for her to answer. 'Can you?'

She pushed him playfully. 'Are you lads truly asking us that question? In Ireland every girl can dance. We're taught at school and practise in the pubs. Music is the heart and soul of Ireland. From jigs to ballads, it's in our blood, our bones, our very being. Why, even our cows tap their hooves to the rhythm of a good fiddle tune!'

Lachie squeezed her shoulders. 'Now I really want to see this.'

'Get ready to have your mind blown, Lachie,' Morag

said as she drank some more beer. 'We'll Irish dance circles around you till you're dizzy.'

'Well, don't just talk about it; show us,' Jasper said. 'Name a tune and I'll get it playing.'

The two girls put their heads together for a while and then looked at the crowd who were all waiting to see what was next. Kat's eyes met Lachie's, a mischievous smile on his face. She spoke loudly, the group listening as she declared, 'Ladies and gentlemen, esteemed guests and lovers of fine music, allow us to commence our musical journey with the melodious strains of *Molly Malone* and the sprightly beats of *Tell Me Ma*. Prepare to be thrilled by the graceful dancing of Morag Maloney and myself, Kat McCullagh. These timeless jigs hail from the rich tapestry of our folklore, promising to whisk you away on a spirited journey through the hills and pubs of the Emerald Isle.' She stopped talking and tried to hold back her laughter as Morag grinned at her. Taking another swig from a can of beer Lachie passed her, she finished her introduction. 'We trust that you all shall find our performance to be nothing short of a splendid delight. Prepare yourselves for a spectacle beyond compare!'

The crowd erupted into cheers and applause, as Kat and Morag gracefully stepped into the centre of the lush grassed stage. As everyone quietened and fell into a silent anticipation, Kat couldn't shake the profound sense of connection to her ancestors, as if their spirits were casting a gaze upon her from the heavens above. Maybe it was the amount of beer she had drunk tonight, but a bitter-sweet ache tugged at her heartstrings as she thought of the countless moments she had stood just like this, eagerly awaiting the music's embrace.

Under the stars of the southern skies and with a balmy still night air surrounding her, she found herself enveloped in a profound sense of belonging, as if every step she took was guided by the gentle whispers of those who had danced before her.

Australia and Ireland had always had strong connections and Granny had often talked about relatives who had come out to what was deemed such a faraway land in the early 1900s. They had lived in bark huts where no one from their kin had been before and stayed in places that were dusty, dry, and full of thick brown snakes. Now Kat was in a different part of the country. A place that had the most beautiful ocean, islands covered in thick rainforest and beaches with the whitest sand in the world. She glanced up at the night sky one more time before grinning at Morag who stood with her hands on her hips waiting for the music to begin. Kat grinned and pointed her toe. 'Ready?' Kat said as she also put her hands on her hips and pointed her foot in front of her.

Morag replied boldly, 'Let's give them a show they'll never forget.'

When the tune started, she and Morag danced in unison to the songs they had grown up with, Kat forgetting about the others standing around watching. Light from a fire behind them flicked sparks up to the heavens, its glow offering a natural spotlight to their show. The lively music stirred in her heart, the quick steps in perfect time with Morag's as their arms intertwined. They swung each other around, their feet dancing faster and faster.

When the first song finished, they rolled quickly into the next one; *Tell me Ma*. The lively melody had their feet moving quicker, their laughter mingling with the cheers of the others. This song brought back so many memories. Dancing with Granny in the small cottage, spinning each other around and clasping hands while singing aloud. Jigging and singing at the pubs with her sister and friends, the room smoky and warm, the aroma of the burning wood on the open fire blended with the smell of beer and food cooking from the pub kitchen. In Galway there were always buskers in the streets, rolling music festivals, and lively parties where the music played until the sun came up. Tonight, just like other nights in the past, she let herself go and forgot who and where she was.

The songs and dances were a testament to the spirit of Ireland and as they paid homage to the jigs and reels of generations past, she felt like the soul of Ireland touched her spirit. Even here, so far from home, the timeless energy of Irish tradition could be found.

When Morag clasped her hands and they spun and whirled for the last part of the song, the tears flowed. So far from home yet amongst good friends.

When the music stopped, they took a bow and although the crowd cheered and yelled, 'more' they decided they'd had enough. 'It's fair boiling hot,' Morag said, her loud voice echoing across the lawn. 'That was mine and Kat's dance of celebration, of friendship, and of the unbreakable incredible bond forged, on the dance floors of our youth. We are the soul of Ireland itself. Amen.'

Lachie came towards her and put his arm around her

shoulders. His eyes sparkled and he squeezed her tightly. 'That was bloody amazing. You girls are brilliant!'

'She pulled away from him, aware that she was covered in sweat. 'I'm sweaty as anything.'

'I don't care.' He pulled her in tightly and the excitement of the dance and his body next to hers was overwhelmingly the best feeling in the world. 'You never told me you could dance like that. The two of you danced brilliantly. Amazing.'

'Every girl in Ireland can dance like that.' She wiped her eyes and took a glass of cold water that Jasper offered her. 'Thank you. That was great. So much fun and for a moment I thought I was back home dancing in the pub.'

Morag came towards her and they hugged. 'Soul sister,' Morag said. 'That was terrific. I needed that. I miss home and the music, something shocking.'

'So do I,' Kat said. 'I pined for many weeks and at one time even thought about going home. But there are so many things here to experience. I'm starting to settle in after months of homesickness.'

Lachie leaned over, 'You'd better settle in. I don't want you going anywhere.'

The night wore on and soon most filtered away back to their cabins, or some to sit on the beach to talk and drink some more. Kat stopped drinking after the dancing. Cold water had gone down nicely and she didn't want a hangover tomorrow. Besides, now the crowd was going wild over Jock and Morag doing some Scottish dancing. She watched their silhouettes jigging and jumping in front of the fire, their movements reminiscent of warriors wielding swords, albeit with palm fronds serving as substitutes.

When she told Lachie she was going to leave, he said he would walk her home. It was quiet once they left the party area and she was glad he was with her in case she encountered any wildlife on the path. After a while he took her hand and they walked in silence, his warm grip sending sensations rippling through her body. When they reached her front door, he turned towards her and took both her hands. 'I had a really good night tonight. I loved seeing you dance and best of all, to see you smiling and laughing so much. When I first met you, I didn't see you smile. You always seemed serious. I knew when I did see you smile it would be something special.'

'Until I settled in, I was terribly homesick. I also didn't really let my true self be. It's different when you're out of your comfort zone. For so many years back home, you're with the people who love you, your family and friends. When you come to a different country you feel a bit like a foreigner. I haven't really let my hair down until, well until, that day you took me swimming on the reef. Now I have a good job, some friends, and you.'

'And do you think of me as just a friend?' he asked, his voice low and his face coming closer to hers.

The words stuck in her throat and she tilted her face and looked up at him. When both his hands gently touched her face, she closed her eyes. Warm lips met hers and she kissed him back, her body leaning in close. They kissed for a long while and she gripped his arms to steady herself. The feeling made her giddy. Giddy for more kisses, giddy for his arms to hold her and giddy for love.

When he pulled away, he looked at her, his gaze steady. 'Goodnight, Kat. I'll see you tomorrow. Sleep tight.' He kissed her again and she stood leaning against the door frame as he began to walk away. When he reached the part where a path led off to his cabin, he turned and waved. The flares that lit up the area were still burning and she could see the look on his face. It was a look of longing. She blew him a kiss and he blew one back. 'Goodnight, Lachie,' she whispered, before closing the door behind her.

Chapter Fifteen

For the next few weeks, Lachie continued to ask her to come with him walking or to snorkel in the bay. At night she would often go to his place and sit out on the front lawn or down on the beach and talk. Sometimes Jasper joined them, but more often than not he was with his mates, having a good time in the pubs of Airlie Beach. Usually, it was just the two of them. Now that she had got to know Lachie more, she felt like she could tell him anything and she noticed he was also confiding in her. He talked a lot about where he had grown up on Stradbroke Island, which was further south and near the city of Brisbane. Although he loved the Whitsundays, Stradbroke was home and he said he would love to take her there one day.

When he walked her home, he kissed her goodnight at her front door and then went back to his own cabin. After a few weeks she decided to change the routine.

When he went to kiss her goodnight, she pulled back

a little. 'Why don't you come in? Come in for the night or as long as you want to stay.'

When she opened the door, he followed. They stood at the doorway to her bedroom, holding hands and looking at one another. 'If we're going to sleep together, it means we're starting a proper relationship. Is that what you want?' he asked.

'I never thought I would say this. But with you, yes.'

'I'm in love with you Kat. I love everything about you.'

She didn't hesitate to reply. 'I feel the same. I didn't really want this to happen. I mean we come from different sides of the world and different backgrounds. That scares me a little.'

'Those differences don't worry me. As long as our feelings are the same, everything will be okay. I just know I want to be with you all the time.'

She pulled him into the room. 'Me too. Welcome to my bedroom. *Vivre* Cabin 25.'

* * *

As he lay on his back the following morning, he ran his hand over his chest. Kat lay with her head nestled into his arm, her long hair a beautiful sight as it spread out across the pillow. When she worked, her hair was usually up in a ponytail or messy bun. Last night had been made special when she loosened the clip holding her long strands together and let them fall down to their full length. He peered down at her naked body, her chest rising slowly up and down as she slept. Running his hand along her arm, he kissed the top of her head.

Meeting an Irish traveller and falling in love was not something he had ever expected. But here he was. Holding the one person that now meant more to him than anyone, in her bed and both naked.

She stirred and he pulled her in tightly. Who knew how this would work out? All he knew was that he would make sure that it did.

Chapter Sixteen

achie and Kat were quickly inseparable, and if she wasn't staying at his place, he was at hers. Christmas was not far off, and the resort was full of people keen to travel after being restricted for so long by travel bans. She was kept busy working at the resort reception and being with Lachie for the rest of the time. There wasn't much time for painting or even snorkelling these days, but they were both happy with the way it was. That was the nature of hospitality. You had to put in the hours while the work and guests were there.

So far she hadn't mentioned much to her family back home about Lachie. While she kept their relationship a secret, it meant she didn't have to answer any questions or give Grace any details. She liked it the way it was, and life at the resort was like living in a bubble. Free from the concerns and worries of the outside world.

On Christmas Day she worked in the morning, then spent the afternoon with Lachie and Jasper. They were also missing family, although both had plans to visit down south in the coming months. At least their family were not that far away. The phone call to family in Galway that day had been difficult and she had tried hard not to cry. It was snowing back home and she envisioned the moors covered in white, trees dripping with icicles and the sight and sounds of what she missed the most; the excited noise of youngsters as they played outside. All the children would be outside, making snowballs and shrieking as they threw them at each other. Others would be riding their sleds down the hills, laughing and calling out as they tumbled into the soft snow at the bottom. She was missing the hot toddies, traditional turkey and vegetables, the gravy and varied spread of hot food. She could almost taste it and imagined the smell of the trappings that went with an Irish Christmas dinner.

Her family had found it hard to believe that today on the island, the temperature had reached thirty-five degrees, the humidity at ninety-five percent. Kat could hardly move from where she sat with the boys, drinking beer and feasting on cold prawns, ham and salad. Dessert consisted of ice cream and apple pie with some cold sparkling champagne to wash the meal down. Now she realised why everyone had looked at her strangely when she questioned why no one was cooking turkey or roast vegetables.

Lachie's cabin had a bigger bed and a better view so they had decided to stay there over Christmas time. They usually alternated between each other's cabin and she wondered how long she would continue to swap clothes or run back to her cabin for something she had forgotten from her place.

For New Year's Eve, they left the celebrating on the mainland to Jasper, the two of them opting for watching the sunset and a quiet dinner on the beach. With the festivities well and truly over, work continued and guests came and went. As she became more confident in the reception role, she started to rearrange the furniture and large prints that hung in the foyer. 'I haven't seen you paint since that first one I saw you do one of the rainforest,' Lachie said one day. 'Why don't you do a painting for the reception entrance and I'll buy it from you. Yours are just as good as the ones we have hanging up there now.'

'Well, a few are getting a bit faded and dated, I guess. I could paint some seaside scenes to replace them.'

'Just do whatever you think. I'll put some money in your account to get a couple of good-sized canvases and paints. Once you're finished you can let me know how much the paintings are to buy. Don't undercut yourself either.'

'I have savings. You don't have to pay me anything.'

'I want to buy them. Make it a business deal. I'd rather pay you money for a decent piece of art than buy one from someone else.'

So far she hadn't had a chance to order what painting supplies she needed. She would have to go online and get them delivered to the resort's post office box in Airlie Beach. For now, work was keeping her busy. Tonight was Lachie's birthday and they were going to eat at the restaurant, then he was going to stay at her place. She needed to start early in the morning and it was easier for her to start the day if all her clothes and other essentials were there.

* * *

Dinner was amazing and even though it was his birthday, he insisted on paying for the meal and drinks. Not only did he order the best food on the menu, but also the most expensive wine and port. 'It's not every day I get to share my thirty-first birthday with the most beautiful girl in the world.'

She blushed. It was strange being waited on and treated like royalty, when once she had been the one serving the food to these tables. Although she felt like she hadn't changed since she arrived at the resort, she knew she had. Lachie was right and now she did smile all the time, her homesickness barely there. She was happy when she was with him and nothing else mattered.

That night when they got home, she gave him his present. A set of beer glasses with a Celtic design on them and a penny keyring that she had bought at the local markets the last time she had gone into town. 'The lady who was selling them told me a penny brings good luck. It's a 1962 one. I think you said that was the year your mother was born. I remember because my mum is born the same year.'

He held the keyring in the air and twirled it around; on one side an embossed kangaroo and on the other the head of Queen Elizabeth II. 'It seems strange to me that you still have the British queen on the back of your coins and on your notes,' she quizzed. 'You think you would have your own symbol or an Australian person on there.'

'Crazy, hey. We still have the Union Jack on our flag also. Thank God we have our own anthem.' He examined his present. 'I love this keyring. My father has a similar one that my mother found on the beach at Stradbroke and gave to him when they were teenagers. It hangs on their wall at home still. They also said it's supposed to bring good luck.'

'This coin isn't valuable. I checked the years and I'm sure the lady would have also. There are some years that are worth thousands. Not that money or belongings are important to me. One of my mum's favourite sayings is 'A thief may have a full purse, but they'll always have an empty heart'. We were brought up with the firm belief that lying and stealing were the darkest of deeds, sins held in the highest disdain. In Irish folklore, there's a belief that if you steal something, bad luck will befall you. Taking what doesn't belong to you can anger the fairies and that might lead to a string of disastrous events, or worse still a curse upon the person who stole, and their entire family. We Irish are a very superstitious lot. Pennies are good luck. Don't lose it.'

As they walked to the bedroom, Lachie thought what a perfect birthday it had been. The penny keyring and Kat's story about stealing, fairies and curses reminded him of the conversation he had overheard the first day they met. Her sister had accused Kat of stealing something and told her not to lie about it. Maybe one day he might ask her what they were talking about. Surely if it was that important, she would have told him about it by now. They shared everything. Not only their bodies and beds, but also their thoughts and ideas.

Lachie had started to drop more and more hints about how he pictured a life with her in it for a long time to come. Until they grew old together, he thought. Sometimes she held back with her response, not saying too much about the future but telling him she was so happy she just wanted to live in the present. Was the concern there in the back of her mind about where she would end up living? Coming from different parts of the world could prove to be a problem. He didn't think he could move to Ireland. It was too cold and how would he surf and fish in winter? There were obviously big conversations they needed to have down the track, but for now, they both needed to sleep. He snuggled into her naked body, her hand resting on his chest. He had never loved someone so much.

Chapter Seventeen

The next few months flew by. The resort was busier than usual and as the heat of summer bore down, Kat was grateful to be working in the air-conditioned reception area. It had also rained a lot, but that didn't seem to cool anything down. It was the tropical wet season and she was surprised by the intensity of the heavy rain; huge splats that thundered onto the tin roofs of the cabins at night.

When she thought it must be time for the weather to cool so that they would be able to get out in the boat more, a cyclone formed in the Coral Sea. As it moved towards the Whitsunday area and then hovered off the coast, she began to recall the stories she had heard about ferocious cyclones that had crossed the coast in previous years. Only six years earlier a cyclone named Debbie had blown in from the same area. Wind gusts of two hundred and sixty kilometres an hour had been recorded on Hamilton Island, which wasn't too far away. Airlie Beach and Proserpine had suffered the brunt of the storm, and with roofs blown away, trees uprooted, and flooding widespread, the cyclone had been one of the worst that locals could remember. It had taken years for the area to recover and people at Dingo Beach had told her that only now, years later, was the vegetation returning to some sort of normality.

Now as the air seemed to become thicker and dark bruised clouds clustered on the horizon, they all waited to see if this cyclone would continue on its track towards the Whitsundays, or veer away in a different direction. She stood with Lachie at the shoreline, watching the waves whip up a storm, the coconut trees bending over with the ferocity of the wind. All of the resort guests had left and most of the staff had been given time off to go and stay with friends, or wait the storm out in hotels at Airlie Beach. Lachie asked Kat if she was still okay to stay. 'You'll be safe here no matter what happens. The cyclone structures we have built are like bunkers. You might never get to experience a cyclone again.' She decided he was right. There was hardly anyone around and with no one coming and going and all travel to and from Airlie Beach cancelled, it was a good time to paint and catch up on some reading.

Lachie and Jasper took the time to clean out the office and some of the other rooms. Those who were staying held their breath, trying not to look at the skies too much, but all waiting to see what direction the cyclone would go. After a week of rain and wind, the swirling mass of storm started to move away from the coastline and head further southeast. 'Off to annoy someone further south,' Lachie said. 'Our weeks of quiet and solitude might be over. There's supposed to be good weather coming behind it. That will be good for business. We need our guests and our staff back.'

That night Lachie cooked dinner for her in his cabin. Jasper was playing cards with Jock and some of the others who had opted to stay. The area was quiet with only the noise of the wind and waves to be heard.

'It's a special night,' Lachie said, as he served her a meal of pasta and meat balls.

She smiled at him. 'It's always special when someone cooks for you. Thank you.'

They sat around his small kitchen table, a candle in the middle flickering as snippets of wind snuck in through tiny gaps in the window and door frames. 'It's still wild outside,' she said. 'I'm glad the cyclone didn't come this way. I'm not sure I'd like to be here if one of them passed directly overhead.'

'There're special safety areas in the resort where you'd go if it was going to hit. We've also had all that extra work done to cyclone-proof the cabins and some of the other buildings. Cyclones are a part of life up here, although I also have trouble thinking what it would be like if one hit us like Cyclone Debbie did. We don't really get them further down south. They've usually petered out by the time they get to Stradbroke Island, although some of our worst floods have come from the lows that the cyclones turn into once they cross land.

The weather intrigued Kat. The interest of everyone was similar to how it was in Galway. When you lived near the water, no matter where you were, you were always waiting to see what the weather was doing. She and Lachie talked non-stop about storms and cyclones and when they finished the spaghetti, he poured her another glass of red wine. 'Such a special night Kat.' He reached behind him and opened one of the cupboards. She gasped when he brought out a present wrapped in birthday paper and tied with a green ribbon.

'How did you know?' she said.

'Your birthdate is on your staff details. You're not getting away with not celebrating it.' He leaned over and kissed her. 'You're sneaky not to tell me.'

She took the present. 'It's no big deal. Just another birthday.'

'Well, it's a big deal to me. I hope you like what I got you.'

When she pulled the paper away, she stared at what she held in her hand. It was a framed photo of her and Lachie standing on the beach in front of the boat. Above them the sky was blue as could be and the sea a mixture of blue and emerald. Diamonds glittered on its surface and a couple of palm trees gave a splash of green in the foreground.

She wore denim shorts and a bikini top, while Lachie wore his favourite board shorts, the faded pattern indistinguishable on the fabric. He wore a straw hat she had bought him from the markets at Airlie Beach and on her head was her favourite hat of Granny's; the white top and rim vivid against the brightness of the water. She ran her hand over the blue stitching that Granny had lovingly sewn on the rim. How she would have loved this photo. For Kat, the picture was the embodiment of her life since she had come to the Whitsundays. Not only the ocean and the beautiful sunshine that beat down on them, but also Lachie.

'Thank you. This means the world to me. I love it. I'll treasure it always.'

* * *

That night they lay for a long while talking. They made love in the early hours of the morning, a storm raging overhead. Lightning flashed like fiery tendrils across the darkened sky and thunder rumbled so loud the ground and the cabin shook. As they lay talking about the weeks to come, he must have seen the look of concern in her eyes when they discussed the distances between their homelands. 'Shh, don't talk anymore.' He put his finger gently on her lips. 'Let's enjoy the moment. We can't look too far ahead at the moment.'

She snuggled in. 'She had been worried where the conversation was going. It wasn't going to be easy if the romance continued. Her home and family were a long way from here. She fell asleep, wondering where the road ahead was going to take her.

Chapter Eighteen

Normal life resumed on the island once the storm had gone and the water and wind calmed. The staff returned from Airlie Beach by boat, eager to get back into work after a week of partying and drinking. Morag swore she would never drink again. 'We stayed at the backpackers in the main street. There were people from everywhere there making sure to hunker down somewhere safe. All the workers from the other islands gathered there also. Seemed like a grand party at the time. But I feel like I need to dry out and eat some proper food.'

* * *

Jock had been kept busy for the next month, tidying up the grounds and cutting back branches that were dangling dangerously from where they had snapped, but still hung in amongst the limbs of trees. Kat came across him as he wheeled a barrow full of branches, along the path. He stopped to talk. 'How are you going, Kat? I'm nearly finished with the clean-up. I can't imagine what it would have been like if that storm crossed land around here. Hopefully one day I get to be in a cyclone. It sounds exciting from what Jasper told me.'

'It sounds like you played a lot of cards while the weather was bad,' Kat said, giving him a gently shove.

'Aye, we did. I'm a fair bit richer than I was before. I need more cyclones. I could become a millionaire. These fellas think they're good at cards, but they'll never beat a canny Scotsman like me.'

'Well, that's one way to make money.'

She pulled a face and he looked at her quizzically. 'Are you alright? he asked. 'You've gone pale.'

She grimaced. 'I've had a stomach bug for a couple of days after eating some leftovers that I shouldn't have touched. Thankfully I've come good today because Lachie and I are going fishing this afternoon. He's been waiting for me to feel better before heading out. I'll bring you some fish tomorrow.'

They talked for a bit longer before Jock looked at his watch. 'Lunch time for me. Catch you soon and don't forget your promise of some fish.'

I'll see you later, Jock. I'm going to ring my sister. We haven't talked in a while.'

Strolling along the path back to her cabin she thought about the friends she had made here on the island. Every day it felt more and more like home. She picked up her pace, thankful that she was feeling better and that her afternoon was planned; phone home and then get ready to go fishing.

As she pushed the button and waited for her sister to answer, she pictured the countryside in Ireland. Here, at least the weather was cooling, and after the cyclone had passed by, the humidity had eased. At home though, with tomorrow being June, the weather would be getting milder and the days longer. If they were lucky, in Galway the sun should be shining and the flowers blooming in the parks and in people's gardens. It was the festival season and there would be music, art and camping festivals in full swing in the county. She sighed and waited.

'I thought you were never going to pick up,' Kat said as Grace answered the phone.

'You made me run,' Grace retorted. 'I was on the loo.'

They chatted for a while about what was happening in each other's lives. Kat said very little about Lachie, only talking about him as she did any of her other friends. Grace knew her sister too well, though.

'You seem to be hanging around this Lachie lad. You're not keen on him, are you? Mum and Dad said you mentioned him when they rang for your birthday.'

'No. No. He's just a friend. There's a crowd of us here and we all hang out together. I'm too busy working to worry about things like that. Have you seen any of the old crew at home?'

Grace talked faster, as she did when she was excited. 'Funny, you should say that. I was at the pub last night. It was a big night. Everyone was out and about with the music festival going on. I ran into some of the crowd from school. They said to say hello. Here's something of interest. They told me that Seamus and Kiaran are travelling to Australia.'

Kat made a strange noise. 'Surely not.'

They said those two had been asking a lot of questions and found out from someone that you were working on a private island out from Airlie Beach. It was Belinda that I spoke to, your old friend from year nine. She said Kiaran mentioned they might visit you. A friendly family call, they said. I wouldn't worry too much, though, those two are always full of shite.'

Chapter Nineteen

Kat thought no more about the story of Kiaran and Seamus. There was always plenty of gossip going around and someone had probably made that up just for something to say. Life was too busy to worry about those two idiots. Tonight, Lachie was going to stay at her place and she was going to cook a feast for him. She had been into Airlie Beach a few days ago for supplies and even splurged a little on herself, buying some sexy underwear. She couldn't wait for the night. Life was exciting and with loving her job and spending every spare second with Lachie, she really thought she was in heaven.

Dinner was, in Lachie's words 'superb'. 'I didn't know you could cook that well. Even my mother's lasagne is not that good, although don't tell her I said that.' They talked about cooking for a while and then for some reason the subject veered to the subject of past relationships.

'Nothing much for me to report,' Kat said. 'A few boys at high school and then one or two I dated during uni. No one I ever really got too involved with. I think all I could think about was coming to Australia and travelling. How about you?'

'I was in a long-term relationship with a girl called Prue. It ended a year or so before I came back up here to the Whitsundays.' He looked pensive and she waited for him to continue.

'What happened?' she asked.

'It just faded out.'

'Do you still think about her?'

'No, not at all. It's in the past. I haven't seen her since and I don't intend seeing her again.'

By the time they finished dinner, the conversation had changed back to other topics, and Kat was pleased that Lachie hadn't been too curious about the years before she met him. What was in the past was best left there, and she certainly didn't want to share too much more information beyond the few details she already had.

She wondered about this Prue girl though. He had sounded a bit preoccupied when he spoke about her and she considered if he still had feelings for her. Her concerns were quickly put to the side though, when she felt his lips moving up and down her neck. Lachie stood behind her and with both her hands in the warm water in the sink, there was nothing she could do except squeal and wriggle in delight.

The washing up did not get finished and he ignored her protests about cleaning the kitchen before going to bed, instead lifting her into his arms and carrying her into her bed.

* * *

As always, they had made love like there was no tomorrow. He wondered how something so sweet and romantic could also feel so invigorating, filling him with a sense of renewed energy and vitality. He lay on his back, with Kat's leg thrown over him. Her hair stretched across his body and he closed his eyes, hoping that this moment would never end. When she snuggled into him, he held her close and fell into a deep sleep.

The next time he woke was to a pounding on the front door. Kat was stirring beside him as he opened his eyes and looked around. The clock showed seven o'clock so they hadn't slept past when they were supposed to start work. She jumped up and wrapped a silky nightgown around her body. He had bought if for her last time he was in town. As he watched her move and then glimpsed her legs as she strode towards the front door, he wished she would ignore the knocking and come back to bed. Sighing deeply, he also got up and threw a towel around his waist. The knocking was loud and persistent. Whoever it was, wanted to see them.

When Kat opened the door, he was right behind her. Surely Jasper wouldn't wake them this early. Maybe something was wrong? He looked past her to see who was banging on the door. In front of Kat stood two burly, ruddy-faced men, neither of whom he had seen before. As soon as they opened their mouths though, he knew they were Irish and he pulled himself up straighter and came to stand beside her.

'Sweet God, Mother Mary, Joseph and the baby

Jesus,' Kat exclaimed, her hand flying to her mouth. 'Seamus and Kiaran O'Rourke. What the feck are you doing here?'

The men straightened their posture, and Lachie noticed bands of sweat staining their T-shirts under their arms, and collecting on their foreheads. 'We might ask you the same, Kat McCullagh. They said you lived here, but they didn't say anything about *him*.'

'Who are they?' Lachie asked Kat.

She pointed to the man with black hair. 'That's Seamus,' she said, then turned to the man with red hair. 'And that's Kiaran. They're both my cousins, and I cannot believe they're here on my doorstep.'

Seamus ran a handkerchief across his brow before gesturing at Lachie. 'Who's he?'

'None of your goddam business,' she shot back at them. 'You've no right turning up here. What do you want?'

Kiaran pushed forward and tried to step inside. 'We want what you pinched and what rightfully belongs to us. And now, finding you here with another fella, we're keen on knowing what your husband, Johnny, will make of you being with someone else when you're still married to him.'

Lachie had heard enough and pushed forward, shoving both men back. 'Get back. You're on private property and if you don't remove yourselves, I'll have the police here in no time.'

He had recoiled a little at the mention of a husband, anger and confusion rolling in his mind as the words hit home. What the hell? She was married? His head was spinning, but right now, figuring out Kat's marital status wasn't as urgent as getting these two guys off his property.

Before he could intervene, Kat stepped closer to them. She tilted her face up at Kiaran's, her hands on her hips as she shouted. 'And what is any of this to Johnny? What in the hell has he got to do with anything? He's just looking to try and get some money and if he's encouraged you to pursue the matter than you're all as stupid as each other.' As she continued to speak her words came out faster and Lachie had to listen hard to decipher what she was saying. 'You've no right to be here stirring up trouble, and you know it well. It's hard to believe you've come all this way just to be a thorn in my side and try and get something that doesn't belong to you.'

'The ring just like all the other jewellery, belongs to us and you're nothing but a thief and a liar.' Kiaran said as he took a step backwards.

Lachie took a step towards them. 'Get the hell out of here and make your way to the jetty. You can both get on a boat back to the mainland. There's a fella down there who can take you back. Otherwise, I'm going to have you charged for trespassing.'

Both men were very overweight, but it was the largest man, Kiaran who seemed the most aggressive. He pointed at Kat. 'She is a crook and a liar. She is well known to the police back home for numerous offences and now she's wanted for theft. Also,' he smirked towards Kat, 'did you forget to tick the box to say you were married when you applied for your visa? You can go to jail for that. Johnny's not happy with you and he also wants to know where the ring is. Everyone knows you've stolen it. The police will be knocking on your door next. We're doing you a favour coming here first and warning you.'

Lachie looked from one to the other. 'Kat?' he asked. 'Is this true? Are you married? Did you steal a ring?'

When she didn't answer he repeated both questions, his hackles rising at the thought she hadn't mentioned either point to him.

Her chest heaved with anger and her eyes glared hard at him. 'I am. I was. But it's not real. It's a joke, and the marriage was supposed to be annulled.'

'Do you think you should have maybe told me that you were married?'

'It's not important to me.'

'Well, it might be to me.'

Seamus drew in close, his breath almost touching hers. 'You fancy yourself, but Johnny mightn't have seen to them annulment papers. Did you ever bother to look?' Now you're sleeping around with anyone,' he tipped his head towards Lachie, 'and you have a million-dollar ring. We want it and Johnny wants you.'

She pulled herself up and pushed her face closer to Seamus's. 'Do you know what, you idiots? You've come a long way for a few hundred quid. The ring is not worth anything. It's a reproduction. I've had it valued and it's not the same as the one on the antique show on the telly. That one might have been worth a lot of money, but the one I have isn't. If you want it that bad, I'll give it to you. Read my lips, you idiots. It's a replica. I've had it checked by experts both in Ireland, London and in Australia to make sure. You've travelled around the world for nothing.'

'You're spinning lies. If it's not worth a penny to you, then hand it over. We won't be shifting until you give over the ring. The will clearly states that the jewellery is to be passed on to the O'Rourkes. Let us be the judge if it's worth anything or not. Why should we believe anything you say. You've always been a liar.'

Lachie was shocked when Kat quickly turned and disappeared inside the cabin. He stood his ground, both men standing with their hands on their hips trying to outstare him. He was just about to go back inside and shut the door behind him when Kat returned, in her hand a small box that she held onto tightly.

She strode past him and held the box out. 'Do you know what? I've had a gutful of hearing about you two looking for me and all your carrying on. And now you're here, intruding on my life. I don't want anything to do with you or see your ugly faces ever again. I'll give the ring to you but if you ever come and try and find me again or bother anyone in my family, I'll make your life hell. There's plenty back home who would join with me to see you both lying with concrete blocks on your feet at the bottom of Galway Bay.'

'You wouldn't dare,' Kiaran said.

She pushed closer to him, her eyes flashing. 'Try me. I have some handy contacts who will do anything for a bit of money. It'll come when you least expect it. So don't you dare stop glancing over your shoulder if you ever come pestering me again. I'll make sure I end this.'

Lachie stood in silence, in shock at the vehemence in her tone and her brazen body language. The quiet, smiling, demure Irish girl he thought he knew had turned into a person who was making even him scared to move.

She took a step back. 'Granny gave this to me a long while before I left for here. It was always meant to be mine and she said she would send a letter saying so.'

Seamus interrupted, 'So where's the letter? You know you've always been the same. Big mouth, no action.'

'Where the letter might be is none of your business. It never made it here. I know that the ring is not yours but if you want it that badly, you can have it. Like I said I've had it valued and it's worth nothing much. It only has sentimental value to me and I have more in my memories than this ring. Something neither of you will have. Granny will be watching you both from up there and you want to watch yourself because she'll take matters into her own hands.'

'She's dead,' Seamus said. 'Dead and gone.'

'Watch your backs. I'm sick and tired of your harassment.' She thrust the box towards them and Seamus quickly took it. He opened the box, inside a gold ring that looked ancient, the dark green stone in the middle, waxy and looking like it had been around for ever. Kiaran took the ring out and held it in front of his face, turning it in different ways to look at it. 'This is it, Seamus. There's no doubting it. There's the little dent where Emily bit when she was a kid. I'd know this ring anywhere. We all used to play with it. It was always to come to our family.' He put the ring back into the box and pushed it into his trouser pocket. Jutting his chin out, he snarled, 'You're nothing but a thief. A common thief.'

'You've got what you came for, now go,' Kat retorted.

'Don't ever come near me again.' With that, she walked back inside and slammed the door behind her.

* * *

Jock and another worker arrived on the scene, the yelling and talking loud enough for them to know that something was not as it should be and maybe some help was needed. Before long the overweight and unfit Seamus and Kiaran were escorted onto one of the motor boats and promptly hurried back to the mainland. Jasper appeared not long afterwards to see what was happening. Lachie was still standing outside Kat's cabin, pacing back and forth trying to get his head around everything he had just seen and heard.

'I saw Jock push those fellas into the boat and then he jumped in and took off towards the mainland,' Jasper said. 'They looked like trouble. What the hell is going on?'

'You tell me and we'll both know. It seems like not only is Kat married, but she also had in her possession a ring worth a million dollars that those men, who were both her cousins, are saying she stole.'

'That's quite the tale. Very interesting. Well, you two have a lot to talk about then,' Jasper exclaimed.

By now Lachie had time to think and also assess Kat's reaction. Why hadn't she been honest with him? He had shared parts of his life with her that he had never told anyone else. She had lied to him and he wasn't sure he wanted to talk to her. He looked at the closed door. For some reason he didn't want to go back in. Returning to his own cabin seemed like a better option.

Feeling overwhelmed by the situation, he considered it best to allow things to settle for a while. With little understanding of what was truly unfolding and the sudden flood of new revelations, he really felt like he was out of his depth and that suddenly she was a stranger to him. It was best to allow her to navigate her own dramas.

Chapter Twenty

Lachie waited for Kat to come to his cabin after she finished work. But she didn't. There was no sign of her on the beach or pathways so he assumed she had gone home straight after her shift. As much as the thought annoyed him and he would rather forget the incident had happened, there was no way what he had heard could just be swept under the carpet. He needed to talk to her.

* * *

She was sitting in the kitchen having a cup of tea when he knocked on her front door. There was no response or call to come in, so he opened the door and walked through the cabin.

When she looked up her eyes were red from crying and she turned away when he tried to hold her gaze. 'I just wondered if you had anything to add to what happened this morning,' he asked.

She pretended to drink her tea. 'No, nothing really. You heard it all. Once I was married to someone called Johnny.'

'What about this ring those two were talking about? The one you gave them.'

'That's my business really.'

'Did you steal it?'

Now he caught the flash in her eye as she looked up and glared hard at him. 'How dare you. How dare you even accuse me of such a thing. Why can't you just trust me? Why do I have to explain my background or what I own? I don't ask you about any of your belongings, or your past.'

'This is different. Two men have come here and accused you of these things. They came a long way and seemed sure that it rightfully belonged to them. I'm also confused as to why you would just hand it over if it really was yours. Now I'm dragged into the situation also. I want to know if you're telling the truth. The last thing I want is drama in my life.'

When she stood up, he thought he felt the ground shake. Although many had told him that the stories about the temper of Irish redheads were a myth, Kat had often spoken about her sister's temper, and now he felt the full brunt of hers. Words flowed out of her mouth so quickly that he could hardly understand what she was saying. Her hands waved in the air and she was in such a livid state that she dropped her teacup, the delicate china scattering all over the floor. When he tried to calm her down, she became angrier, and in the end he gave up and backed away. If she couldn't trust him and tell him the truth, or talk sensibly about matters, what hope was there for them together as a couple?

'I'll only ask one more time and then I'll leave you be. Was the ring stolen? At least be honest. From what I can gather, the ring was left to them but you had possession of it. I also remember a conversation I overheard with your sister, the very first time I met you. Please Kat, this is your last chance to tell me the truth.'

'Get out,' she said, tears streaming down her face. 'Go. How can I be with someone who doesn't trust me and thinks the worst of me? I don't want to see you again. You're no better than those two. Everyone's blaming me and dragging up the past, accusing me of all different things. You can all go to hell and back for all I care.'

With that, she stormed past him and pushed through the side gate onto a path that led to the beach. He watched as she walked and then ran, through the rainforest and onto the sand. She never looked back. She just kept running. His head ached and for a split second he thought about chasing her. She was angry though, so angry. And so was he. Fuming, defeated and also heartbroken. The girl he thought he was going to spend the rest of his life with, did not trust him enough to share important parts of her life. She was married and accused of theft. He was done.

It was all too much to get his head around. When he added everything together that he had overheard and how she had reacted to his questions, the accusations seemed to carry some truth. A ring with an emerald stone that strangely he had never seen her wear before, a husband called Johnny, and two fat Irish cousins who turned up unexpectedly at her front door. The intensity overwhelmed him. He'd pack his bags and be gone in the morning. Back to Stradbroke Island for a while. At least long enough for what had happened to simmer down. By then Kat would have either moved on to another job, or gone back to Ireland.

The girl he thought he knew had revealed herself to be someone entirely different. The layers of her personality had unfolded like the pages of a complex novel, each story revealing new depths and complexities he hadn't expected. He felt as though it had happened to him before. Prue had been similar, with a drama always either happening or threatening to. She also had been a different person than what she portrayed to him. Was he a bad judge of character and lacked the ability to truly know another person?

Chapter Twenty-One

By the time Kat arrived back to her cabin it was dark and she stomped up the path. If there was a snake or centipede in her way she didn't care. She'd smash it with her bare feet and throw it into the garden. She was so angry she felt like she could crush a snake with her hands, or kick a toad into the trees and then tramp on it until it was dead. Fury bubbled inside her and she had no way of dispelling her angry mood. She was in this by herself. No family to guide her, no friends to confide in and now no Lachie to talk to. After raging around the cabin for ages she threw herself onto the bed. Damn those idiots, Seamus and Kiaran. She needed to make sure they were gone and never coming back.

* * *

To her surprise she slept solidly. Maybe she was so exhausted from the distance she had run, that she had exhausted her energy. Her shift started at seven this morning so she didn't have time to go and see Lachie. Was she ready to face him yet? She was still angry and he hadn't experienced her ire before.

At home, her tirade would hardly be a cause for concern. Outbursts like these were a familiar part of the landscape, blowing like a storm and then eventually subsiding. Perhaps it was prudent to allow a day or two to pass, or perhaps he would make the first move to reconcile.

When her shift finished at four, she made a beeline for his cabin. Jasper was gardening outside and she waved to him before going up to Lachie's front door and knocking loudly. When he didn't open the door, she turned around to find Jasper staring at her.

'I need to talk to Lachie.'

Jasper stood up and came towards her. His face was sad and she wondered how much Lachie had told him. 'He's gone. Left. Packed up this morning and went.'

'What do you mean he's gone? Gone to Airlie Beach?'

'No. Back home to Stradbroke. Said he'd be away a few months and to put Georgia into his job while he was gone.'

A heavy feeling descended on her. He had left without saying goodbye or hearing her explanation. 'Oh. Right. I see.' She crossed her arms and looked at the ground, trying to stop the tears from coming. When she looked up at Jasper she knew she had failed and he passed her a tea towel that was on the table nearby. 'Please don't cry. I can't explain why he left, but he was angry and upset. I don't know what happened between you, but I wish he'd talked to you before going.'

She wiped her eyes. 'He did try to talk to me but my temper got the better of me. It's fine Jasper. It's not your fault. It's not anyone's fault.' Not anyone's except Seamus and Kiaran's, she thought. 'Can I talk to you for a moment? I have a couple of favours to ask. Just some things that I need looked after.'

'Of course, we can talk, and I'll help you any way I can, no questions asked.' Kind and thoughtful Jasper, she thought. He took her word without the benefit of the doubt. Why couldn't Lachie have done the same?

They talked for a long while, and then she returned to her cabin. After a while, she came back with a parcel and gave it to him. 'Thank you, Jasper. I know you won't breathe a word of this to anyone. I'll talk to you once the other problem is dealt with.'

Jasper nodded and she saw a glint of excitement in his eye. He was up for adventure and if he kept his word, he'd have a bit of fun chasing away those two idiot cousins of hers. Airlie Beach was a small place and he would have no trouble finding where they were staying.

* * *

With the first matter out of the way and in Jasper's control and the second matter being dealt with within the week, Kat set her mind back to work. If Lachie didn't want to be with her, then there wasn't much she could do about it. She certainly wasn't going to go begging after him, not after he accused her of being a liar and a thief.

He could go to hell, she told herself. I'll just forget about him and move on.

When the paint and canvases that she had ordered arrived, she threw herself into her artwork. Taking on every shift she could, she worked hard and saved her money. At night she cooked a light meal rather than eating with any of the others, and in her spare time she painted. Although she kept to herself most of the time she wasn't working, the weeks passed quickly.

Morag often came to visit at night and she loved to sit and watch Kat paint. 'You've really got a talent,' Morag said. 'You should try and sell some to the art galleries in town or maybe you could have a stall at the markets. Do some little ones of dolphins or whales. The tourists would love them.'

'Do you really think so? Would you come with me? Maybe you could be like my agent. You're better at talking and selling stuff than me.'

Morag did not have a creative bone in her Irish body, but she was brilliant at marketing and selling. 'You're right,' Morag said. 'My mother always said I could sell a glass of water to a drowning man.' Kat laughed. 'It's good to see you smile again, Kat. I don't know the full story of what happened between you and Lachie but it seems a shame. You made a grand couple.'

'Never mind, Morag. You win some, you lose some.'

'Talk about losing some. Did you hear what happened to those two fat Irishmen? I think they're your dreaded cousins that Jasper had fun with. He found where they were staying and shouted them drinks in Airlie Beach. Got them full of beer and then talked them into going out diving with him on the reef. He promised to take them sightseeing to one of the tiny islands where no one lives and tourists rarely get to go. Said there was a bar there, up in the rainforest where you just helped yourself to the beverages and could have as much as you wanted.'

'What happened?'

'He left them there. Overnight. Told them he needed to go back for more fuel to take them to another beach. Then he drove the boat away and left them standing there on the beach. There's no reception there for phones so they were well and truly stuck.'

'Holy mother of God. Please tell me they didn't get eaten by a crocodile. I mean they deserve that, but I don't want Jasper to be in trouble for anything.'

'No, nothing like that. He went back for them the next morning. Told them he ran out of fuel and that was the first he could get to them. Took a couple of the lads with him in case there was any trouble. Apparently, they were sunburnt and covered in mosquito bites. Starving, dehydrated, and terrified from all the creepy crawlies. He took them back in the boat, waited until they collected their belongings and drove them to the airport. Waited there he did, until he saw them get on a plane bound for Brisbane. I reckon they won't be rushing back anytime soon.'

Chapter Twenty-Two

Lachie knew that his mum, Evie, would be surprised to see him arrive home a month earlier than he had planned. He had driven straight through from Airlie Beach and only stopped a couple of times for coffee and something to eat. When he arrived back home his parents were sitting on the front deck having a cup of coffee. The family home was at Point Lookout on the eastern side of Stradbroke Island. The pole house, where they had lived for over thirty years, was set high on a hill overlooking the Pacific Ocean. For Lachie, it would always be home.

He leaned down and kissed his mother on the cheek, before giving his father a boisterous hug. 'Good to see you both. I'm a bit earlier than expected.'

'I'll make you a coffee,' his mother said as she got up and gave him a long hug. She never seemed to age, he thought. Her hair was still dark brown with only a few strands of grey poking through, and her skin was glowing and kissed with the golden radiance of a Queensland tan. It helped that her father was Italian and she had inherited not only his olive skin but his vivid green eyes and dark eyebrows. 'Mum, you look great.' He gave her another hug. 'It's good to see you.'

'I'll be back,' she said, disappearing into the kitchen.

His father also looked well. 'You both look so relaxed. Have you been taking it a bit easier?' Lachie asked.

'We have,' his father replied. 'Easing back on work and just enjoying being together. We've been fishing a lot off the beach, walking, and going away in the van sometimes.' His father looked him up and down. 'You look like shit, might I say. What's up?'

Lachie ran his hand through his hair, reaching out with the other to take the coffee from his mum. These days his dad's hair was short and receding a little. It was still blonde though and when Lachie looked back to answer him, he shook his head. Sometimes, it was like looking in the mirror; his dad was just an older, more tanned version of himself. 'There's got to be a reason you've come back early. Is it a girl?' his dad asked.

His mum sat down next to him on the outdoor couch. 'Jasper said you were getting on well with a young Irish girl.'

Lachie took a sip of his coffee and looked out over the ocean. Stradbroke Island never seemed to change. Although there were a few more houses on the hill and new businesses opening up down on the road opposite the beach, the essence of the island stayed the same. Cut off from the mainland by Moreton Bay and only accessible by boat or a ferry, it still had the same atmosphere as when he was a kid. The days were long, the pace slow, the beaches isolated and not frequented by that many people, apart from in the holiday seasons.

The ocean was sparkling today and flat as far as the eye could see. The water was a different colour than the Whitsundays and there were no islands further out to break the line of the horizon. He pointed out towards the northwest. 'There're a couple of whales out there. They're spouting.'

The three of them stood up and went to the railings. He pointed again. 'I see them,' his mother said. 'It looks like two adults and maybe a baby.'

His father grabbed a pair of binoculars off the table nearby and held them up to his eyes. 'Look further south. A way back from the lot you're looking at now. That's a white whale.'

He passed the binoculars to Lachie. 'It's white alright but I don't think it's big enough to be Migaloo.'

His mother took the binoculars next. 'I've seen Migaloo a few times over the years, from this spot, but I think you're right. It's white, but maybe only half the size of Migaloo.'

They watched the whales for a bit longer. His mum sat down on the couch and patted the seat beside her. 'Okay, Lachie. Back to the Irish girl. Tell us what's been happening.'

His dad leaned forward on his chair. 'You really don't look yourself. It's not like you to let anything get under your skin. You usually carry on, no matter what.'

'That's because I run from whatever it is that's

causing ripples in my life. I'm good at that.' He wrapped his hand around the mug of coffee. 'I've come to realise that unexpected problems don't sit well with me.'

'That's not a bad thing,' his mum said. 'I'm the same. I run a mile from confrontation or upsets. It stems back to my first partner. Arguments, problems and violence. I've told you about it before. I can't deal with any of it anymore.'

'You two always seem to see right through me,' Lachie said. 'I wasn't going to say anything. I thought I could just forget about everything that's happened. The girl's name is Kat. She's Irish and I thought she was the one. As in, the person I wanted to spend the rest of my life with.'

His father clapped his hands together. 'I never thought I'd hear you say that. Now there's going to be a 'but' isn't there?'

'Yep. A big 'but'. She's lied to me. She never told me she was, or had been married. It appears that she is married. I'm still not sure about the story behind that. And two of her Irish cousins came all the way out here to retrieve a ring, supposedly worth a million dollars that she stole off her Granny before she left Ireland.'

His dad's eyes were wide. 'Um, that's considerable drama. Does she have the ring?'

'She did. When they turned up on her doorstep, she said she'd had enough of running from them and gave it back to them. I think she knew she was defeated and they weren't going to give up. They'd been chasing her for a while and said the police would also be turning up. When her Granny died, the jewellery and contents of the house were left to these two fellas' family. It sounds like this ring was rightfully theirs. There was a huge confrontation between these two cousins and Kat. I felt like I was out in the cold because I knew absolutely nothing about any of it. The entire episode made me feel distant from her and that I didn't really know her at all. She'd never mentioned any of this to me and I'd never seen the ring. She certainly never wore it.'

'She just handed it over?' his mum questioned.

'Yep. Gave it to them and told them to leave. It was like she snapped. I think she knew they were never going to leave her alone until they had it.'

'And did she steal it?' his mum asked.

'I don't know. It sounds like she did. She told them it had been left to her before she left Ireland but she didn't say she had anything to prove that. They seemed to think it should have been with other jewellery that was left.'

'Did she admit to you she stole it?'

'No.'

'Did you ask her?'

'I tried, but she flew off the handle and went crazy. Started yelling at me and accusing me of not trusting or believing her. Intense and emotional. I'm telling you. I couldn't deal with how she reacted. I saw a completely different side of her.'

His mum pulled a quizzical face. 'So, you left?'

'Yep.'

'You never gave her a chance to explain herself once she had calmed down.'

'I left early the next morning. Georgia will look after the office. It's all too much for me. She's married and is involved in this million-dollar ring thing. I told you, I like my days to run smoothly. No commotions.'

'Well, son,' his dad intervened, 'we'd all like our lives to run smoothly, but it doesn't always work out that way. I'm thinking that you don't really love this girl if you took off like that. I wonder how she's feeling?'

Lachie stood up. 'I don't really care. It's over. If she couldn't tell me the truth or be upfront about all of this before it blew up in her face, then I can't trust her. And that's no way to be in a relationship. I've learnt that from experience.'

They talked for a bit longer about what had happened but then he asked them just to forget about it. 'I really don't want to talk about it anymore. I just want to put the events behind me. I'll be fine.'

* * *

The next day he went to what they called the home office. Many years ago his father had built in under their house to use for the business. It was a spacious area and had everything an office needed. Here he could immerse himself in his work and keeping busy would stop him dwelling on past events. The *Vivre* business had over ten surf stores in Australia and five overseas, so there was always work to do. There was also the island bait shop that was his mother's pride and joy.

Their main office was in Brisbane, but working online from home was fine by him. He didn't feel the need to socialise, and tucking away at home was perfect at the moment. In his spare time, he could surf and fish.

His parents were pulling back from some of their previous roles in the business and over the next few weeks his mother handed more work over to him, so there was always something to deal with. Occasionally he spoke to Jasper, but Lachie never asked his brother about Kat or what was going on at the island. Jasper had tried to broach the subject about him leaving so suddenly and not saying goodbye to Kat, but Lachie made it clear he didn't want to talk about it. Jasper knew him well enough to know when he dug his heels in over something major, there was no changing his mind.

Throwing himself into work was the best remedy to forget about everything. It was better to put it all behind him and look forward. Look forward to what, he didn't know, but there had to be something, or somebody, out there for him.

* * *

He had been home over a month when his mum informed him that she was going north to the Whitsundays to sort out some office procedures with Georgia. She wondered if he would like to travel with her. 'Sorry, Mum. I'm happy here. Jasper will love to see you though.'

His stomach lurched when he thought of going back to the island. It would be easy enough to check the staff lists to see if Kat was still working there, but he controlled himself and didn't look. He had not heard from her since he left and he wondered if she had gone back to Ireland, or maybe she was working in a different part of the country. No doubt he would find out when his Mum returned from her trip. For now, he had another problem to contend with. Prue was back on the island and had rung him several times, asking him to meet for dinner. She was persistent, and eventually he agreed to meet her at the pub.

* * *

He couldn't help but smile when he saw her, waiting at the entrance to the Point Lookout Pub. Although she had driven him crazy, especially at the end of their relationship, they'd had some good times together and travelled to a variety of places overseas. She had been living in California since they split up, but now she was back.

When she kissed him on the cheek, he got a whiff of her perfume. Chanel No 5, he remembered. Always her favourite and one he had often given her as a gift. 'You look so tanned and well, Lachie. I've missed you,' she purred, her voice soft and elegant.

'You look great, Prue.' He kissed her on the cheek and smiled. It was true. She was stunning to look at. Long tanned legs, immaculate black hair and makeup, and wearing a stunning black dress that revealed much of her body. When she leaned in towards him, her large breasts pushed up against him, the touch of her hand on her arm reminding him of the many intimate times they'd had together.

She laughed and pushed her thumb across his cheek where she had kissed him back. 'Lipstick. You know you're still as gorgeous as ever.'

For a while they stood and stared at each other. 'It's

good to see you,' he said. 'Let's go and have a drink before dinner.'

They sat outside, overlooking the ocean. The sun had already set, but the colours heralding the end of the day were painted across the sky. The sand and sea were still glowing and the sky was a mixture of pinks, orange and violet. It was the perfect setting.

'Just divine,' Prue murmured. There was a lot to catch up on and she filled him in on her stay in California. 'You know, Lachie. I thought that was where I wanted to live, but after a while I just wanted to come back here. I longed for the beach and missed Brisbane so much. I'm happy now to live in one of the inner suburbs in the city. My ideas have changed and I've realised I'm ready to settle down.'

Her last sentence was not lost on him, although he was still pondering her words about missing the beach. When they had lived together here on Stradbroke, she had only gone to the beach a couple of times to walk. Even then she had complained about the wind and sand between her toes. She spent most of her time sunbaking on a sun lounge in the front yard, soft mown grass under her delicate feet, well away from the beach.

'That's great Prue. I'm pleased you've worked out what you want.'

'What about you Lachie? Have you come back here to settle down also? Have you got a girlfriend?'

'No. No girlfriend and I'm happy working, and going fishing and surfing.'

A man came up beside them. 'Lachie McIntosh. Great to see you.'

It was Cameron, the reporter and photographer from the local newspaper. Lachie had gone to school with him and fished with him on the beach last year. 'How's Yvonne and the kids?' Lachie asked.

'Great. Yvonne is busy with the family but loves being a mum. The kids are all growing too quickly. Six, four and two and now another one on the way. They keep us on our toes.'

They chatted for a bit longer and Prue added a few comments. Positive and sensible, he thought. Perhaps she had changed. She seemed more settled and friendly, displaying a different attitude than when they had dated. So far he hadn't noticed the usual pouting and trying to get his attention all the time. Cameron had his camera hanging from his neck. 'Listen, can I get a photo of the two of you? Just for the social pages.' He looked around the pub. 'You two certainly look the picture of island locals. I'd love a photo of you both. It'll be in the local paper's social pages and if I'm luck, The Courier Mail.'

Prue quickly moved her chair closer to Lachie and he instinctively wrapped his arm around her shoulder. She loved nothing more than to pose for a camera and she moved in different ways, delighting Cameron. He talked to them for a bit more before moving off to find the next models for his photos.

During dinner, Lachie and Prue engaged in easy, light conversation, laughing as they reminisced about her holiday escapades. He playfully jogged her memory about their shared adventures across Asia, the year prior to their separation and there was more laughter and reminiscing. He remembered her favourite wine and they shared a bottle, the cool liquid relaxing his angst that lately always seemed to be there. During dinner he found himself staring at Prue's fingers that were elegantly wrapped around the crystal wine glass. Her long nails were painted a vibrant red, evoking a flood of memories from the nights they had spent together.

She must have caught him staring. 'Do you ever think about me, Lachie? About all the good times?'

'Sometimes,' he replied. 'You've changed, Prue. You're not so uptight.'

She sat up straighter, and her eyebrows lowered. 'I was never uptight, just practical about how things should be. You often needed reminders, or someone to point out how you should approach certain matters.'

Something in the back of his mind punched at him. There was that tone. The one he hated. The tone she used when she wanted to put him down, or try to control what he did. He swirled the wine in his glass. 'Wrong choice of word. You just seem more relaxed.'

Her face took on its earlier happy look and she leaned back in her chair. 'Someone told me you were going out with an Irish backpacker. Is that true?'

Frowning he took another long sip from his glass. 'Who told you that?'

'It doesn't matter. But I need to know. You know, if us dating is to go any further than tonight. Let's be honest. We're attracted to each other. It would be great to hook up or see each other again. I'd like to know how long it is since you were in a relationship though. I haven't been with anyone for several months, so I'm ready to plunge in again with you, if that's what we both want.'

'I'm single,' he replied cautiously. 'But I'm not in a hurry to date again. Dinner is nice tonight but let's leave it at that.'

She laughed. 'Oh, Lachie. Sometimes you just need a push along. Have a little think about it.' She stroked his arm, running her nails along his skin. 'I'll give you a call in a few days. We can talk more about 'us' then.'

Chapter Twenty-Three

Kat was hanging a painting on the foyer wall when a lady whose face she thought was familiar but couldn't place, walked in. She tried to work out who it was but she couldn't remember where she had met her. 'Won't be a sec. I'll just put this down,' she called out as she descended from a ladder.

She brushed her hands on her uniform, the light blue dress pressed and clean. She took a lot of pride in her role working in the reception area, and even though her heart was broken and pangs of homesickness had kicked back in, she worked hard and made sure she did the best job possible.

The lady walked over to her. 'Oh, my goodness, those paintings are exquisite. Where did you get them from?'

Kat looked up at the four large paintings that hung across the foyer walls. They were all done from photos that she had taken around the island. A sunset, a sunrise and two scenes as if you were standing on the beach and looking out across the ocean. Palm trees, white sand and blue skies with puffy white clouds made for the perfect painting and the pieces looked amazing on the white stucco wall.

Kat reached up and straightened one of them. 'They're actually mine. I painted them. They're all places here on the island.'

The lady peered closer at them, walking between them and then back again. 'You've captured the essence of *Vivre*. I don't think I've ever seen any as good as these and I've been to many different galleries.'

Kat sighed. 'I do love them. But really you can't go wrong with the scenery around here.'

When the lady turned to her, Kat noticed her green eyes and attractive face. She must have been in her fifties but her skin, although tanned, didn't have the usual wrinkled sun damaged look that many of the locals her age had. Kat guessed she was from the Mediterranean or maybe Brazil. 'Are you checking in?' she asked her. 'I have a few people arriving this morning.'

Kat admired the lady's style. She wore crème linen pants that swung elegantly on her body and a black singlet top showing off a slim and well-toned body. She followed Kat as she went back behind the desk and started looking at the computer, checking her bookings. When Kat looked up, she noticed her looking at the small painting that was hanging on the wall next to where she sat.

'Is that one of yours also?' she asked, gesturing to the painting.

'It is. It's home. Galway County. My Granny's cottage,' she murmured, her heart swelling with a familiar ache as her gaze lingered upon the small painting. The cottage stood proud, its whitewashed walls and thatched roof, set amidst lush meadows, contented cows and the beach beyond. She could almost taste the crispness of the air and envision wisps of smoke curling from the chimney in winter. Tracing her fingers gently over the puffy clouds depicted in the painting, she wondered what the weather was like there today. She mused aloud. 'The days will stretch on as the warmth settles in. The sun will be shining and everyone will be out and about, with music from the festivals filling the air. Everyone will be enjoying the sun.' She sighed and then suddenly realised she was talking aloud. 'Oh, I'm so sorry. I was lost in my thoughts.'

'Please don't apologise. You sound like you're homesick. I can understand why. I've spent some time in Ireland. We loved it, especially the pubs. We've always said that one day we'd go back.'

'There's so much to see. The pubs are the best. Full of music and dancing and, of course the beer.'

The lady's next words took her by surprise. 'I should introduce myself. I'm Evie McIntosh. You must be Kat.'

Kat's hand flew to her mouth. 'Jesus, Mary and Joseph. I thought you were a guest. What a surprise and here I am prattling on. I'm pleased to meet you. I've heard so much about you.'

'And I'm pleased to meet you also. Nobody told me you were an artist. Have you done the rest of the decorating in here. This area looks amazing.'

'I hope you don't mind.' Kat hesitated and thought for a moment before she spoke. 'Your son told me to play around with the foyer area and that I could hang my paintings in here.' She didn't add that she had been secretly doing the paintings to give to Lachie as a present. Their argument and then his departure had put an end to that surprise and she had instead hung the paintings in the foyer. 'Are you here to stay for a while?' she asked. 'Jasper did mention that you were coming up to do some bookwork.'

I'll stay for about a month and make sure the office is running smoothly. I don't work too much these days, but I like to keep my hand in and know what's going on. It keeps my mind active.'

'You sound like my mum. She and Granny always said that age is just a number and to ignore it. That attitude kept them going strong through the years.'

'You must miss home. Ireland is so different to here.'

'I miss it terribly. Like you wouldn't believe. The people, the food, the music, well just about everything there is about home. I came here to see the world though, and to get away from the cold. The Whitsundays are beautiful also and I love the warm weather.'

As she finished talking, Jasper burst through the entrance door. His arms were outstretched wide, his face radiant with joy at the sight of his mother. 'Mum. You've surprised us. You've snuck in. How did you get here without me knowing?' He wrapped his arms around her and lifted her off her feet. She laughed loudly as he swung her around. 'God, it's good to see you,' he said.

When he put her down, she reached up and held his face, her hands either side. 'Let me look at you. Have you been eating properly and looking after yourself? I hope you haven't been partying or drinking too much.'

'I have been taking care of myself, Mum. I promise. Ask Kat here. I see you two have met. Now, how did you sneak in without me knowing?'

'I was going to ring and get you to pick me up but the chef at the café where I had breakfast said that there were guests arriving back in this morning. A lovely young Scottish boy called Jock who dropped the guests at the wharf, gave me a lift back. It was a beautiful ride over and we even saw a whale on the way. He's a great kid. You want to hang on to him. He tells me he's the gardener.'

'Jock is one of the best workers you'll find,' Kat said. 'He's saved me numerous times from the gigantic bugs you have here. He arrives from wherever he is within two seconds of me ringing. He is a bit hard to understand, though. Thick Scottish accents are difficult to decipher sometimes.'

Evie laughed. 'I have to listen carefully to yours. I do love an Irish accent though.'

'Well, you'll get to hear more of her. Come for dinner with Mum and I tonight, Kat,' Jasper asked.

'Oh, I'm busy. I don't want to intrude.' The alarm at having further interaction with Lachie's mother was overwhelming and she tried to make more excuses not to join them. What had he told her? That she was married and had stolen a ring? Who knew what he was saying.

Evie placed her hands on the counter. 'I'll not take no for an answer. See you at Jasper's at six. We'll let him cook.'

Chapter Twenty-Four

Never had she been so nervous about what to wear. Although she had bought some new clothes, her wardrobe was still limited. Settling for a summery floral dress that was short, but not too short, she twirled in front of the mirror. She had taken an instant liking to Evie. Not only because Evie had admired her paintings, but because she seemed direct and had a no-nonsense attitude. She also had a carefree, almost Bohemian charisma, and Kat decided that she was more like Jasper than Lachie.

Although Lachie had tried not to worry about things and be laid back, she had detected that underneath the calm exterior, he stressed about minor incidents. Now it was also obvious that he couldn't deal with a few hurdles in his life. Admittedly the sight of two burly Irish lads turning up unannounced and shooting accusations was an unusual event. There was also the added complication that she had flown off the handle and expressed her feelings very loudly and vocally. But it was the way they did it in her family.

It was not a rare occurrence for a McCullagh Christmas lunch, with all the family attending, ending up dissolving into a yelling argument. Usually with comments and accusations thrown back and forth that would have been better left unsaid. The next day though, everyone would carry on as if nothing had happened. There was no sweeping of problems or arguments under the carpet, or hiding your feelings in her family. It was all in and open slather.

After encountering Evie, the epitome of poise and grace, Kat couldn't shake the feeling that the McIntosh clan likely operated on a different wavelength than her own family. Lachie's mother exuded charm and radiated composure, and going by the sound of her voice summoning Kat to dinner, it was clear she wasn't one to be trifled with. Kat made a mental note to tread carefully; despite Evie's amiable demeanour, she was the boss of *Vivre*. Tonight, Kat would have to mind her manners and be cautious, especially if the conversation veered towards the complexities of her relationship with Lachie.

Kat made sure she arrived for dinner on time. As she walked down towards Jasper's hut she could see that a table had been set up on the lawn and flares flickered in the gardens nearby, lighting up the area. Stars glittered above the coconut palms and a full moon hung low over the water, its glow creating a shimmering ribbon of gold laid out across the ocean; a stairway to heaven. As she approached the table she could see the others already seated and she was excited that Jock was also invited for dinner. Everyone greeted her and she sat down on a seat beside Evie. Glancing at Jock, she threw him a cheeky wink and a nod of approval. He had worn a tartan tie over the top of his white T-shirt, his curly mop of red hair also brushed and neat.

'I see you've worn your special tie, Jock,' she joked.

'It's the only formal attire I have,' he answered. 'It's not every night I get asked to a fancy dinner with the big boss.'

'I wouldn't say it's fancy,' Jasper said as he placed three large bowls of crabs, prawns and oysters in the middle of the table. 'It's more like a, use your fingers, peel your own sort of night.'

Kat was starving. For some reason she hadn't eaten lunch and she thanked her lucky stars that Jasper had laid out a feast. 'Laughter is brightest where food is best,' she quipped. 'Thank you for inviting us. I'm sure Jock feels the same. It's a special night to finally meet Jasper's mum.'

'Looks like a right treat,' Jock said as he reached over and offered one of the bowls to Evie. 'In our house my dad always makes us wait until my mother is served. After all she's the one who does all the cooking.'

Evie smiled around the table and raised her wine glass. 'To family and good friends. You're both a long way from home and your families. I can tell from talking to you, that you have a close connection to your families.

Thank you for both being such good workers. You are valued here at *Vivre*.'

Kat felt special. It was nice to be recognised and appreciated for her good work. There was so much to talk about that the night had gone quickly. They had all travelled to similar places but agreed that it didn't get much better than here on the island. 'The best part for me,' Kat told them, 'apart from the glorious weather, is the lack of people. I don't like cities or crowded places. It will be interesting how I'll go whenever I go back, because I'll probably have to live in one of the cities if I want a decent job.'

Evie made Irish coffees to finish off the night and the four of them sat on deck chairs positioned on the sand. Small waves lapped against a couple of sailing boats anchored out further and a mallee hen called from the bushes to the side of where they sat. Other than that, the night was still and quiet.

Jasper regaled Evie with funny stories of incidents that had happened on the island and repeated the story of how Kat and Morag and then Jock, had danced at Jasper's party. 'She can sing also,' Jock said, as he came to sit next to Kat on her wooden recliner. 'She has the voice of an angel.'

Kat gave his arm a friendly pat. 'Well, now, isn't that the pot calling the kettle black? You've got a grand voice. Grace us with one of your own tunes.'

She knew he could sing also. He always sung or whistled while he was working.

Evie turned to Jock. 'I would love to hear your sing.

That would really make the night something special for me.'

When he cleared his voice, stood up and looked to the stars, Kat knew they were in for something special.

He bowed before he began and then announced. 'I give you, *Flowers of Scotland*. The unofficial national anthem of my home.'

It was as if the waves and the mallee hens knew to be silent. You could have heard a pin drop, as Jock, with hand on his heart, sang in his beautiful deep voice the most beautiful song about his homeland. When he finished, he bowed again and with tears in her eyes, Kat stood up and took his hand. She started singing the song again with him. She had been around enough Scottish people to know the words by heart. Her heart lifted as their voices joined in unison, the lilting tones of the beautiful song a fitting tribute to his homeland. When she looked at Jock, tears streamed down her face and she wiped them away to continue singing. Her voice lifted in melody with Jock when they sang the last lines – '*And sent him homeward, to think again.*'

Evie and Jasper clapped and both wiped tears from their eyes. For a moment all Kat could think about was that she wished Lachie was here also. She noticed Evie staring at her and their eyes locked. Kat knew that her thoughts were transparent. She looked to Jasper who was shaking his head in amazement.

Now Kat had started she didn't want to stop. 'Could you sing *Galway Bay* with me, Jock?'

'Aye. I know the chorus. You start and I'll come in.'

Taking a sip from her wine before she started, she

looked out across the ocean. 'This one's for you Granny. From one bay to another, across the oceans.'

Her voice was clear and crisp in the night air and as she sang, she put her heart and soul into the tune. The first lines came out a bit shaky, but once she pulled her emotions into check, she sang with gusto. '*If you ever go across the sea to Ireland. Then maybe at the closing of your day.*' She gestured for Jock to join in, but he, like the other two, appeared mesmerised by her voice. She surprised herself. Her voice was level and full of sentiment. She knew it was because of the raw emotions that lately were always simmering just under the surface. As Granny would say, a voice without passion or insight is as empty as a pot without a drop of gold at the end of the rainbow.

When she belted out the song the second time, Jock joined in and their voices blended beautifully, the rich harmonies giving the best to the tune. When she finished, she hugged Jock, but then turned around to face the ocean. Tears rolled down her face and she wiped them away with her hand before turning back to the others.

'Excuse me. I'm very emotional. It was good to sing. Thank you, Jock. Sometimes I don't know what I'd do without you.'

Evie stood up and put her arm around her. 'That was beautiful. I feel like I've been at a concert and heard the Celtic singers or someone famous. You can't get any better than both your voices.'

'Jock laughed. 'Next time I'll bring my fiddle. Then we'll have some toe-tapping music.'

The night wound up not long after and Kat was sorry to say goodbye to the other three. It had been an emotional night and one she would always remember. When she lay in bed that night, loneliness crept in and the tears flowed again. This time not for the music or missing home, but more for the loss of Lachie and his arms around her. She pushed her face into the pillow and willed herself to sleep. Work started at seven in the morning and she needed to be bright and early to the office. As much as Evie had been friendly and appeared to like Kat, she was still the big boss.

Chapter Twenty-Five

Lachie was buttering his toast when Jasper rang the next morning. 'How are you going, brother?' Jasper asked. 'We miss you up here.'

Lachie put the phone on speaker so he could continue what he was doing. 'Good, Jasper. Great. How about yourself?'

'Couldn't be better.'

They talked about the business, fishing and the weather. Lachie purposely steered the conversation away from anything that could remotely relate to Kat. It was too early in the morning for those types of conversations. He hadn't heard from his mother since she left over a week ago. She had stayed with some other friends on the journey north, and he hadn't been sure what day she was arriving at the island. Jasper filled him in on what she had been doing and how good it was for him to have her there. 'Mum arrived yesterday and I had her over for dinner last night.'

'That would've been good. Any crabs? She loves them.'

'Yes. We had a feast of them, and prawns and oysters. Demolished the entire lot. Only the shells left. I asked two of your other friends as well. Jock and Kat.'

He had wondered in the back of his mind, whether his mother had met Kat yet. 'How was that?'

'You should've been here, mate. They talked and ate and everyone got along great. It was a fun night. I wish you'd been there.'

'Well, I've been keeping busy here with work.'

'You should have heard the music, Lachie. Jock and Kat sang together. Under the stars, on the beach. It was something else. They sang ballads and their voices even made me cry. You should've seen Mum's face. She was in seventh heaven listening to them. You know how she loves music.'

'That's great.'

'And, I saw her looking at Kat. You know that look she gets on her face when she's scheming something. That look like she's got plans ticking in her mind and she's not going to let anyone else know. You want to watch out, I could practically see the gears turning in her head. You're a goner, Lachie. Mum loves her.'

* * *

Evie had not wasted any time. The next afternoon she was waiting for Kat when she finished her shift. 'I thought we could take a walk along the beach together. It's a beautiful afternoon and I'd like to show you a small waterfall that not many people know about. Have you seen it?'

'I haven't seen any waterfalls here on the island. I'd love to walk. Just let me slip home and throw some shorts on.'

Evie was waiting on the jetty, her hand shading her eyes as she looked across the ocean. 'Dolphins,' she said, pointing to the north. 'A large pod of them. See, there they are.'

Kat looked out. A couple of the dolphins leapt out of the water and danced on their tails. The water was flat and calm so they were easy to see. 'We get dolphins in Galway Bay. There are some large pods and the locals have even given names to some of them. The water here seems much bluer than at home, probably because the sky is usually blue here, which I love. I must admit the heat does get to me in summer though.'

'You'll have to come to Stradbroke Island one day. It's cooler there but just as beautiful. When I was younger, I lived further up north, past Cairns. That's even more tropical. Wet, humid and hot. Also a beautiful place though.'

'How did you end up down south?'

Evie walked down the jetty and Kat followed her onto the beach. 'That's a long story. For a short version of those years, I would say that I moved back down south to escape a bad relationship. I was fortunate that some good people helped me get back on my feet. Eventually I met back up with Chris, who I had gone out with when I was a teenager. We've been together for over thirty years now and I wouldn't change a thing. I'd follow him to the end of the world, and he would say the same about me. Anyway enough about me. C'mon and I'll show you this waterfall.'

They talked as they walked and Evie asked a lot of questions about Kat's home and family. She nodded when Kat described the chaotic, raucous gatherings and how everyone in her family often argued and told it how it was. 'Sometimes it's just one calamity after another. We always manage to come through to the other side unscathed, but at the time it's unbelievable and can't get any messier. No wonder my mum has so many grey hairs.'

'I knew another Irish girl once and her family was the same,' Evie said. 'She said there was always a barney or something happening. Our family is the opposite of that. I think it's because I can't stand arguments or confrontation. It's probably because I put up with a lot of things I shouldn't have when I was with my first partner. I run a mile from any arguments or issues.' She paused for a moment. 'And so does Lachie.'

Evie bit her lip and kept walking. She didn't want to get into the complexities of Lachie's personality. She knew what mothers could be like. If Evie was anything like her own mother, she would stick up for Lachie come hell or high water.

Kat's brother, Ronan, could do no wrong in her mother's eyes and Kat had often tried to convince her to rein Ronan in, or to stop him doing something he wasn't supposed to. He was the biggest calamity maker in her family. If there was room for trouble, he would either create it or find it. Mum's favourite saying rang in Kat's ears. 'Your brother is as pure as the morning dew on the shamrocks, bless his little heart.' What a load of rubbish, Kat thought. Claiming that her son could do no wrong was like claiming there was no rain in Galway.

Luckily the conversation didn't continue in that direction because they came to where Evie wanted to go. As they ambled along the sandy shores, a meandering creek greeted their path, snaking its way from the inland to meet the ocean. Following its gentle banks, they ventured a short distance into the rising hillside. Here, the landscape transformed into a picturesque scene straight out of a fairy-tale. Water tumbled gracefully over a rugged rocky ledge, forming a sparkling cascade that descended into a crystal-clear pool below. Surrounding this oasis were clusters of small boulders draped with delicate ferns, creating a tranquil sanctuary hidden beneath a lush canopy of trees, their branches inter-locking to form a protective shield against the sun's rays.

'The water comes down from the mountain in the middle of the island, along with any rain that soaks through the hillside. It isn't always running. When it hasn't rained for ages, it's been known to dry up. We swim here sometimes in summer, but we don't tell the guests about it. Better that it's not overrun with tourists. There are plenty of places for them at the beach and in the ocean. I'm surprised no one in the family has ever brought you here.'

There it was again—a little hint, at what, she wondered. Evie took a deep breath. She knew that sooner or later the questions were going to come. They talked again, and Evie told Kat about the history of the small island and how they had come to buy it. It sounded like they owned more property than Kat thought, and she was in awe of how someone could own an entire island.

When they left the shaded area and turned back to the beach, the sun was low in the sky. The afternoon light filtered through the clouds and seabirds flew above them, diving into the water every now and then, in search of small fish. Evie's question came abruptly, like a sudden gust of wind.

'Why did you and Lachie part ways?'

Closing her eyes for a moment she thought about the best way to put it. Without insulting Lachie. 'It just wasn't working. We're too different.'

'I don't want the formal explanation. I want what really happened.'

Kat stopped walking and so did Evie. They looked each other in the eye. 'Why?' Kat asked. 'What does it matter to you? I'm not going to harass him or chase after him, so you don't have to worry about that. I won't say anything bad about him. You're his mother and I know what mothers and sons are like. I have a brother. My mother will take his side every time.' She took a breath, feeling her face burning and a tone of anger in her voice. 'I just want to keep working here for a while. I'm looking for another job so that when Lachie comes back, I'll be gone. I don't want it to be awkward for him.'

She jumped when Evie gently grabbed her arm. 'I know my Lachie. I know his good points and his bad points. I just want us to be honest with each other. The reason I want to know, is because I like you and I think he's made a big mistake running from you. He might have come back to his family at Stradbroke and he says he's okay, but he's not. He's lying and I can see the hurt in his eyes. Surely you can tell me the full story. I promise you can trust me. I won't repeat anything you say if you don't want me to. Not to him, not to anyone.'

Kat hesitated only for a moment. It was time she offloaded on someone and for some reason she knew Evie was that person. There was something about her that let Kat know she could trust her. 'I need a drink,' Kat announced. 'Let's go back to my cabin and have some wine. I haven't told anyone the real story about any of this.'

Chapter Twenty-Six

When Kat opened the door an hour later to let Evie in, she was happy to see that she had arrived with hot chips in hand. 'I got them from the restaurant and this bottle of wine,' Evie said. 'Jasper is filling in for one of the barmen who's sick, so we're on our own which is good.'

They sat at the wooden kitchen table, chips spread out on the plain paper they had been wrapped in and a glass of wine each. Kat's offer of plates and cutlery had been dismissed. 'There's only one way to eat takeaway chips and that's like they're a takeaway,' Evie said as she spread the meal out in front of them. 'I had to find some paper in the office for the chef to put them on. They don't usually serve them this way.' She giggled. 'Maybe that's something new we could add to the menu. I tell you what, Kat. I feel like a young girl again. Eating chips and drinking wine with a young person who's travelling the world. It's a while since I've done this.'

'You don't seem older to me. Age is irrelevant anyway

when it comes to women and conversation. My granny was also my best friend. The fifty plus years between us meant nothing when we got together and yacked.

'I have two daughters of my own so I'm used to being with young ones and helping to solve their romances. If you could hear some of the stories my girls have shared. As my father would say, it would make your hair curl.'

'Are your parents still alive?'

'They are. Dad is eighty-two and Mum is eighty. Mum remarried many years ago, so I also have a step-father who happens to be Chris's father.'

Kat tried to work that out. 'So, your mother married Chris's father?'

'Yes. Another long story, but Chris's mother had passed away and my mother and father had separated. My mum, Maya, and Chris's father, David, had always been keen on each other. True love prevailed and they ended up together. They live in a retirement village in Noosa. Both happy and healthy.'

'And what about your dad?'

'Oh, my beautiful father who I adore. His name is Carlo. He's Sicilian, hence my features. He lives in Sydney still. He has for a long time, since him and Mum split up. He's gay and was with the same partner, Matteo, for many years. Matteo passed away a few years ago and Dad has taken a long time to get over the loss. They loved each other. When I was younger there were times when I didn't see my father for a long while. He was sort of forced to live in Sydney as there was a supportive gay community there at the time. Brisbane had a small-town mentality back then and it's sad to say but my dad never came back to Queensland to live because of that. That's my story in a nutshell. There's a lot more to it than that, but that gives you the picture.'

'Families. There's always so many layers. I couldn't even begin with mine. Large families with lots of different personalities, some good and some not so good.'

Evie filled up their glasses. 'Right. I want to hear your entire story. Don't leave anything out and I swear that anything you tell me stays in this room.' She settled back in her chair. 'I once had an old friend, she's passed away now, but she and I had secrets. We never told anyone. Between you and me, if we had, one or two of us could have ended up in jail.'

'Granny and I were like that. I told her lots of things I never told anyone else, and she was the same with me.' She took a big breath and a large gulp of wine. 'I'll try and make this easy to understand. I'm only telling you this because you're not connected to my family and now that Granny and Grandad are gone it doesn't seem so bad to share her story. If I start with my Granny, I'll leave the marriage thing to the last.'

Evie raised her eyebrows but didn't flinch or say anything. 'Start. I'm all ears.'

* * *

'Before Granny was married to my Grandad, she was a housemaid for one of the richest families in Galway. They lived in a castle in the hills and the views were so spectacular Granny believed you could see halfway across the county. It was a long way from her home and she used to tell me about how homesick she got. The family who lived in the castle had seven or eight kids and typically there was a lot of family feuding, and troubles that happened. Granny was only about fifteen so she knew how to stay out of it all and keep her nose clean. Sorry, that means to be honest.'

Leaning back in her chair, Evie's eyes were sparkling and it was obvious she was interested in the story. 'Go on,' she encouraged.

'She worked there for two or three years. With those sorts of positions you lived in the servants' quarters at the back of the property and sometimes she said it would be over a year before she saw her parents and siblings. Over time she became friendly with some of the family she worked for.' She stopped, unsure if she could continue. Granny had entrusted her with her secrets and, as far as she knew, no one else in the family knew about the times she was talking about.

Evie must have sensed her uncertainty. 'It's okay if you don't want to tell the secret part. If you've been sworn to secrecy, I understand.'

Twirling the stem of the wine glass in her hand, Kat thought about how to word the next part. 'Let's just say that there was a romance with a younger member of the family, a pregnancy, and an offer to buy the newborn when it arrived. After that the person would leave the employ and no one would be any the wiser. The head of the family had a younger sister who could not have children. The unfortunate event would be hidden and kept secret and the sister would solve the dilemma of what to do with the baby.'

Evie sat forward in her seat, her green eyes flashing with interest.

'So, her parents never knew?'

'No, she said they never found out. She visited them when she first discovered she was pregnant and then again after she had the baby, which of course had been removed from her as soon as it was born. That's also when she returned home and a year or so later, she met my Grandad. No one knew about the baby, except probably the head of the family and his wife.'

'How much money was involved?'

'There was a small amount of money but the bulk of the compensation or purchase was paid for with a ring. A ring that had been handed down through generations and was said to be made of the finest gold, and bearing an emerald that she was told had come from the jungles of Colombia. They told her that the ring would be more valuable in years to come and she could keep it for a long time and no one would ask any questions. It would be suspicious if she returned home with a large amount of money, so it was better to have the ring and then down the track, once a certain amount of time had passed and no suspicions could be aroused, she could sell it. They even gave her a slip of paper with a description and words that showed they had gifted her the ring as a reward for her good ework while she had been in their employ.

Granny said that the lady of the house had a trinket box full of similar rings and other jewellery. She overheard her telling her husband that the one they had given her was the least valuable and only worth a few shillings.

Granny always hated the ring and I'm not sure why she didn't throw it away. She never wore it and it was always kept with her discarded badges and bits'n'pieces that she let us kids play with when we were little. Of course we all loved the emerald ring, because it was such a vivid green and the stone was huge. We'd dress up, all of us cousins, and pretend we were rich and living in a manor house.'

'Your poor granny. Life must have been so hard for any of them back in those days. So many with very little money.'

'Granny said that living with the family she was working for taught her that money did not buy happiness. She said that, even though she disliked the ring and she never forgot the baby, the lessons learned after she left the family stood her in good stead for the rest of her life. Years after she left, she learned that a large part of the castle had burnt down and the parents and two of the children had died in the fire. She was never one hundred percent sure, but the story was that the family who had taken the baby had also perished in the fire. It was Christmas time and they had all been together to celebrate.'

Evie's voice was quiet. 'Did the baby die too?'

'She tried to find out but couldn't come up with anything. No one knew and she said it was more than likely that they had all been together. No one will ever know.'

They both took long sips of their drinks. 'It's a sad Irish tale,' Kat eventually continues, 'and I'm sure many things like that happened to others during that era.

Anyway, the ring was forgotten about for a long time and as we grew up, no one really bothered with it. I had however always liked it. Granny told me several times to take it. I remember her saying she wasn't sure why she had never thrown it out. I started to wear it and I liked to put it on when I went to university. I lived with her for a while then and studied online, as Covid had started and there weren't many live lectures.

One day she asked me if I still had the ring. She had watched a show on the telly. An antique show where people are invited on to get their antiques valued. A lady had turned up with a ring that looked exactly like the one Granny had given me. It was worth a million pounds. A rare green emerald from Colombia.

That night we sat and stared at the ring for a long time, passing it back and forth between us and looking at the way the light played on the emerald. Being old gold and quite soft, there were a few chips out of the band and some dents where one of the baby cousins had chewed on it once. We drank a bottle of wine while looking at it and then also tried to work out what to do next. It was that night she told me the story of it. She had never told anyone her entire life. She'd kept that secret, nearly to the grave.'

'You must have been very close to her. She obviously wanted someone to know the story.'

I think she told me, not only because she wanted someone to know, but also because she wanted me to have the ring. And if I was to have the ring, I needed to know that story and learn the same lessons she had. She wanted me to know that money doesn't buy happiness.'

'What happened then?'

'She didn't want to get the ring valued in case people found out about her doing so. Wherever you go near home, someone will know someone and sooner or later, if it was worth anything, everyone would know. She said, 'I don't want money at my age, but I want you to have money. You're young. You could travel the world. Go to Australia for me. I'm too old now but you could go. Sell it. It means nothing to me and I don't want anyone else getting it if it's worth something. You must promise though not to tell anyone you have it. No one, you hear me. Money causes trouble and especially so if someone else is wanting it.'

'How did you find out if it was the real thing?' Evie asked.

'I'd gone to university with a lad whose father had a jewellery shop in London. They were nice people and I knew I could trust them. Before I left for Australia, I flew to London and went to this particular jeweller. He couldn't believe it when I showed him the ring. He had been in the business for a long time and had some connections with the valuers on the antique show. He talked to them about the ring they had on there, that was similar to mine.

They told him there had been three emerald rings made for a royal family in Europe in the early 1900s. The stones came from Colombia and were rare. Only one ring was known to be in circulation and the question of what happened to the other two rings had remained an unsolved puzzle for many years. It was assumed they had been hidden or lost during World War II. The one the lady on telly had meant that there were now two known in circulation. That meant there was only one missing. The one I have is larger and more exceptional than the one that was on the antique show. They call them untreated Colombian emeralds. The jeweller was one hundred percent sure that the ring I had was the third ring.'

'Wow.' Evie's eyes were wide and she blinked rapidly. 'Go on. Go on.'

'I went away and thought about what I was going to do. When I went back to see him, I asked how long it would take him to make me a replica ring.' He didn't ask any questions as to why. He was very professional and his son had already told him that my Granny had given me the ring years ago. Within three days he had made me a replica ring. The day after that I flew to Brisbane, with both rings coming with me. I wore the real one and hid the reproduction one in my luggage.

Unfortunately, everyone in my family, including my cousins, also saw the show. It's such an unusual ring and we had played with it so much as kids that even my idiot cousins, Seamus and Kiaran, recognised it. They harassed Granny but she told them she no longer had it and it had disappeared years earlier. She must have been worried about them though, because she rang my sister, Grace, and checked my postal address had not changed from the last time she wrote. At the time I was working at Dingo Beach Pub. You can get mail posted to the store there. It acts as a mini post office.'

'Yes, yes. I know where you mean,' Evie interrupted. 'So she posted you something?'

'I'm presuming so from what Grace said. Granny told her to let me know that something important was coming in the post. Tell her it's the rights to our Irish secret,' she said. 'She'll know what I'm talking about.'

When Grace told me, I knew it would be something to say she had given the ring to me. Mum had told me the cousins were harassing her about it and she asked if I knew its whereabouts. I kept Granny's secret, and said no.

It was only a week later that Mum rang me to tell me Granny had passed away in her sleep. She had been staying with them in Galway for her birthday, and she slept in my bed.' Kat wiped her eyes. 'She died in my bed, with her and my favourite patchwork quilt she had made me, over her. It was like it was meant to be. I never went back for the funeral. She'd already told me that if she died, I wasn't to return. Go to the top of the nearest hill and sit and think about me, she said. I'll be there listening. You can always tell me your secrets still.'

Evie poured another glass of wine for herself and Kat stood up and went to the fridge. 'I need chocolate. Nothing better than wine and chocolate.' Evie agreed and they broke large bits off the block of dark chocolate and sat munching one piece after the other.

'That's a sad story,' Evie said, in between bites. 'How beautiful that she died in your bed. She would have been thinking about you and your adventure here in Australia.'

'She would have. The day after she died, the will was read and my cousins cleared her place out. They must've been searching for that ring because my dad said they tore the floorboards up and even put huge holes in some of the walls looking for secret hiding spots.

Their family was left all the contents of Granny's house and some money she had in the bank. Nothing else though. My family was left the house.

Those two were after the ring though. They had it in their heads that it was worth a lot of money and they presumed I had it. Seamus rang me a few times, being all nice and asking me questions about where I was and had I seen the ring recently. He kept ringing and eventually accused me of taking it. I hung up and blocked his calls. They pestered Grace though and also some of my other friends who still kept in contact with me. Eventually they found out where I was living and came all the way out here to try and collect what I guess could have rightfully been theirs.'

'Well, not really. If she gave it to you before she died, I would think that would mean it's yours.'

'That's what I think too. The problem is I'm the only person who knows the truth. I told no one else because she asked me not to, not even my mum or sister, and the jeweller only took my word for it also. Nothing would stand up in a court of law.'

'What happened to what she posted to the Dingo Beach Pub for you? Isn't that enough to show you own it?'

'I don't have it. I continually went there, but they said there was nothing there. The place is messy and disorganised. They probably threw it out.'

'That doesn't surprise me. I know the lady there. She's lovely, but running a post office is not her strong suit. So where is the ring now? Lachie said very little when he came back home. When I pushed him for more information, he said that you had taken something but now you had given it back.'

Kat gritted her teeth. 'That is exactly why we argued. I took nothing. I gave the reproduction one back to Seamus and Kiaran. I told them it was a reproduction. I never lied. I just didn't tell them I had the original. They'll get it valued and soon find out it's worth very little. I doubt very much whether they'd be smart enough to think that I had a replica one made.'

'So where is the real Emerald ring?'

Kat took a deep breath and looked straight at Evie. 'It's in your son's safe. I gave it to Jasper to put it in his safe under the floorboards in his cabin.'

Chapter Twenty-Seven

By the time Evie left to go back to her cabin it was after midnight. They finished off with several cups of tea and some stale biscuits that Kat found in the cupboard. 'I think the marriage story will have to wait for another night,' Evie said as she hugged Kat and said goodbye. 'If it's as complicated as that one, we'll need a lot more chocolate.'

'Nowhere near as interesting. It's boring, actually, and something I never really think about. A drunken night and a dare. I'll tell you the rest sometime.'

When she lay in bed that night, Kat's head was spinning. Through her window she glimpsed stars twinkling brightly to the south. At least Evie now knew the truth. She could trust her and it was best that someone knew exactly what had happened, just in case those two buffoons returned and tried to get nasty. Sometimes she wished she hadn't accepted the ring from Granny. She was never going to wear it. It was worth too much money, plus Granny had disliked it. On the other hand, it would be good to hang onto the ring like Granny had wanted her to, and in the years to come she could sell it and use the money to maybe buy a house or something important like that.

* * *

It was a relief to have it tucked away safe and sound in Jasper's keeping. For too long, it had been a heavy burden, her mind fraught with worry about whether it was stashed away well enough. As she finally succumbed to sleep, her dreams swirled with whispers of secrets she had held close for countless years. In the midst of it all, Granny's gentle face graced her visions, a warm smile lighting up the shadows. With that comforting thought, Kat drifted into a deep, peaceful sleep, awakening only to the raucous calls of black cockatoos greeting the morning outside her window.

* * *

The next week flew by and Kat let Jasper have some time with his mum alone. Evie had called into reception quite a few times to talk to her, and they had gone over a few of the parts of the story that Evie was confused about. 'I think we should go and have another look at Dingo Beach for your letter. The lady at the shop, Myrtle, knows me and it's worth a try. If you had a piece of paper to say the ring was yours, it would fix any problems later on, in case those two ever work out what you've done.'

'You know, Myrtle? The lady at the Dingo Beach store?'

'Yes, she and I go way back. You wouldn't believe it but she's a technology guru. When we set up the computer system here, we had a few glitches and she answered my call for help on the local Facebook page. Fixed it straight away. No problems, and hardly charged me anything. Don't worry, I've been to her shop and I know it wouldn't appear that she's organised and could do that sort of work, but she's one smart cookie when it comes to tech. I'm sure if I rang she'd agree to let us have a good look for the letter.'

'I guess it's worth a try. As long as you don't mind spending the time going there and looking for it.'

'We could have a girls' day out. It would be fun. I haven't been to the pub there for years. They do a good lunch. I also think you should ring Lachie. It's not up to me to say anything to him, but surely it's worth talking to him. If he knew the real story, I'm sure he would come around.'

'I'm sorry, Evie. I'm still so angry with him for not believing in me. It's not my fault I've carried around that emerald secret for so long.'

* * *

The following week they arranged for Jasper to take them to Dingo Beach in the boat named after Evie. Sitting on the bench seats brought back memories to Kat of the first time she had gone snorkelling with Lachie. They had made many other trips in this boat, and she tried not to look at the couch in the cabin, the heat rising in her body when she thought of the times they had made love in that spot. Back then her skin had been lily white and she had been paranoid about the sun and everything else that came with the Australian way of life. She looked down at her legs which were tanned a little. Her concern about the sun might have dwindled a little, however her fear of the bugs and reptiles had not. Twisting her hair, which needed a good cut, she tied it back in a ponytail. It was down to the middle of her back and for a second the thought crossed her mind to get it cut short. Really short. 'Keep it long while you're young,' Granny had always said. 'Especially with the cinnamon colour. You've been blessed.'

Holding her hat which was threatening to fly off, she looked towards the mainland. Dingo Beach was not far north of where they were and with such calm weather and clear skies, it was what Lachie would have called the perfect day. A variety of different-sized boats plied across the water, some of them heading further out to sea to the outer reefs and small islands where the bigger fish could be caught. A couple of tinnies were anchored nearer the shoreline, the occupants waving to them as they passed. Soon the houses of Airlie Beach had disappeared and only a few houses could be seen dotted amongst the thick vegetation that bordered the water.

Steep red cliffs plunged into the sea and spray from a few small waves splashed onto her face as she stared at the incredible colours. The cool water was refreshing and the scenery amazing. When she glanced upward she caught sight of an eagle gracefully circling above. Its massive wings were spread wide as it glided on the thermals before looping back around the boat. Eventually it landed on one of the tall pine trees that leaned out from gullies in amongst the cliffs. Above them a blue sky shone brilliantly, the heat of the day yet to come. As they rounded another headland the boat sped across a couple of bays, the small village of Dingo Beach soon coming into view.

She had been back to the store several times to ask about the letter, but each time Myrtle said there was nothing there. No doubt this time the result would be the same. Still, it was an excuse for a day out on the water and to be in the company of two people she had come to like a lot. Jasper was always up for an outing, especially when it involved food or a beer. They had not gone into details about the visit, instead telling him they just wanted to check there was no leftover mail for Kat. It would be a good opportunity to sit and relax as well as have a meal. As usual he didn't ask questions. He was just happy to be out and about with his mum and Kat.

At first Myrtle was not very helpful, but when Evie persisted and asked if they could go through the numerous boxes and shelves themselves, she huffed and puffed a lot before agreeing. 'Must be bloody important this letter. Don't make a mess otherwise my husband will get the shits. He's the one who cleans up in here. I'm only letting you have a look because I know you from the computer work you gave me. I certainly don't have time so go right ahead.'

It didn't appear that anyone had cleaned the office part of the store for decades. Kat held her tongue though and smiled sweetly. Luckily Evie was diplomatic and stubborn, as well as possessing a canny knack of persuading someone to do what she wanted. Myrtle showed them into a back room, kicking a box full of papers out of the way and clearing a space on the bench for them. She then left them to it.

Jasper had decided to try his luck at fishing around the island that lay across the passage. They had agreed to meet back at the pub in an hour. 'We'll have to watch the tide here,' he told them before dropping them off. 'I'll just have a go at fishing around Gloucester Island and then I'll anchor up and we can have a feed. We'll have to get back out before two o'clock, though. There's only a narrow channel to get in and out.' Both of them kept an eye on the time. As lovely as Dingo Beach was, neither of them wanted to spend the night there.

Evie organised the areas where they would look. 'You start with those boxes and I'll look through these. We can both check the shelves. A letter could have easily fallen down the back of these tables. I can see envelopes and even some parcels under the bench there. Right at the back.'

They had looked through everything for half an hour before Evie yelled out. 'Bingo. There is a small parcel here. Look under this washing basket full of towels. It's addressed to you.'

They grinned at each other as Kat took the parcel from Evie, too excited to think properly.

'Open it,' Evie said. 'See what it is.'

They both peered into the wrappings as they were unfolded. Inside was a new hat and a birthday card from her Granny, but no paperwork to say the ring belonged to Kat. 'She posted this not long after I left. She must have been worried either that she wasn't going to be still around in January, or that the post would take a very long time.'

Evie looked at her watch. We have half an hour still. I think we should keep looking.'

It took another ten minutes before Kat pulled a heavy box away from the wall to reveal a bundle of letters that had fallen down behind it. She undid the band that held them together and started looking through them. She gave a squeal of delight. 'Can you believe it. This one is addressed to me. I can't believe that two of my letters were lost here. If we hadn't looked, I would never have known.' When she opened the envelope, she knew they had found what they were looking for. She held it high in the air. 'We did it. You helped me find it, Evie. Thank you.'

* * *

During their midday meal, the trio delved into the contents of the discovered letter. Evie provided Jasper with the backstory of the ring, omitting the intricacies of its acquisition by Granny. A tremble coursed through her hand as she unfolded the paper inside the envelope. Granny's script evoked poignant memories, conjuring images of the old woman painstakingly penning the note, then sealing it with a lick and a firm press.

Kat read aloud.

To my beautiful Kat, my kindred spirit, I hope this gets

to you before I go. Just know wherever you are in the world, when the breeze brushes across your face it will be me by your side. The ring is yours and the rest is our Emerald secret. Granny Mae

'It looks like she's had someone word the rest of the letter for her,' Kat said as she prepared to read it aloud. 'This last part is her writing but the wording is more formal than she would have used.'

'Look at that beautiful calligraphic penmanship,' Evie said. 'It's certainly official though. See the embossed wax stamps down the bottom on the signatures?'

'What does it say?' Jasper said, 'I can't stand the suspense. This is better than a movie.'

She laughed and began to read again.

To whom it may concern,

This testament serves to affirm that the Emerald ring, distinguished by a prominent central stone and encircled by a cluster of diamonds, is hereby designated to be inherited by Kat MacCullagh

I, Mae Joyce, of sound mind and body, have consistently desired for this ring to be bestowed upon my granddaughter, Kat. Enclosed is a depiction of the ring, and given that no other jewellery in my possession is comparable, it is of no consequence to any party other than Kat that she is to be its rightful possessor. Therefore, I hereby bequeath the Emerald ring to her, with full liberty to do what she wants with it. She may choose to retain ownership or opt for its sale.

Kat put the letter down on the table so they could all see it. 'See here, that's Granny's signature and this is Mr. O'Connor's, a retired judge. He must be nearly a century old, but his faculties remain intact. Everyone in the vicinity can vouch for his soundness of mind. She's meticulously followed all the proper procedures. It's as though she foresaw potential complications.'

'No one would have bothered with any of this if it wasn't for the antique show,' Evie said.

'I know. Fancy the ring sitting there amongst all the play jewellery for all those years. I think Granny would have liked the way this story has unfolded. She was always up for adventure and loved nothing more than a bit of argy-bargy when trying to get rid of someone. If you had asked her, she would have probably said that Jasper should have left Seamus and Kiaran to rot on that little island.'

The other two laughed. 'We'd better finish these meals and get going,' Jasper said. 'The tide'll be starting to go out. Kat gazed northward, where the ocean danced under the blazing afternoon sun, its surface sparkling like diamonds as tin boats traversed it in pursuit of prime fishing spots. Casuarina trees cast dappled shadows along the shoreline, providing shade for holidaymakers relishing the respite from the sun as they reclined on blankets and chairs. A gentle breeze swept across the coast, momentarily diverting their attention as it playfully lifted a light chair and a lady's hat. In the sandy car park opposite, the breeze conjured a whirlwind, causing a couple of stray items to dance, before finding refuge on the grass.

The breeze seemed to pick up strength as it pushed towards where they sat. She could sense its caress upon her skin, a refreshing zephyr borne from distant shores. It carried the essence of the sea, with its emerald luminescence, connecting her to Ireland and to Granny.

'Calling Kat. Calling Kat,' Jasper joked.

'You're a million miles away,' Evie said. 'Is this closure for you? Affirmation that you're in the right, although you always knew you were anyway.'

She turned back to them. 'In a way, yes. And you two believed in me. Thank you, Evie, for helping me. This letter might have never turned up if it wasn't for you. And thank you, Jasper for asking no questions, but for just trusting me.

Chapter Twenty-Eight

Plans were made to have copies made of the letter. Evie would keep the original one with her as they all agreed that was the best option when Kat was travelling. Kat would keep a copy, as would Jasper, who said he would keep the document with the ring in his safe for the meantime.

After more discussions on the boat on the way home, Kat laid out her plans for the safe storage of the ring. 'It's worth too much for me to wear and I have no idea what I'm going to do with it yet. I don't need money at the moment. I do fine on my wage and live simply. I have enough savings put away if I needed to go home or if anything expensive crops up. I think I'd like to put the ring in a bank, like in a safe deposit box. Maybe in Brisbane. That way I don't have to worry about it. Could you help me do that, Evie?

'I could. But how are going to get it there?'

'I'll take a trip down there. If I could have three or four days off, that would be grand. I'll fly down and back and just spend a few days looking around and I can also go to the bank. I'll wear the ring. No one knows how much it's worth except us.'

'You must come and visit at Stradbroke Island. You can stay with us and ...'

Kat put her hand on Evie's arm, both of them bouncing up and down on the seats as they rounded the point and Airlie Beach loomed ahead. 'I don't think that's a good idea.' Kat answered quickly. 'I don't want to make anything awkward for Lachie.'

'I think of you as another daughter now. You're not getting out of visiting that easy.'

'I'll see. Maybe I might give him a call before I go down there and see what's what.'

She didn't miss the look that passed between Jasper and his mother. Those two were plotting. She knew it, and whatever it was they were planning, it wasn't what she wanted. If Lachie had forgotten about her, then there was no use pining after him. She now had other things on her mind.

The most pressing question was, should she work longer on the island or move somewhere else? Morag was getting ready to travel to Perth on the other side of Australia. She had asked Kat to go with her. It was tempting, particularly as sooner or later Lachie would return to *Vivre*. Possibly next month, by the sounds of what Jasper had told her. Once she had the ring and her letter settled into safekeeping, she could go wherever the wind blew. The world, or at least Australia, was her oyster.

As she lay in bed that night pondering her next destination, a sense of weariness settled over her. Despite perusing the glossy brochures Morag had left, showcasing the scenic coastline of Western Australia and the allure of Perth's beauty, none of it ignited a spark of excitement within her. Something seemed to be missing, but she couldn't quite pinpoint what it was. Was it the familiarity of the places in the brochures, their picturesque landscapes seemingly blending into one another in a haze of sameness? Or perhaps it was a lack of connection to places that were on the other side of the country.

She yearned for something more, something beyond the glossy pages and tourist attractions. She longed for a destination that would stir her soul and create lasting memories. As she tossed and turned in her bed, the image of Granny's emerald ring flashed before her eyes, a reminder of her roots and the ties that bound her to Ireland.

Was it the old homesickness creeping in again? That aching torture that had gnawed at her soul for the first few months after she left Ireland? This niggle felt different though; an emotion that cut deeper, like a heartache; a broken heart. This was about Lachie. Nothing had seemed right since he left. Fleeting glimpses of joy were soon replaced with lingering doubts and regrets. Finally, she had solved the emerald secret, but still, there was no definite sense of closure, no wave of euphoria to wash away the turmoil that seemed to be bubbling just under the surface.

The last night before Evie and Kat were to leave for Brisbane, they strolled along the beach in the late afternoon. Black cockatoos that had been eating berries in a large tree on the shoreline flew into the air as they walked underneath. Their black wings spread out like an eagle's; the bright red patterns underneath, stark against the clear blue sky. Their squarks echoed across the water and Kat stood shielding her eyes from the sun as she watched them glide along the beach and then back into some trees further up.

'You know, I'll never forget the sights and sounds I've experienced since I've been in the Whitsundays. This place is like nowhere else on earth.'

'You've been lucky to come to this area and particularly this island. There aren't too many places in the world so pristine and clean, and lacking the crowds. We like to keep it that way. Have you rung Lachie yet?'

'No. I'll leave it until tonight. I've booked my hotel in Brisbane and if he seems okay, I'll come and visit. I'm not promising anything though.'

'You know, I made a mistake once when I was young. A mistake that changed the course of my life and threw me into the path of a life and a man who nearly killed me. I was only fifteen and Chris and I were going out. We loved each other even back then and I had my entire life planned out in my head with him. I overheard a conversation from someone in his family who I thought was telling the truth. The trouble was he was only guessing at what was going on and it turns out he was wrong. He said that Chris was sleeping with another girl, so I broke the relationship off. Mum and I left town not long after and I was so angry I didn't contact Chris again. It was a huge mistake. Our lives went in different directions for many years and I lived a shitty life, hardly in contact with my parents and with no friends except one old lady, Matilda.

The bloke I was with was a drug addict, a dealer and user and although I didn't touch the stuff, I got dragged into his murky life. If it wasn't for Matilda, I'd probably be dead by now. She saved me, and eventually Chris and I found each other again.'

'Wow. I can't imagine you being involved with anyone seedy or with drugs. You don't seem like that sort of person at all.'

'It was the late seventies, early eighties, and anything went. We were all young and stupid and I was rebelling against losing Chris and my parents splitting up. There were a lot of other factors that contributed as well. Now I have a gut feeling about everything that's happened for you lately and I just know you'll regret it if you don't contact Lachie. You two are meant to be together. I can feel it in my heart.'

'You're such a romantic. You remind me a little of my Granny. She said she had a premonition that I'd find a husband when I came to Australia. My folks and my siblings joke about it all the time. Every time I talk to them, they ask if I've stumbled across a husband yet. But truth be told, it's all just a bit of fun, for I've no intentions of walking down the aisle. That leads me to another stupid thing that I did in my life. The marriage.

Some might say I'm married but it isn't real. It was a wild day, the kind you'd only find in the heart of Ireland, spent at the local pub, with everyone egging us on. The day turned to night and we were still drinking. Johnny was standing next to me and someone dared us to get married. We accepted the challenge. All I needed to do was to say 'I do' to Johnny, a boy who I grew up with. He was never even a boyfriend and I should have known better because he was a friend of my cousins. Everyone threw money on the table and said we wouldn't go through with it. But we did and both of us pocketed a tidy sum, a hundred quid apiece.

Down at the registry office, you could pay a bit and get hitched. There were others there doing the same thing, except their marriages were for real, not like ours. We queued up, with the whole pub looking in through the windows and doors. I don't know what the official was thinking, letting us go ahead with our obviously bogus vows. He must've had a pint or two himself, I reckon, and the more couples he married the more money he got paid.

Of course, in the days following, once we were sober, we realised how stupid we'd been. I signed some papers, and Johnny was supposed to do the same and send them off. They call it a void marriage. It's supposed to be a simple fix once the paperwork's in. But I never bothered to check that he finalised it all, did I? But now I'll have to follow it up. I was stupid to get so drunk and do something like that just for a bit of money. I don't know what I was thinking. Now that one night of stupidity has turned around to bite me.'

'We've all done things when we were young that were stupid. Your misdemeanours do make for a good tale though. It's a shame Lachie doesn't know the full story.'

'Please don't tell him. I want to talk to him and then, if he'll listen, I'll tell him myself.'

'Don't worry, I promise to keep out of it. I'm not about to meddle. It's up to you both to sort it out. I hope it all works out because I don't want to lose contact with you.'

Kat put her arm around Evie's shoulders. 'You won't. I promise. You're like my Australian mum and a good friend. I'll always keep in contact with you wherever I am.'

'You're not thinking of going home, are you?' Evie asked, her face full of concern. 'You haven't seemed yourself since you found the letter.'

'I'm not sure what I'm going to do. I don't think so, but I'm taking it day by day. Let's just see where the wind takes me.'

Chapter Twenty-Nine

Picking up her phone several times and then putting it down, Kat went over and over in her head what she was going to say to Lachie. A knock at the door gave her some relief from her procrastination. It was Jock. 'Can I come in for a second,' he asked.

'Sure. Come in. sit down. Do you want a beer or a cup of tea?'

'No. No. Nothing. I want to ask your advice.'

'Me?'

'Yes?'

'What's up?'

'My mum rang a few days ago and after we talked for a while she mentioned that my dad had gone in for some tests and it wasn't good. She said Dad had sworn her not to say anything to me. It's cancer, and he has to have treatment.'

'Oh that's terrible, Jock. What are you going to do?'

'She made me promise not to come back home, but to wait and see. I have a terrible feeling in my gut though and it won't go away. It's like an invisible rope is pulling me back there. I know you suffered homesickness when you were first here. Maybe it's just that.'

Jock's eyes were red and she could tell he had been crying. 'If you have the feeling that you need to be back there with them, then you should go. If it were me and one of my family was sick like that, I'd be on the first plane out of here. You only get one set of parents and if anything were to happen, you'd never forgive yourself. And maybe you being back home will give your dad a lift, especially if he's having treatment. Just go. That's not homesickness you're feeling. That's knowing where you need to be.'

Brushing his hand across his eyes he took a deep breath. 'I think I just needed to hear you say that. The longing is so bad it's like nothing I've ever felt. That's a bloody big ocean between us, and now it seems endless. You know when you're off and travelling it's like living in a bubble. You don't have responsibilities except for looking after yourself and making sure you know where your next feed is coming from. It's well over two years since I've seen the family. I was supposed to go home for a visit and then Covid came along. We talk all the time but now I need more than that. I feel like I'm lost, drifting on another planet, in another universe to my mum and dad.'

'It sounds like you know what you need to do.'

'I'd have to give short notice here. If I was to go, I should leave as soon as I can. I feel bad though because there's a big crowd coming in a couple of weeks and I promised I'd have everything ship shape. I'd be letting them down. They've been good to me.'

'Talk to Evie. I know what she'll say. She's very close to her father and she'll understand. Do you need any money? Have you got enough to get you back home?'

'Aye, I have. I always have a backup in the bank, just in case of something like this. I've been lucky. All the years I've travelled and I've never had to dash back. You're a good friend, Kat. I hope we meet again one day, somewhere on this planet. Hopefully you and Lachie will work out your differences too. You made a grand couple.'

'Thanks, Jock. Take care and we'll meet again, I'm sure. Ireland and Scotland are not far apart. Our paths will cross again, I have no doubt.'

She sat at the table, staring at her phone. Eventually she picked it up and pressed Lachie's number. She let it ring for a while, but no one picked up and she breathed a sigh of relief. He either didn't want to talk to her, or he didn't have his phone with him, wherever he might be. As it rang out, she put her feet up on the chairs opposite her. She jumped a few minutes later when her phone rang. It was Grace.

It was grand to hear her sister's voice. Grace was also excited and launched straight into what had been happening at home. Their brother Ronan had gone to Dublin for the weekend. 'You wouldn't believe it, Kat. He's met someone who has stolen his heart. She's an Aussie girl who came over here to travel and work. He says he's head over heels in love with her. He wants to marry her, and he's only just met her. Unbelievable. I've never seen him in such a state. Eileen, of course, is the opposite with her head down studying. You know her, always serious and with a clear path in mind. She's so efficient and her life runs ship-shape. I reckon she's more mature than you and I. Mum and Dad have gone up to Granny's cottage for a few days' rest. Seamus and the rest of the O'Rourkes have cleaned all the contents out and the paperwork is through that says the house belongs to our family. The O'Rourkes can no longer set a foot on the property. The finalisation of the will also means that they are not entitled to anything left behind. They've removed all the belongings they wanted. Mum said they had a stall at the markets and sold Granny's stuff. Eileen sent a heap of her friends down there and they bought anything that they thought we might want. I've kept you some bits and pieces. Those idiots left all her old timber furniture in the shed down the back. Obviously couldn't be bothered moving it out. So at least we still have all of that. The old dresser, the china cabinet, the kitchen table and some other pieces are still there.'

'That's grand, Grace. I'm so glad the furniture stayed. Did any of them mention the ring? I found the paperwork that says Granny left it to me. The letter was at the post office. The envelope had fallen down behind some boxes and I found it and another parcel Granny had sent just before she died. Can you tell Mum and Dad that for me?'

'Oh, Kat. That's grand news. All this time and you finally have something that says it's yours. What was in the parcel?

'Typical Granny. Always worried about me getting sunburnt or skin cancer. She sent another hat, sunscreen and some other creams she would have bought at Tesco's. It brought a smile to my face anyway.'

'Oh Lordy be. She was always going on about the sun in Australia. No doubt she would have thought our Irish creams would do a better job than the ones you can buy out there. I thought you were going to say she sent you something sentimental.'

'No. Just a hat and cream. What's the word on the O'Rourkes?'

'Idiots they are. Seamus and Kiaran came back here bragging about their trip to down under. Said they'd swum with sharks and crocodiles and had to fight off the girls who were chasing them.'

'Chasing them for what? Those two have tickets on themselves. They mustn't look in the mirror.'

'Well you should have seen them. They'd only been back a day or two when I saw them. They looked a bit worse for wear and covered in bites all over their arms and faces. Thank God they had trousers on and I wasn't subjected to seeing their legs. Kiaran told everyone he had scratched so much he ended up with infections in his leg and needed to go to the doctors to get fixed. He's a right mess. I heard them down at the pub. I also heard them saying that you had immediately given them the ring when you saw they meant business. Dot who works at the bar told me later they told her the ring wasn't worth anything. It's a reproduction. They've had it checked by two reliable jewellers. All that time Kat and you really did have it. You never told me. I knew deep down you did, but you never said it.'

'I know. Granny made me promise not to tell anyone.

And the valuers they took the ring to were correct. There was no value in the ring I gave them at all. At least they're off my back now.'

'I know you too well Kat, and I have a sneaky feeling that there's more to that story than you're telling me. Perhaps a chunk missing?'

'There could be, but you'll have to wait until the day I come home to tell you.'

'We miss you Kat. Mum and Dad are looking a bit tired lately. They're getting older you know. They're talking about trying to give up work. They might either sell Granny's cottage or move in there. They're undecided and I wish you were here to nut it out with them.'

'Sell it? Oh, they can't. I'll phone them and talk about it in a few days. I've got to go down to Brisbane for a quick visit and when I'm back, I will need to decide if I'm going to stay here in the Whitsundays or move on. One of the Irish girls here is going to Perth and wants me to go with her.'

'You don't sound that excited.'

'I'm not.'

'What happened to the lad you were keen on?'

Kat had only briefly mentioned Lachie to Grace not long before they split up, but her sister never forgot any gossip. 'It's over. Finished.'

'I saw your husband Johnny down at the pub the other night also.' She laughed, the frivolous sound echoing over the phone. 'He said to tell you he's done with you. The lads told him that the ring's worth nothing and he's found himself a new bride so he needs everything put in order. The paperwork has gone in for the marriage void.'

'Jesus, it took him long enough. Him and those other two have caused me no end of trouble. I see no one is interested in me when there's no money involved.'

'No. It's a grand thing to be broke.'

'It is. I'd better go, I've got a phone call to make. Tell Mum I'll give her a call in a few days.'

'Love you Kat. Come home one day won't you.'

'Love you too Grace, and I will come home one day.'

Chapter Thirty

race's words hung in her mind. Now that all the stolen emerald business was behind her, it would be easy to go home and see everyone. She had been gone for over a year and the thought of her parents selling the cottage reminded her that she needed to be with family to work things like that out. As the eldest, she had often sat at the table and gone over budgets, or worked out how to save more money to put the younger ones through university. Sure, they were all standing on their own two feet now and contributing to the family income, but it was time for her mum and dad to stop work and enjoy life a little. How she would love to bring them out to Australia. Her father would be amazed at the colour of the ocean and her mother could walk along the beach. How would she ever be able to get them out here? They'd say it would cost too much and was too far away.

Always so many decisions, she thought as she hit the button on her phone that was next to the name Lachie

McIntosh. This time he answered straight away. Maybe he had seen the missed call and had been waiting for her to call back?

'Hi, Lachie. It's Kat. I just thought I'd call and say hello.'

'How are you, Kat. It's nice to hear from you.

There was an awkward silence and she tried to calm the nervousness in her voice. 'I, I, well I'm coming down to Brisbane next week to tidy up some business stuff. Actually, I'm flying down with your mum. I'll be staying for a few days and then I'm coming back up here. Your mum wanted me to come and stay with her at Stradbroke and I just wanted to check what you thought about that.'

He coughed and if she didn't know better, she would think he was stalling for time; thinking about what he would say next. It took him a while to reply. 'That would be fine to come and stay. You'll love the island. I won't be here, but Dad and probably my younger brother and sister will be. I'm going to Bryon Bay surfing with some mates. I'll have to catch you another time. Also, I don't know if you noticed, but I put money in your account for those paintings you did for the foyer. I noticed them in the new brochures that just came out.'

'Really? Why did you do that? I never look at my balance or get a statement. How much did you put in there? I don't really want it.'

'It's a business deal and I've already paid. Anyway, I need to go. I've got another call. Like I said I won't be at home when you're down this way, but the others will be.'

She tried to keep the disappointment out of her voice and to not burst into tears. 'That's a shame. I really wanted to see you. I also wanted to explain all the trouble there was the other month, you know about the marriage to Johnny and the ring.'

He laughed and the sound of the false merriment instantly changed her mood. Was he laughing at her? 'No worries, Kat. That's your business and obviously not information you wanted to share. It's no concern of mine.'

'But I want to tell you the entire story so that it all makes sense. And so you know I wasn't lying to you.'

'Like I said, it's your business and there's no need to tell me. Listen, I have to go. Have a great time and enjoy Stradbroke. Seeya Kat.'

Her throat constricted, as if words were trapped, unable to escape. Was this the end? Would this be the last conversation they would share? The realisation of what she needed to do struck her like a bolt of lightning— by the time Lachie returned to *Vivre*, she'd make sure she was long gone. There was no way she could go through another parting from him. It was too much anguish and her heart ached every time she thought of him. Now she was certain. It was time to move on. Find another job in another location.

Chapter Thirty-One

Although the plane was delayed and they waited at the airport for over an hour to board, the flight from Proserpine to Brisbane took less than two hours. Evie and Kat talked the entire way. Lachie's mother was interested to know what her son had said. Kat was blunt. 'He didn't want to talk to me at all. I said I'd explain and then he could see I wasn't lying, but he didn't want to listen.

'He's bloody stubborn. Always has been and once his mind is made up about something it's very hard, if not impossible, to change it.' Her eyes narrowed. 'I'm sorry Kat, but I don't trust his excuse. He never goes to Byron Bay to surf. I don't believe that for a minute.'

'Well, that excuse just goes to show he really doesn't want to see me. It's okay Evie. I'm fine. I'll get over him. It wasn't meant to be.' She kept her ideas of moving on from the Whitsundays to herself. She would need time to work out exactly where she was going, and what she would do for work.

When the plane landed, they looked at each other. 'Thank God,' Kat said. 'I thought my days were numbered then, when the plane came down, nearly landed and then went back up again. Maybe there were some cows on the runway.'

Evie laughed. 'I'd say it's the weather. No cows here.' They both looked out the window. 'You're in the city now, and the weather is dreadful.'

The rain was torrential and after such a bumpy landing, Evie was grateful to share a taxi into the city. Evie walked Kat to her hotel which was in one of the main streets. Even though they had tried to stay under cover, both of them were soaked and as they stood under a metal awning, the rain continued to thunder down around them. People rushed back and forth, their umbrellas doing little to protect them from the heavy downpour. Evie talked loudly to be heard over the rain. 'I'm getting picked up further up the street and I'll just make the last ferry back to the island today. I've checked the weather reports and it looks like there's more really bad weather coming. It's more than likely they will cancel the ferries to the island. It's rare for them not to run, so it must be really wild weather. You've picked a terrible time to be here, but the shops and cafes in town will keep you busy.'

'I'll be fine. I have some books to read and I'm looking forward to walking around the city, even if it's raining. I'm used to it.' Kat sounded more confident about getting about in Brisbane than she felt. A wave of homesickness washed over her. As she looked along the footpath, she felt as if she was somewhere she didn't belong. It wasn't a pleasant feeling and she tried to push it away, but all she wanted to do was get away from the city and feel like she was in the right place for once.

She looked at Evie, another strange feeling sweeping over her that this person was also leaving her and she might not see her again. Too many goodbyes and too many worries about tomorrow, and the day after that, and the day after that. Staring at the people hurrying along the street, she was snapped back to the present when Evie touched her on the arm, a worried look on her face.

'Don't worry about me, Evie. I'm used to travelling by myself and in all sorts of weather. We wouldn't go anywhere back home if we didn't go out in the rain. She held her hand out. I also have to fix this up and get it safely tucked away.'

They both looked down at the emerald ring on her finger. The green was darker in the dullness of the grey weather and the diamonds glittered under the lights that hung from the awning above. Kat wiggled her finger and touched the ring with her other finger. 'It is beautiful but it makes me nervous wearing it. I'll be glad when it's taken care of.'

They hugged for a long time. 'You're family to me now, no matter what Lachie wants. Keep in contact because I don't think you're going to get to Stradbroke Island this trip. You only have a couple of days as it is and if those ferries stop running there's no way to get there. The way the weather is, it won't be safe for any boats to cross Moreton Bay.'

* * *

As Kat stood alone beneath the awning, the rain continued to cascade down and puddles pooled at her feet. She couldn't help but shiver against the chilly wind that suddenly swept through the street. Rain blew horizontally and wet her clothes even more. Her wet hair hung down her back and she pulled it back, wiping the water from her face. She watched as other people's umbrellas turned inside out, their owners struggling to wrestle them back into shape. The breeze caught the hem of her dress, threatening to lift it skyward, prompting her to hastily press her hand against the fabric to keep it in place. The street resembled a turbulent wind tunnel, and in the midst of the downpour, the air held a coldness. Loose papers danced about, propelled by the gusts and she quickly pushed open the door of the hotel to get out of the weather.

As she stepped inside, another sudden gust caught the door and clipped her heel, sending a sharp jolt of pain shooting up her leg. Limping toward the reception, she felt her grip slip on her bag, the contents spilling out across the glossy tiles. With a sinking feeling in her chest, she watched as her wallet, coins, and various belongings scattered across the floor.

The receptionist was preoccupied with another guest, leaving Kat to hastily gather everything. In that moment, with her heel throbbing, her wet clothes clinging to her, and her belongings strewn about for all to see, she felt a sense of clarity wash over her. Enough was enough. She couldn't continue to run from her unhappiness, nor could she escape the ache of a fractured romance by fleeing to the other side of Australia. There was only one thing to do. She needed to return home. To her true home where she belonged. To Galway.

Chapter Thirty-Two

The inclement weather had worsened by the time Lachie opened the front door and let his mother in. A strong gust of wind followed her as she entered and her hair, damp from the rain, clung to her face and neck. 'It's wild out there,' she said as she gave him a welcoming kiss on the cheek. 'What are you doing here? I thought you were going to Byron.'

'I changed my mind at the last minute. And it's pouring down there. There's a low off the coast and we're in for a spell of bad weather.'

He looked behind her as if expecting someone else to be there. 'Where's Kat? I thought she was coming to stay.'

His mother put her bags down and took off the light jumper she was wearing. 'No, she's staying in Brisbane. She was going to come and stay for a night, but now the ferries have been cancelled. I doubt she'll get here.' She looked at him curiously. 'I didn't think you were interested in seeing her.'

'Well. I wasn't. But, I don't know, I'm just a bit mixed

up at the moment. I don't really feel like talking about it. I was hoping to see Kat though.' Disappointment washed over him. 'How's Jasper?'

'He's fine. Listen, I'm going to have a shower and dry off. I'll talk more when I'm cleaned up. I will say one thing though.'

'Yes, Mum.'

'Kat's a wonderful girl and I've become very close to her. It won't matter what you decide, because she and I are friends regardless. You need to think hard about your choices and actions, Lachie. I find the situation disappointing. Not that's she's said much to me, it's more what I've heard from Jasper. I expected more from you. Anyway, I'll talk about it later.'

Her words cut deep, leaving a lingering sting. Though she hadn't voiced it directly, he could sense her displeasure. Over the years they had seldom argued, but the weight of her unspoken disapproval right now was palpable. He stood silently, gazing through the glass doors leading out onto the deck. In the distance, the rolling waves, stirred by the weather, were barely visible through the heavy rain. Like the storm outside, his insides churned with a feeling of unrest, as unanswered questions pressed heavily on his mind.

* * *

A large bathroom with a deep bathtub had been a perfect spot for Kat to soak off the events of the day and go over her decision, which had seemed very clear at the time. Bubbles to soak in and a warm drink, she thought. Why not? She had made herself a cup of tea and she took small sips, placing it back carefully on the ledge next to the bath. It was tradition to always have a cup of tea when there were big decisions to be made. When Ronan had fallen down the stairs and broken not only the stairs but also his leg, her mother had made a cup of tea while she waited for the ambulance. Another time, only the year before Kat left Ireland, Grace had somehow got her finger caught in the plughole of the kitchen sink. While they waited for the plumber to arrive, they made a large pot of tea and along with the rest of the family who all happened to be home at the time, they sat around the kitchen table and made jokes about plug holes and fingers.

At one stage her dad had laughed so much he had fallen off his chair and they had all laughed even more. That was everyone, except Grace. It hadn't ended up a laughing matter because the plumber couldn't help and the firemen who eventually came had to nearly destroy half the kitchen to remove the sink and plug; still with Grace's finger attached. It had been a good ending though and at least four pots of tea later and maybe some whisky that the firemen might have also shared, Grace's finger was freed, unharmed.

She laughed to herself when she remembered that night. All of them in the kitchen that always smelled of either a cake baking or a pot of stew bubbling on the stove.

It would be grand to be back there sitting and sharing a pot of tea.

Taking another sip of her drink, she thought hard.

The decision was made. Tomorrow she would go to the bank and do whatever business she needed to. For now though, she picked up her phone from beside the tub. She was going to book some flights.

* * *

The room remained dark because of the weather and she slept in, surprised to see that it was nine o'clock by the time she got out of bed. Looking through the bedroom window she watched as workers scurried along the streets, their formal city attire vastly different to the work gear worn on the island. For a moment she wondered about what job she would be able to get when she got home. Pushing those questions to the back of her mind, she reminded herself to focus on the 'now' not the 'what ifs' or 'when'.

Breakfast had been included in the accommodation price so she ate at the hotel's restaurant, feasting on bacon, eggs and avocado along with coffee and cake to finish with. There was no hurry today, and a newspaper that had been left on her table gave her something to read. The headline, *Extreme Weather Event*, screamed out from the front page. The paper was called The Courier Mail and she sifted through it, picking out pieces of information that she found interesting. There were quite a few articles about the 'Ekka', which was in ten days' time. Alongside photos of people eating ice cream with strawberries on the top, was an article that explained that the annual event was really called the Royal Queensland Show. It brought the city and the country together for a celebration of agriculture. There was a picture of a boy eating a dagwood dog, which Kat had previously learned was something like the corn dogs they ate back home; a battered Frankfurt on a stick, with lots of red sauce plastered on the top.

She read with curiosity about the different events that would take place over the nine days the show went for. There were woodchopping competitions and giant vegetable displays, as well as pavilions full of cattle, cats, dogs and other livestock to look at. Some of the photos reminded her of fetes back home, with carnival rides and games as well as showbags full of goodies that you could buy from the different stalls.

She read some other articles in the following pages. People were worried about flooding that might occur because of the weather, a politician was in trouble for using taxpayers' money for private use, and then there was a long story about overseas workers and immigrants settling in what they called the 'Sunshine State'. Someone was bleating on about cutting workers' visas so Aussies would have more jobs. She laughed at that. They couldn't even get enough workers to fill the jobs they had vacant now. If it wasn't for the backpackers and overseas students who all worked in roles that no one else wanted, the country wouldn't function. 'Sure, she said aloud. 'Send us back home. Then see how you go.'

The back part of the paper was not very interesting and she didn't stop to look at the sports, racing, or real estate sections. There was a social page however, and she gazed at the women, who all looked so glamorous. She wasn't one for worrying about what was in fashion, but it was interesting to look at the stylish clothes people wore when they went out. Her heart nearly stopped when she looked at the last photo down the bottom of the page. It was Lachie and...she read the caption. *Lachie McIntosh and his partner Prue Washton, enjoying a meal at the Stradbroke Island Hotel.* Slamming the paper shut she blinked several times before opening it back up again, flicking hurriedly through the pages until she found it again. So, he had a new girlfriend, or was it an old one? The name Prue rang a bell and she was sure that was the name of the girl Lachie had said he once dated. The photo was the final nail in the coffin. Her decision was right. 'Galway, here I come,' she said aloud.

Chapter Thirty-Three

It had not been difficult to organise to leave Brisbane for the Whitsundays the following afternoon. She switched her flights and made it to the airport just in time. The terminal was busy. Several flights had been cancelled and passengers were scrambling to try and re-book, or to find an alternative. Luckily she had been able to book a ticket back to Proserpine. 'Might be the last one,' the attendant said, as she walked down the aisle checking everyone's seat belts. 'Could be a slippery take-off. I'd make sure to buckle up.'

Great, Kat thought, nothing like a bit of confidence from the flight staff.

* * *

By the time they neared Proserpine, the rain eased and she looked down as they descended over the cane fields to the south of the town. It never ceased to amaze her just how big Australia was and she wondered if she would come back and explore different areas in the future. Visiting small towns and the Whitsundays over the last year had given her a taste of what life was like in the northern parts of Queensland. It was an experience she wouldn't forget and she was grateful for the opportunity. However, the urge to travel and have adventures had diminished. It's actually disappeared, she thought. Even though there was so much more to see, there were no second thoughts or doubts about the decision she had made.

* * *

Jock was waiting for her at the airport. When she rang him early this morning he said it would be fine to pick her up. He was going in to Proserpine to get a pump fixed, so it was perfect timing. It would be easy to swing through and get her. He also was getting ready to leave for Scotland, and although he was surprised when she told him about her decision to go back to Ireland, he understood. 'I think you know when it's time to go back. You have to trust your instincts and your heart.' He put his hand on his chest. 'Family. That invisible umbilical cord that draws you back. I'm not telling my lot that I'm coming,' he said. 'It's going to be a surprise. Are you going to let your family know?'

'No.' she smiled, imagining their surprise when she walked in through the front door of their home in Galway. 'I would have flown straight out from Brisbane if I could have, but I thought I should do the right thing and come back here and tidy my cabin and get my stuff. Not that I have much. Morag would have packed it and sent it over, but I wanted to say goodbye to you and Jasper and the others. It's been a grand time.'

'It has,' Jock said. 'And no doubt with plenty more to come for the two of us.'

Chapter Thirty-Four

The rain had flooded large parts of south-east Queensland, and with roads inundated, ferries cancelled, and large parts of Brisbane under water, the area had come to a standstill. For many, there was no way in or out, and it was just a matter of staying put and waiting until the rain eased. Lachie had been standing where he seemed to spend a lot of time lately, leaning on the railing of the deck and looking out to sea. He was searching for answers, his mind whirling as he grappled with what to do next. As each day passed, the dullness in his body intensified and he found no joy in anything he did.

It continued to rain and his mood matched the colour of the sky. When his mother came to stand beside him and also looked over the top of the bush to the ocean beyond, he put his arm around her shoulders. 'You think I've made a mistake, don't you.'

She gripped his hand that rested on her shoulder. 'I don't think, I know.'

He turned to her. 'I struggle with conflict, and you know that, because you're the same. I just don't want any dramas.'

'I know.'

'But,' he paused for a long time. 'I can't get Kat out of my mind. I think about her when I go to sleep and when I wake up. I hear her Irish voice in my dreams and those green eyes, they seem to be there watching me every-where I go. I almost feel like I'm going mad. Like someone put a spell on me and all I can think about is her.'

His mother raised one eyebrow.

'And then I go over everything that happened and how I didn't get back to her that same day we argued and let her tell me her side of the story. I should have trusted her. Listened. Even if she was married or did steal the ring, I'm not sure I care. I just want to be with her.'

It was as if once he started talking, he couldn't stop. 'I feel like I'm dying inside. Nothing means anything. I've tried. I've tried everything to keep busy and ... I've gone fishing, swimming, surfing and even walked in the rain yesterday. All I can think about is Kat and that lilting voice of hers. I even imagine I hear her singing, or tapping her foot.'

He turned to his mother who hadn't interrupted, instead just listening. Now she looked like she had some-thing to say. Her voice was quiet. 'I got a message from Kat. She's gone back up north. She only stayed a day in Brisbane and then she took off back to Proserpine. Her message said that she'd done what she needed to do in Brisbane and there was no use staying any longer with the weather the way it was. She was worried the flights would get cancelled. Her next message said that she was safely back in the Whitsundays.'

A heavy despondency settled on Kat once she arrived back on the island. A new girl that Georgia had employed a couple of weeks earlier was doing a good job in the reception area. Kat had been training her to fill in while she was away in Brisbane and she was pleased that there was someone to take her place, now that she was going to leave for Ireland.

It had only taken a couple of days to pack her belongings and say goodbye to everyone. She asked Georgia not to mention to Lachie's family that she was leaving until after she was gone. Luckily Jasper, who had been away camping with some mates, returned back to the island the morning before she left. At least she would get to say goodbye to him. Jock would take her over to the mainland in the boat in an hour or so and then drive her to the airport in Proserpine. She had connecting flights organised, with international flights leaving from Brisbane. The timeline was rushed, but there had only been a couple of options available at such short notice.

They stood together on the sand, Jock holding the boat ready for her to board. Morag wiped tears from her face as she hugged Kat. 'I'm leaving too and I won't see you for ages. Next time we meet, it might be in a pub in Galway or Dublin. Then we can dance and sing and bring the house down again.'

It was hard to say goodbye and Jasper also sounded emotional. 'Mum is going to kill me for not letting her know you're going back to Ireland, but I promise I won't say anything until you've left.' She had made him swear on his grandmother's life that he wouldn't tell Evie, or anyone else that she had gone until he had to. Lachie had been given enough chances. At least now she knew exactly where she stood with him.

Morag and Jasper stood on the sand, waving until she could no longer see them. As the boat sped over the waves, she lifted her hat and let the wind blow through her hair. There was a stiff breeze today and white caps flickered over the top of the waves. A seagull tried to fly alongside them, but soon took off in the other direction when the wind became stronger. 'Hang on,' Jock called out. 'There's a rough patch here. You might get a bit wet.'

As the spray washed over, she relished the salty water on her face. It was warm water, unlike the North Atlantic Sea. The funny thing was, she thought, it was all the same ocean. It was all connected and before long she would be flying over the endless ocean, back to home.

She whispered into the wind. 'Goodbye Whitsundays. I'm not sure I'll be back this way, but thank you. You are beautiful.'

Chapter Thirty-Five

By Tuesday, the rain started to ease, and so did the doubts in Lachie's mind. 'It might take you a while to make your decisions, son,' his father said as he sipped his morning coffee, 'but you get there in the end.'

Lachie was energised and his voice full of optimism. 'The ferries are starting back up tomorrow and I intend to leave straight away. I'll catch the first one in the morning. I've booked it to make sure. It's time for me to go back up north for work anyway.'

'And Kat?' his mother questioned.

'Yes. She's the real reason I'm going. I want to work out our differences and let her know how I feel about her. I've made a mistake. I shouldn't have been so stubborn.'

His father thumped his back. 'Good decision.' He gestured towards the kitchen. 'That's your phone ringing, Evie.'

'I'll be back,' his mother said. 'You've made me very happy, Lachie.'

'Now that you're sure about your feelings,' his dad continued, 'everything else will fall into place.'

The two of them talked about a few work processes that Lachie needed to sort out that day and some other plans that Chris wanted implemented once he got to the island. 'It'll be great having you working up there again and I'm sure Jasper will be pleased too. That's the beauty of online work. If there was one good thing to come out of Covid, it was remote working.

Evie reappeared and they both turned as she walked toward them. She had a strange look on her face as she looked from Chris to Lachie.

'Is everything okay,' Lachie asked. 'You look like you've had bad news.'

'There's no easy way to say this. That was Jasper on the phone. Kat's left. She's gone home to Ireland. Jasper had been away camping and only came back the morning she was leaving. He said she flew out yesterday and he wasn't supposed to tell us she'd left until after she'd gone. Her connecting flight left last night from Brisbane. He said it wouldn't have mattered what anyone said anyway. She'd made her mind up when she was in Brisbane that she was going. She only went back to the island to gather a few things, tidy up her work duties, and say goodbye.'

Lachie stood up. 'What? Shit. Really! Back to Ireland. Jasper should have rung me straight away. Why didn't he let me know?'

His dad frowned. 'And what would you have done? You're down here and she's up there. It sounds like she didn't want you to know. I'm surprised she didn't tell Evie though.'

Lachie slumped back in his chair. 'She obviously thought Mum might try and talk her out of it, or tell me. I can't believe I've missed her. I thought I had time. She must have really wanted to get away from here and me. Did she leave a message? Did Jasper say anything?'

'No,' his mother replied. 'She just told Jasper to let me know next time he was talking to me. She was adamant he was not to tell us. He was only to mention it the next time we rang him. Her message was to thank us for everything we'd done for her, and that leaving was an easy decision. Jasper said her words were, it was time to return.'

The trio lapsed into a heavy silence and the weight of unspoken regret hung in the air. Lachie rose from his seat and leaned against the railings. The rain, having dissipated, left behind a radiant rainbow stretching across the ocean. It was a moment of reflection and the stark realisation that he might not see her again settled over him like a heavy blanket. He had made a mess of things, and now there was no undoing it. All he could do was move on and leave the past behind, much like Kat had been forced to do when he left from up north. The bitter irony wasn't lost on him — the deserving taste of karma hitting him with startling clarity.

Chapter Thirty-Six

The flight home for Kat was, as usual, long and tedious. A five-hour stopover in Singapore added to the length of the trip, but she was pleased to get the first leg out of the way. When she boarded the next plane that would take her directly to Heathrow and another connecting flight to Dublin, she was thankful that the lady next to her put earplugs in and closed her eyes. It was a pleasant relief after the chatty Australian businessman who had told her everything he knew about Ireland on the first flight. I just want peace and quiet, she thought, as she also closed her eyes and tried to sleep.

When she landed at Heathrow airport she was greeted by grey skies and drizzly rain. Typical, she thought. It was supposed to be summer in England but it was freezing and she shivered in the light jacket she wore. She had a two-day stopover in London, so perhaps she could find a coat in an op shop and another pair of boots. The flimsy tops and tiny shorts she had worn for the last year on the island wouldn't stand a chance in this weather.

It had been fun to walk around the area of London where she was staying, which wasn't too far from the airport. London had been a regular travel spot when she was younger and she remembered where some of the op shops were. It didn't take her long to find a good one that had plenty of cheap clothes to choose from. A lady called Lisa served her and helped her find what she was looking for. Lisa had backpacked around Australia when she was younger and they compared travel stories, laughing at the unusual Aussie sayings and comparing stories about snakes, cockroaches and spiders.

'I don't know how many cans of insect spray I went through in that year,' Kat said, laughing at the memory. 'I'd spray the entire can if necessary, until I was sure the wretched things were dead.'

'And what about the toads,' Lisa said, wrinkling her nose. 'The people I worked for used to put salt on them, then watch them blow up and die. Disgusting.'

They chatted for a bit longer as they searched through the racks of clothes. Eventually, they found two coats and a nearly-new pair of boots for Kat. 'You'll take a while to get used to the weather again,' Lisa said. 'No more endless days of blue skies and bright sunshine. You're back in the northern hemisphere now. Do you think you'll ever go back to Australia?'

Kat pulled the coat on and took the shoes she was wearing off and put them in her bag. When she put the new boots on, they were warm and comfortable. The weather was icy and she needed all the protection she could get. 'I'm not sure. I met a lot of nice people along the way. I'll miss some of them for sure, and the weather.'

'I met my husband over there in Australia. We fell in love and have been together ever since. That's fifteen years ago and three kids later. Luckily, he's Welsh, so there were no problems about where to live, really. He doesn't mind London and maybe when the kids are older, we'll move to Wales. Who knows? As long as we're together, we don't care.'

They chatted a while longer before Kat bid her farewell and strolled back to her modest hotel. Lisa's tale lingered in her mind that evening. Ah, sure, plenty of travellers found love in far-off lands, but there were likely just as many who returned home, content to resume life in their own corner of the world. Life wasn't always a fairy tale, after all.

As she lay in bed, she imagined her own storybook ending. Maybe it wasn't about finding a prince, or a pot of gold at the end of a rainbow. Perhaps it was about the journey itself, the people she met along the way, and the memories she would cherish forever. Rolling over, she closed her eyes. One more day and she'd be home in Galway.

Chapter Thirty-Seven

Although she had let her parents know she was coming, she had sworn them to secrecy. They weren't to tell anyone else. Once she had made her mind up to leave Australia, she phoned her mum and dad and they had a lengthy chat over the phone. Both were surprised, but said as long as she was sure about coming back, they were happy. They'd have a grand party the night she got back. And they wouldn't tell the others. It would be a surprise.

* * *

The welcome home party had been just as Kat imagined. When she walked in through the door, her siblings screamed and yelled and there were a lot of, Jesus, Mary and Josephs, loudly exclaimed. Grace did not stop hugging her, and Eileen and Ronan kept staring, as if she wasn't real

'I can't believe me eyes, seein' you back,' Ronan

exclaimed, as their father slid another pint across the table to him. 'It's like a mirage, you know? Like you're here, but ya ain't really here, if you catch me drift.' He chuckled, taking a sip of his beer. 'So, spill the beans, what's happening? What's been going on in your world?'

'Well, I'm real and I'm here.'

'So, did you find a husband?' Eileen asked, her eyes widening with curiosity. Her hair—which was the same colour as Kat's but curly as a woolly sheep's—bounced up and down as she spoke. She jigged around in her seat, all the while asking for one plate after another to be passed to her. Mum had put on a grand feast and everyone was making the most of it.

'This meal is the best, Mum,' Kat declared. 'After airport and plane food, it's pure magic, and no, Eileen. I did not find a husband, nor do I want one. I've come back to pursue my art and find a good job. There's more to life than men.'

'Agh, you say that now,' Ronan said. 'But wait until you meet the right one. Like me. I've met a girl so beautiful and smart that the stars themselves seem to pale in comparison to her radiant presence. She possesses a wit as sharp as the Cliffs of Moher and a kindness as warm as a peat fire on a chilly evening.'

They all laughed and talked loudly over one another. 'You got that out of a book,' Grace said as she playfully punched her brother.

'I hear she's from Australia,' Kat exclaimed. 'I can't wait to meet her.'

'He's full of shite, he is,' her father, Patrick, said, shaking his head as he looked at them across the table.

Eileen sat up straight and talked the loudest so everyone would listen. 'I don't know why you're all so wanting to be with someone. I'm never going to lose my independence or my heart for that matter. Women can be single these days and still have the grandest time ever. You're all searching for the wrong things in life. Just be happy doing what you do, and forget about the romance.'

Patrick reached over and squeezed Eileen's hand. 'It's so good you have your head screwed on right. No man would ever be good enough for my Eileen anyway.'

Grace and Kat looked at each other and rolled their eyes. Grace spoke even louder than Eileen had. Kat had forgotten how the loudest voice won the floor and she revelled in the familiarity of a family dinner and noisy competitive conversation. 'I pity the poor man who ever wants Eileen,' Grace said. 'He'd never get over the front tread anyway. Dad'd be there with the broomstick waiting for whoever wants to court his special daughter, Eileen. No one would ever be good enough.'

'Well, she is the baby of the family,' he replied.

'Maybe an older man might be more fitting for you, Eileen,' Kat added. 'I don't think anyone your age, or even a bit older, would be sensible enough.'

'If I was looking, I'd need to find someone who is highly intelligent and knows exactly what direction they're taking in life. And might I add, they would need some money behind them.'

'What about their looks?' Ronan chimed in, giving a playful flex of his arm as if muscles were magically going to appear.'

'Looks mean nothing to me. In fact, someone who is

too good-looking should not be trusted. Anyway, it's all irrelevant because I'm not looking, and I never will be.'

Kat's mother added in. 'What about our handsome Ronan here? No one is as good-looking as my son, and he can be trusted. Well, with most things anyway.'

They all laughed and Kat remarked. 'I reckon you're onto something with your philosophy, Eileen. There's a fair share of idiots out there, and most aren't alright for a night out, let alone dating.'

'So, you never stumbled upon someone you thought was alright or grand?' her mother enquired, a knowing glint in her eye as she held Kat's gaze.

It was always this way with their mother. She had the same intuition as her own mother, Granny Mae. Kat couldn't pull the wool over their eyes. They could read her moods and mind, despite her best efforts to conceal what she didn't want them to know.

'Ah, I may have, but that's ancient history now. No, I'm not needing a man. All of you will keep me busy enough,' Kat replied with a wink, gesturing to her family gathered around. 'Sure, with all the banter and love we have here, who needs a fella?' she added with a grin, raising her glass in a toast. 'To family, and to being home with you all.'

Chapter Thirty-Eight

Once Kat was home, she stuck to her dreams and found a job that involved art. The art gallery she worked at was in a small town called Clifden, which was over an hour's drive from Galway. She worked there three days a week and stayed in Granny's cottage, which was within walking distance from the gallery. On the other days, she taught art classes in Galway, and then stayed at the family home. The arrangements seemed to be working fine, although she was getting tired of dragging her clothes back and forth between the two places. She would prefer to stay at Granny's but then she wouldn't see any of her friends or go out. The pubs and restaurants in Galway provided an escape for her. Socialising with old friends and spending time with her family kept her busy. There was no spare time to dwell on what could have been.

* * *

As August rolled into September, the sun's warmth began to wane. Outside the gallery where she worked, the trees started to lose their summer attire, their leaves painting the scene with fiery orange and rustic red hues. The display heralding autumn was just outside her window, and she spent a lot of time staring at the scene during the quiet periods. As the leaves gracefully descended to the ground, the pavement transformed into a canvas of vibrant colours, and one had to tread carefully to avoid slipping on the mushy slush that formed underfoot.

Today, as she gazed out the window, watching the rain cascade down the panes of glass, memories of sun-drenched days in the Whitsundays flooded her mind. This time last year, September in the Whitsundays had been filled with sunshine and warmth, a stark contrast to the dreary drizzle outside. The days had felt like something out of one of those glossy travel magazines that she had spent half her life looking through before she travelled to Australia. September was not long after she first met Lachie and she remembered the perfect temperatures, the clear skies, and a whisper of spring in the air. Though the seasons in the north of Queensland didn't vary drastically, there had been a subtle shift, a gentle reminder of the passage of time.

Kat's gaze followed a small sparrow that hopped along the pavement. She followed its movements, her mind elsewhere as she reminisced about Lachie. Her mind conjured images of his sun-kissed blonde hair and piercing blue eyes, clad in his old board shorts and faded T-shirt. She visualised him holding her hand as they strolled along the beach, his hands warm and gentle. If only the warmth and feel of his touch could have travelled home with her. Spring in the Whitsundays had marked the early days of their acquaintance; a time when he had become her friend.

At least Evie still kept in contact via email. From what Kat could gather, Lachie had returned to the Whitsundays and was back working his old job in the office. Evie didn't reveal too much about his whereabouts and Kat didn't ask. Maybe he had taken Prue back up to the island with him. Perhaps she was much calmer, or didn't yell and curse like a banshee when something went wrong.

A hint of a breeze came through a gap in the open wooden window and she jiggled the catch and tried to close it so the cold couldn't enter. Her thoughts fell back to the present and she peered further down the street. Just like the rain, the fallen leaves washed along the pavement and soon found their way into the drains, eventually journeying to the nearby ocean, marking the cyclical dance of nature.

Drawing her eyes away she looked at the clock on the wall. Every lunchtime she locked the gallery front door, flipped the 'out for lunch, be back in half an hour,' sign around and come rain, hail or shine, she would walk down to the esplanade.

Today the ocean was murky, stirred up by the cold blasts that pummelled across the North Atlantic. At least the rain had stopped once she left the gallery. The sun was trying to poke out from behind heavy clouds, a stiff breeze sending them scuttling towards the north. A heavy coat and thick boots protected her from the cold and with winter only a couple months away, she knew it would only get colder as the days marched on.

Gazing across the bay, she thought about the different seasons here in Ireland and the line of her family's generations who had always lived in the area. Her connection to the bay and this tiny town were strong. Somewhere out there on the grey rolling waves, her grandad had perished. It was a comfort to look out and know that his and Granny's ashes were scattered in the waters not far away. She giggled inwardly. Grace and her mother had given her a very detailed description of the scattering of Granny's ashes and, thankfully, lessons had been learnt from the day they spread Grandad's. 'The memorial for Granny was grand,' her mother had told her. 'No mistakes this time. We're getting better at the process. Everyone should be expert by the time it comes to Dad's and my turn.'

A breeze blew across her face and she couldn't help but laugh. The Irish were such a superstitious lot and every time she felt the wind, she remembered Granny's words. *When the breeze brushes across your face it will be me by your side.*

The wind blows constantly here, she thought. It can't be Granny all the time. A fishing trawler caught her eye as it made its way across the water in front of her. The bright red hull and sides were vivid against the colours of the sea, and she watched the boat rise up and then traverse down into the gullies of the waves, making its way out towards the open waters. The fishermen would still be going fishing, even in this rough weather. It had to be a serious storm for them not to work and at least it appeared that the weather was improving. Terns followed the trawler, their noisy squarks rising up to where she was standing, leaning on the rock wall.

She tried not to let the memories of another day spent near the sea, sneak in. She and Lachie had stood in the clear shallow water in front of his cabin. They had used the last of their bait to feed the seagulls, the birds' swooping movements and loud calls vivid in her memory. Lachie had splashed her, and she splashed him back. When he playfully wrestled with her, she gave in, and he had kissed her for a long time as they stood in the cool shallows.

As she lightly brushed her fingers across her lips, the trawler sounded its horn, the noise reverberating across the bay to where she stood. Turning around she looked at her watch. It was time to head back to work. With the fine weather, perhaps the afternoon might bring some tourists in.

The afternoon had been quiet in the gallery and, despite the lingering chill indoors, a sliver of sunshine streamed in through the window. She passed the time by writing an email on her phone to Morag who was travelling around Western Australia with an Australian lad she had met over there. He was gorgeous, Morag's last email had told her. With an Aussie sun-tanned body and a kind gentle soul to match. She flicked through the messages, reading another long one from Morag, just as the bell on the front gallery door rang.

She read the message again, as she hadn't read the last words properly and had missed the part about where Morag and her new fella were planning to travel up

through the northern part of Western Australia and ....
She paused her reading when the person standing in
front of her coughed. For a moment she had forgotten
where she was. Morag's news was so interesting. She put
her phone down and looked up.

Her voice was almost a shriek. 'Sweet God, Mother
Mary, Joseph and the baby Jesus! What the feck are you
doing here?' She turned into a statue in her seat and
blinked rapidly as she stared intently at the man standing
in front of her. This time, her voice emerged as a squeak.
'Lachie?'

For a long while his eyes held hers and then he
walked a bit closer to the counter that she sat behind. 'I
found out where you worked. I, um, thought I'd come and
see you.'

'Are you on holiday here? I never knew you wanted
to visit Galway, let alone Clifden. No one comes here.
Look, no one is here.' She waved her arms around and
realised she was babbling, but holy mother of God, what
was he doing here? 'Where are you staying? Do you have
someone else with you? How long are you here for?'

His face broke into a smile, and she took a deep
breath when she caught the sparkle in his eye and the
familiar lilt of his laughter. 'I'm here alone and I'm not
really on holiday.'

She stood up and frowned. 'Then why are you here?'

Chapter Thirty-Nine

Finding out where Kat was living and working hadn't been difficult. Once Lachie decided to go to Ireland, he quickly pulled up her details from *Vivre's* work files. Unethical perhaps, but this time he was pulling all stops out. When he contacted her mother and explained what had happened and apologised for his errors, he felt like he was halfway there.

Her mother, Orla, sounded much like Kat, although her accent was broader, and he had to ask her to repeat herself a couple of times. 'I knew that girl was pining after something or somebody,' she'd told him. 'She seemed to come back with her tail between her legs, though trying to make out everything was all fine and dandy. But I'm her mother, and I knew straight away. Mind you she wouldn't talk to us about what had happened or who she was yearning for. She did fill us in about Kiaran and Seamus and all the other stuff that went with that debacle.' She paused as if she wanted to say more, but then thought better of it. 'Of course, I'll give you the details of where she works and yes, mum's the word. I won't tell a soul, well maybe her dad. He should know.' Lachie had written down the days, the address and times that Kat worked.

'Or course, Orla. But I'd appreciate it if you didn't tell anyone else. I want to really catch her by surprise. She has every right not to want to see me. I just got mixed up with everything that happened. I'm used to a calm life without any major unnecessary problems.'

A loud chuckle sounded through the phone. 'Well, my lad. You're going to need to change those ideas. Family life, especially here in Galway, is one drama after another. Never a dull moment. Of course, her father will need to meet you once you're here. She's a special girl, our Kat. Patrick might have to approve of you first.'

Lachie had a silent chuckle about that. Here was Kat, now twenty-nine years old and had travelled around the world by herself, yet her mum still wanted to make sure her dad checked him out. 'Of course, Orla. I want to meet him also, and the rest of the family.'

Now as he stood in front of Kat, her green eyes flashing with either anger or excitement, confusion or surprise, he knew for sure he had made the right decision. Her long hair was loose and hung down past her shoulders. Three months back in Ireland and she had lost most of her tan, her beautiful pale skin with a pearly glow that made her even more beautiful than ever. He had not seen even a flicker of a smile though, and that concerned him. He took a couple of steps closer to the counter.

'I came because of you, Kat. I came because I realised I had made a terrible mistake. That I should have heard you out, and no matter what the situation was, it shouldn't have mattered. I know that now and I don't care about whatever has happened in the past. It doesn't matter, as long as we can be together again.'

She stayed sitting, her face unmoving, which worried him even more. It wasn't exactly a welcoming gesture and she hadn't shifted from where she had been when he entered the gallery. Her words were shaky. 'Your mother has told you what happened, hasn't she? The Johnny story and how the emerald ring is really mine. You wouldn't have come otherwise. You didn't listen to me when I wanted to tell you my story. You cut me off on the phone and never gave me a chance. You can't expect me to just forget that you walked away, well actually ran away from me. And now what? You think you can just turn up here like this unannounced, and that I'm going to jump into your arms and say all is forgiven. Is that what you think? Do you think I'm an easy pushover?'

He gulped and took a deep breath. 'I shouldn't have left like I did. I made a terrible mistake and I should have heard you out, or tried to work out whatever was happening. I swear Mum has told me nothing. She said her lips were sealed and I needed to follow my heart. She refused to tell me anything, no matter how much I pestered her. She just kept saying I had made the biggest mistake of my life.'

Now her eyes narrowed. 'You're lying. You wouldn't

have come all this way just to see me. I asked your mother not to tell you anything. If you couldn't trust me then, there is no use now.'

'I promise you. I swear on my life that she never told me what happened. Jasper wouldn't say anything either. They ganged up on me and said I had to sort my own life out. It was like a code of silence. They said they promised you they wouldn't repeat anything you had confided in them. Jasper didn't even tell me you were gone until a day after you left. I promise, Kat. You have to believe me. No one has said anything to me. This is all my own doing and I'm asking you to forgive me.'

Wrinkling her nose, she tilted her head to the side. 'And tell me again why you're here, and how the hell you knew where I worked?'

'I rang your mum and told her what a stupid mistake I'd made. She's a good person your mum.'

Kat pulled a shawl she had wrapped around her shoulders tighter, and he thought how the green of the shawl brought out the green in her eyes. The trouble was that those eyes could quickly turn from laughter to fury. He was careful when he spoke. He knew one foot out of place, and he was a goner.

'You spoke to my mum? She never said anything to me. What else did she tell you?'

'Nothing more than where you worked. Please Kat. I've come directly here to tell you that I love you and I want to be with you. If it means moving here to Ireland, I'll do it. I'd understand if you don't want to be away from your family. I could get a job and we could live wherever you want. If you wanted to live in Australia, I'd share my life there with you. We can go wherever you want. I will follow you to the end of the world and back again. I promise that whatever it is, I will work it out with you. I don't ever want to be apart from you again.' Now he reached into his pocket and her hand went over her mouth with his next words. 'I haven't asked your dad's permission yet, but I will. I want to ask you first though.' He took a deep breath before continuing. 'Kate MacCullagh, will you marry me? Will you let me be with you for the rest of your life, whatever hemisphere or country we live in? I want to be with you. Will you be my wife?'

He waited for her to reply. She blinked rapidly and he held his breath. When she did reply, her answer was not what he expected. This time her voice was even and measured. 'Can you please just turn around and go and lock the door for me. It's closing time and you need to pull that bolt across. The gallery needs to be locked up and there's a back door to exit through. Also turn the *Open* sign around to *Closed*. Thank you.'

Scrunching up his face and awkwardly holding the ring box in one hand, he did exactly as she asked. He twisted the sign around the right way and quickly shut the door. When he slid the barrel bolt across, he turned around and went back to where she was standing. By now she had moved around to the front of the counter. In the same spot, where he had been a few minutes ago, declaring his love for her. His stomach lurched. She had not given him an answer. For a moment he wondered if he had travelled all this way for nothing. It didn't seem that she was ready to forgive him for running in the opposite direction.

Her eyes followed his movements, and suddenly a slight smile crossed her lips. His heart melted, and he put out his hands towards her. She put both of hers in his and stepped in toward him.

He spoke softly. 'Oh, Kat. It's so good to see you again.' He waited but she didn't say anything. 'I know this is all out of the blue, but over the last couple of months I've done nothing but want to be with you again. I love you.' There was still no reply. 'You haven't answered my question.' For a long while they looked at each other and he wondered if he should reduce the pressure and offer to just go out together again, instead of the huge leap of marriage. Maybe he had been too presumptuous and marriage was not in her thoughts. Perhaps she had no feelings for him and, unlike him, had been able to carry on with life. She may not have the same feelings as he did.

Her voice made him jump. 'You say you want to get married? Is that what you're asking me?'

He nodded, his words caught in his throat.

Suddenly she pulled her shawl off and placed it on a nearby chair. 'Well, I've listened to all you have to say. And I'm thinking about all your words. There is one little thing I need to get square with you first. Something that I didn't think I'd ever share with you.'

Now his words gushed out. 'You don't need to tell me about any of the things from before. I don't care about the ring, or if you were ever married, or your cousins. When you're ready you can tell me, but right now I don't really care. It's your business. We can be engaged for as long as you want. You know if there is paperwork that needs to happen or whatever needs to be done, I'll wait. I don't know the story but I don't care. If you're not ready to get married we can start again and just go out if you like. I don't want to rush you, but I want you to know exactly how I feel.' He waited, his next words barely audible. 'I'd like to know how you feel about me. If you don't share the same feelings, then it's okay to say. I just need to know.'

Her eyebrows raised and he thought he saw a flicker of amusement cross her face. He was babbling, but there was so much at stake. When he went to speak again, she shook her head and he stopped. 'Stop, Lachie. I don't want to talk to you right now about any of that. That's not what I want to tell you. I do feel the same about you, and,' tears filled her eyes, 'it's grand to see you.' She reached down and took his hand, placing it on her stomach. For a moment he felt like his heart had stopped. Her words were softly spoken. 'There is more though. I'm pregnant. We're pregnant. You and me. I'm about three months on and due on the first of March.

They stared at each other for a long time, and when Lachie's legs stopped feeling like they were going to drop out from under him and he could find words, he finally spoke. 'Did you just say, *we're* pregnant?'

'Yes.'

'Right.' He cleared his throat. 'That's a lot to take in for me, and well, no doubt for you too.' He took her hands and held them firmly. 'Can you please just answer my other question first. The one when I declared my love for you and held out a ring. I'll feel a lot calmer if I know that first. Kat MacCullagh. Will you marry me?'

She laughed. That sweet melodic Irish laugh that

made his heart soar. This time there was no hesitation. 'I will Lachie McIntosh. I will. God knows where we'll live or how we'll get by. As you said though, as long as we're together, who cares.'

When she tilted her head up and kissed him, his world exploded and he pressed his lips gently down on hers. Her body pressed against him and he wrapped his arms around her. The kiss was the most passionate feeling he had ever experienced and when he finally pulled away, he took a step back and held her hands again. He laughed loudly and then declared. 'It will be grand. I'm not sure what order the events will be in, but I can't believe it. We're going to have a baby and get married.'

Chapter Forty

That night they stayed at Granny's cottage. It had been still light when they arrived, and Kat gave Lachie a tour around the grounds. He ran his hand over the white stucco walls and touched the thick thatch roof that had stood for over a hundred years. He could feel the legacy, the traditions and the soul of Ireland in the building. Now he understood where Kat came from and what made her who she was.

The property was fascinating and had the most amazing view. 'It takes your breath away. It's like nothing I've ever seen before,' Lachie said as they stood together looking over an ancient rock fence. In front of them, the meadows ran away from the house and down the gentle hillside to the sea beyond. Hundreds of gulls wove in and out above them, and the colours of the sunset on the opposite side of the horizon cast magical colours of light pinks and orange across the eastern sky. 'The North Atlantic Ocean,' Kat said. 'It's calmed down a little this afternoon but it can kick up some serious storms.' Fat sheep meandered down to the beach and he spotted a couple of painted wooden row boats tied up to trees, their bottoms roosting in the sand for the night, high above the water line.

I'd like to go for a fish in that ocean, when it's calm. You know Kat, if it makes you happy, we can live right here in this little cottage. I could buy it from your family for you, for us. As long as I'm close to the ocean I can make it work. Do your family know about the baby?'

'Yes, they all know, but no one else does. My mother knew the second she saw me and there's no keeping a secret like that in our house for very long. It won't take long for word to get out. Especially now you're here. You know, I think I know when it happened.'

'I did wonder because you were on the pill, although I believe that's not always a guarantee.'

'It's sort of my fault. When the cyclone was coming, I didn't get into town. My pills were nearly finished and then another week went by before I got into Airlie Beach. I started taking them again though, and I thought everything was okay. The trouble was I got that stomach bug from eating old leftovers, which I think was the end of May. I didn't give it a thought at the time but something like that can mess with the protection you should have from the pill.'

By the time I travelled to Brisbane with your mum, I had a fair idea I might be pregnant because I was feeling sick in the mornings and my periods hadn't arrived.'

'I can't believe you didn't tell me. Imagine if I hadn't come to my senses. I might have never known that we were going to have a baby, or come to Ireland.'

She laughed and snuggled into his arm. 'You're serious aren't you, about living here? Perhaps think about what you're offering. You might say that now, but wait until winter comes and the winds blow for months on end and the snow covers everything in its path. Even the beaches disappear. Where there is sand now, there'll be snow, and those church steeples in town and all the houses you see in town will have ice and snow dripping from them. There's hardly any daylight to get out and about, and the nights are long and freezing. Then there's the rain. You'll spend most of your life at the pub, because that's the only dry place to hang out. It's a far cry from your sunny beer gardens, fishing and surfing life.'

'Let's not make any decision on where we'll live yet,' Lachie said. 'I'd like to enjoy just meeting your parents and family and seeing where you come from. There's so much to see. And,' he put his hand on her stomach, 'I want to enjoy these months also. Let's not put any pressure on ourselves or rush into anything.'

Chapter Forty-One

She had made pumpkin soup for dinner, and they sat with a candle burning in the middle of the table—a table where for many decades, grannies, grandads, mums, dads and kids had come together to sit and talk.

'Thank goodness those idiots left all the furniture in the shed. We've moved it all back up here to the house. Just the way Granny would have wanted it.'

'So, this cottage belongs to your parents?' Lachie asked. 'I was confused when I spoke to your mum, because she kept referring to it as your cottage, but I'm guessing it's your mum and dad's, or it belongs to the entire family.'

'No. It was left to Mum, but now it's mine. I bought it from her. I sold something that was worth a lot of money.' She held out her right hand. He had noticed the emerald ring on her other hand when he had put his ring on her left finger. At the time he didn't say anything. Last time he had done that, it had been disastrous. There was plenty of time to discuss other past events that didn't matter at the moment.

'This is a replica of the ring I sold. Granny's ring that she left to me. It was worth nearly a million, so I sold it and had enough to buy this cottage, pay my parent's house off, give them quite a large amount of money and put away plenty for myself. I even bought myself this lovely shawl from the op shop in the main street of Galway.'

He shook his head. Do all Irish people have crazy family stories to tell? Sometimes, I think we Aussies are a bit boring. We don't have the history you people do.'

'Don't forget half of you came from either here, Scotland or England, originally. I think there's a little Irish or Scotch in many of you. Look at your surname, it has a Mac in it.'

They'd talked a bit longer and she had put the kettle on for a cup of tea. 'Have you got it in you to stay up for a bit longer tonight, or are you too jet-lagged?'

He stretched out on the couch, his feet hanging over the end. 'Sure, I've got it in me. I'm too excited, happy, relieved to sleep.' He turned and looked at her as she finished making the tea. 'You know the first time I met you, I was lying on a couch like this. I heard your voice first. Irish, I thought. Trouble. Trouble with a capital T.'

She laughed and he sat up as she came to sit beside him. 'If my memory serves me right, you had next to nothing on and were extremely hungover. You looked like something the cat dragged in.' She leaned across and kissed him. 'I want to tell you, my story. I want you to know the truth.'

* * *

It was late into the night and they were on their third cup of tea when she finished telling the secret of the emerald ring. 'As soon as I got to Brisbane that day and said goodbye to your mum, I knew I was going to come home to Ireland. I had a fair idea I was pregnant, but I never said a word to anyone. I thought you had moved on and wouldn't welcome such news. I also happened to see a photo of you and someone called Prue at the Point Lookout Pub. It was in the social pages of a newspaper in Brisbane.'

'Oh my goodness. Unbelievable. I'm so sorry about that. She was once my girlfriend and when I returned to Stradbroke Island she asked me to go for a meal at the pub. A photographer snapped a photo of us and I didn't realise it not only made the local paper but also the city one. She means nothing to me. I went out with her that once and that was it.'

'You don't have to explain anything to me, Lachie. It's okay.'

'No. I want you to know for sure that I only went because she insisted and ...'

'Stop.' Kat held her hand up. 'It's alright. I trust you and you wouldn't be here if you didn't want to be.'

'Okay. What happened after you decided to leave? Finish your story.'

'After that, I flew straight back to the Whitsundays, packed up my belongings and said some quick goodbyes. I flew back to Brisbane and then took the long flight home. It was all so quick. I didn't want to involve your mum. She probably thinks the emerald ring is still sitting in a safety box in a bank in Brisbane, but I never went to the bank. I kept the ring and when I got back to London, I returned to the same jeweller I had gone to before I came to Australia. I knew I could trust him. Within a short while he had the ring valued and sold, through one of the top auction houses in London.

He made a pretty penny out of it also, but I was grateful and would have given him more if he had let me. All the paperwork is with solicitors and everything is legal. I got him to make another replica of the ring, so that I still had some connection to what Granny had left me. This ring I wear, actually does have a real emerald, but it's not a very expensive one and the diamonds are zircons. That's the end of that story. And now I have another ring, a beautiful diamond ring, that means every-thing to me.'

'What a story, Kat. And I can't believe my mother knew the details and didn't tell me. I knew you two got on well, but I don't think I realised how close you had become.'

'Does she know about you coming here?' Kat asked.

'No. No one does. They think I've gone up to Cairns, to the islands, to check out a resort up there. We'll ring them once I've met your parents and everyone here knows what's going on. Maybe when things are more in order.'

'Get used to it Lachie. Nothing ever settles down here. Life is always a roller coaster. Wait until you meet the family.'

Chapter Forty-Two

Lachie spent the past days with her in the gallery, as well as getting to know the area. He walked around the town of Clifden and up into the hills, following paths that gave him amazing views of the countryside. She had insisted that she was okay and he should get out and have a better look around, but he would only go for an hour and then return. She could tell he didn't want to let her out of his sight.

'I'm worried you're going to disappear and not be here when I come back,' he said as he held her close and kissed the top of her head. 'You look radiant. Just beautiful.' He ran his hand through her hair and she pushed him gently away, laughing at how attentive he was.

'I'm supposed to be working. Now off you go. Head down towards the sea this time. There're plenty of boats to look at down there.'

* * *

That afternoon, by the time she closed up and locked the front door of the gallery, it was a bit later than her usual finishing time. They were running late, and tonight they were going to have dinner with her family. Her sisters and brother were only expecting her to come. She had let her parents know about Lachie's arrival, and they had secretly ensured that everyone was at home tonight for a special welcome dinner.

The delay closing up made them arrive later than she had planned, and as she opened the front door, Grace was waiting for her. Her sister had been watching the large clock above the mantlepiece. She spun around when Kat entered. 'Where were you? We were starting to get worried. You're late home. Did something happen? I mean, I know you're usually pretty punctual, but today you were just, like, nowhere to be found! And I kept thinking, what if something happened? I mean, I know I tend to overthink things, but seriously, it's not like you to be so late, and I was just here, staring out the window, imagining all sorts of scenarios, like maybe you got lost, or you had car trouble, or—oh, I don't know—I just couldn't shake this feeling that something wasn't right, you know?' Grace rambled on, her words tumbling out in a rush of concern.

Taking off her shawl, Kat walked slowly toward the table where everyone was seated. 'I'm fine. Calm down, Grace. You're all fussing over me too much lately. I'm not the first person to have a baby. You need to relax a little.'

'You should have rung us when you left and when you were halfway home,' Eileen added. 'It's dark and we've been worried sick.'

Even Ronan was anxious. 'I've rung a few times and you didn't answer. The only ones not worried are Mum and Dad. You've had the rest of us on the edge of our chairs. Don't be late like that again. You're looking after two people now. It's not just about you.'

She looked around the table at them. 'Thank you, Ronan, for your concern, and the rest of you. I'm not a baby and I was just a bit late locking up the gallery and organising a few things.'

'Why aren't you taking a seat and you've left the front door open,' Eileen said. 'What is wrong with you today, Kat. And why are you grinning like that?'

'I'd like you all to meet someone.' Lachie had been waiting outside and she went back to the doorway and took his hand. He followed her into the room, and she gave his hand a reassuring squeeze. 'I want you all to meet Lachie McIntosh.'

A stunned silence followed, and Ronan's knife clattered onto the table. 'As in Australian Lachie?' he asked.

Grace stood up. 'Like in Lachie, the father of your baby?'

'Eileen, close your mouth. I can see food in it. Where are your manners,' her mother called out as she stood up and came towards Kat. Her father also stood up, and they greeted Lachie with boisterous hugs and lots of hand-shaking.'

'Wait a minute,' Grace said as she looked at her parents. 'You two seem like you knew about this. You knew didn't you that Kat's fella was here. That's why you weren't worried when she was late. I smell a rat.'

Kat's mum was positively beaming, and her words

gushed out like the most important person in the world was gracing their house. 'We might have known, but we hadn't met Lachie yet. Here, young man, let me take your coat and come and sit down. It's such a pleasure to finally meet you.'

As they came to sit at the table, the room erupted into a million questions. Soon everyone was shouting over each other, trying to work out who knew that the father of the baby had been arriving, and had Kat known, and why weren't they told, and how long was he staying and ...'

In the end Patrick held up his hands and clapped loudly, announcing that, 'Everyone needs to shut up and give the young man a chance to eat his dinner, and then he can answer your questions in his own time.'

As the night rolled on and dessert hit the table, there was a lull in the chat. You could hear the clinking of cutlery and the pouring of port, signalling a temporary ceasefire in the lively banter. Kat took the chance to sneak a few glances at Lachie, trying to gauge what he thought about her madcap family.

Lachie, however, seemed as cool as a cucumber. His nods and smiles, here and there, showed he was keeping up with the banter, and he had laughed loudly several times at some of the jokes along the way. Kat was glad he had siblings of his own; he probably knew a thing or two about dinner table chaos. Maybe not as rowdy as hers, but surely all families had their moments.

As the night wore on and the dessert plates were cleared, her nerves began to settle, and she couldn't help but feel grateful for his easy-going nature and the sense of calm he brought to the table.

When Patrick made a short speech and thanked Lachie for coming to his senses and travelling to Ireland to reunite with one of the three most beautiful, intelligent and kind girls in the world, they all cheered and clapped. 'The other two being of course, Grace and my baby girl Eileen.'

Lachie stood up and raised his glass to theirs. 'I didn't know that Kat was pregnant until I arrived a few days ago, so that was a bit of a surprise. A very pleasant one and I want you all to know that I'm over the moon to think we'll be having a baby. When I arrived at the gallery and told her my true feelings, I asked her a question.' Kat looked up at him, and then her eyes locked on Grace's, who looked like she was about to levitate off her chair.

'No way. You didn't. Did you?' Grace shouted.

'What?' Ronan questioned, looking from one to the other. 'What didn't he do? What did he do? I don't understand.'

'I'm confused,' Eileen said. 'What are you all blabbering on about?'

Lachie waited for them to stop talking, all eyes now fixed on him. 'And I rang Patrick to ask his permission. Then I asked Kat to marry me,' Lachie said.

Kat stood up beside him. 'And I said yes.'

Chapter Forty-Three

Kat continued to work at the gallery until Christmas time. She and Lachie settled into the cottage and he spent much of his spare time renovating one of the small sheds to work from. The small white stuccoed building was sturdy on the outside, its thick walls and thatch roof standing strong as they had done for a century. Inside however, needed a lot of work.

The inside had now been lined, and with help from Ronan, Lachie rebuilt some of the interior walls and turned the shed into an office space. Granny's old wooden chair and a desk that had belonged to Grandad now took pride of place next to a small leather couch and a low table. They had built a metal bench along one wall with a sink and kitchen equipment. Now he could work in the space, and make himself lunch and cups of tea when he wanted. A small fridge and a little pantry with everything needed, filled another corner.

The internet ran through a satellite system and with

plenty of work from his family's business to keep him busy, and now his own space to work in, Lachie quickly settled into life in Clifden. At three o'clock he would shut up the shed and make his way along a path that wound along the coastline and led into the town.

Kat would be ready to close the gallery and they sometimes strolled around town or maybe he would have a Guiness, and Kat a lemonade, at the local pub. Most afternoons though, they strolled slowly home back along the path, talking about what had taken place during the day.

The days were peaceful and slow, and he loved being with Kat and watching her body change. At night they sat together on the couch, his hand on her stomach waiting for the baby to kick. It was a boisterous baby and Kat was only a small build. He wondered how everything fitted inside her and marvelled at how much her skin had stretched to accommodate the growing baby.

'Don't look so worried, Lachie. I'm not going to burst. My body stretches when it needs to.'

'I am worried, Kat. I'm worried about you bursting and nervous thinking about when you'll go into labour. I'm concerned about keeping you healthy and mostly about how that baby is going to come out of you. I'm big and you're only small. It's crazy.'

She cuddled into him as they sat on the couch, watching a game of rugby on the TV. 'Don't worry. Because I'm not. It will all be easy. I can feel it in my bones. It will be smooth sailing all the way.'

He wished he shared her calm approach and confidence about how something that obviously large was going to make its way into the world. Hopefully when his parents arrived for Christmas, he would feel a bit calmer.

Chapter Forty-Four

A hotel in Galway had been booked for his parents, who were arriving the day before Christmas. They would stay for a week and then they were going to travel around the rest of Ireland, Scotland and Wales for a month before travelling down to England and then over to Europe. After that, it would nearly be time for the baby to be born, so they would make a quick trip back to Galway to visit before making the long journey home. There was no way Evie would miss out on seeing the new baby before they returned to Australia.

Orla was beside herself and every inch of the house had been cleaned and scrubbed.

She had spent the past two weeks in the kitchen, a bright green apron tied around her waist as she scurried back and forth from the pantry to the fridge and then back to the table where rows of bowls, saucepans and other plates stood ready for whatever dish she was preparing. A radio that sat on the window sill blared out loud music, and Lachie loved to watch her bustling around as she sang along with the tunes.

In the kitchen there seemed to be sacks of flour, oats and potatoes on every bench and the centrepiece of the Christmas meal, a succulent joint of beef, waited patiently on another benchtop. A marinade of garlic, thyme and a splash of stout was sure to give it an unmistakable Irish flavour. There was an aroma of onions and carrots—coming from the huge pot simmering on the stove—mingling with the smell of soda bread baking in the oven. Orla sang an old Irish tune as she stirred the pot that was bubbling and threatening to boil over.

'Pass me those herbs there, Lachie. It'll be a grand day tomorrow. What time are they getting here?'

Lachie sat at the table, shelling the peas in between sipping a cup of tea. 'If you're going to sit there and chat, you might as well have a job to do,' Orla had told him.

Kat had gone to lie down. She was tired and the bigger her stomach got, the more she struggled with keeping up her energy levels.

'They should be landing about now,' Lachie said, looking up at the large clock that hung on the kitchen wall. 'They'll pick up a hire car in Dublin and drive straight to their hotel. I think they'll be worn out from the long flights, so I said I'd just pick them up in the morning. Best they have a rest, then they'll be ready for a big day here.'

'I know I've thanked you before, but I'll say it again. Patrick would tell you too. We're forever grateful you're staying in Galway while the baby is born and for a while afterwards. We totally respect your decision to move back to Australia after that. I've talked to Kat and I know it's what she wants also. It's important that she's with us for the birth and after though, while that baby is still new. She'll need us as well as you, to make sure everything goes smoothly and there aren't any issues. We'll all make sure of that.'

'She will especially need you, Orla. I know nothing about babies and I'm hoping you'll come to the cottage when you can.'

Orla beamed. 'That's grand that you want me around. I guess I do know a thing or two about babies.'

* * *

After resting the previous afternoon Kat felt revived and while she slept it had been a good opportunity for Lachie to help her mum in the kitchen and have a talk, just the two of them. Now it was finally Christmas Day and everything was ready to go. A crisp white tablecloth covered the dining room table, and Eileen had arranged a bunch of wildflowers that sat in the centre.

Grace had spent hours polishing the silver, and the cutlery and crystal glasses were glistening and set in place. The family were all dressed up and ready for the festivities to begin. Now all they needed was for Evie and Chris to arrive.

For a long while after Lachie's mum and dad walked into the house, no one could hear anything. Everyone talked at once and Kat had trouble getting close to Evie to give her a hug. Evie wiped tears from her eyes when she put her hand on Kat's stomach. 'I'm so glad we're here. The others in the family all send their love.'

The chatter went on for ages and Lachie looked so excited Kat thought he was going to burst. It wasn't until Ronan mentioned it might be time for the first Christmas traditional Guinness of the day that everyone calmed a little and sat down at the table.

Evie and Chris fitted into the family as if they had been there forever and as she sat next to Lachie, Kat felt like her world was complete. Everyone under the same roof at Christmas, and with a storm forecast, it also looked like they would get Evie's wish for a white Christmas.

Chapter Forty-Five

When the food was served, there was noisy chatter and the clanging of utensils as the large bowls of steaming vegetables and creamy mashed potatoes were passed around the table. Bowl after bowl of food followed, and Eileen and Grace constantly got up and down to help their mother bring everything to the table.

'Don't you dare move,' Grace fussed over Kat. 'You look like you're having trouble just sitting there. Get over here Ronan. Yes, I know your job is the drinks, but give me a hand with this meat. This Aussie girl you're so madly in love with must be worth it. I've never seen a Christmas day when you haven't been rolling drunk.'

'I'm a responsible man now. There'll be no drinking and driving. Also, I'm to meet her family tomorrow, so I want to look my best. They've come out to see her for Christmas.

Ronan did a little jig and messed his sister's hair, while cursing and lamenting about the snow that was just starting to fall outside. 'A white Christmas is lovely but I need the roads clear, to get to Dublin tonight to see me darlin'.'

A string of jokes followed and Evie and Chris joined in the laughter. When her father toasted such a grand Christmas day, and that the family was all together, Kat tried to hold back the tears. She was so emotional these days. Her mother passed her a handkerchief as they also toasted those who had passed. 'Thank you, dear Granny and Grandad, for always looking after us and giving us your love,' Patrick said with his glass high in the air.

The lunch continued until well into the night. 'Lunch and dinner all rolled into one,' Lachie whispered in her ear. 'You look a bit tired.'

'I'm a bit uncomfortable. I feel like there's a foot pushing down on me, you know where.'

She moved in her chair as Evie and Chris stood up, ready to leave. It was nearly midnight and everyone was ready to call it a night. As they stood in the doorway waving Lachie's parents off in a taxi, she thanked the heavens for everything working out. It had been a Christmas to remember.

Chapter Forty-Six

The next week flew past as Lachie and Kat drove his parents around Galway and along the coastline. The weather was perfect and they were blessed with still, mild days and calm seas. There was plenty to see and Kat enjoyed going places, many of them she hadn't been to for years. Lachie also loved the scenery and especially the different castles they visited. 'It's an ancient land,' Chris said as he and Lachie stared up at the walls and tower of Dunguaire Castle, a 16th century tower house that sat on a rocky outcrop on the shores of Galway Bay. 'We don't have anything like this back home. I think, Kat, that you Irish take these castles for granted. You're so used to seeing them that they're part of the landscape for you. But for us, they're incredible. Just beautiful.'

By the end of the week, they were all tired from the sightseeing and enjoyed a quiet couple of days relaxing and spending time at the cottage. It was soon time for Evie and Chris to move on and continue travelling around in the campervan they had hired. 'We'll go wherever the wind blows us,' Evie said. 'There's so much to see here in Ireland. Now look after yourself,' she said as she wrapped her arms around Kat. 'You look tired. We've worn you out. Make sure she puts her feet up and rests,' she added as she looked towards Lachie.

'I will Mum. Don't worry. She's not allowed to do anything from now on in. She only has nine weeks to go.'

* * *

A party was to be held for Ronan's birthday on the 28th of January. It was just before Lachie's birthday and Ronan thought it a grand idea that they celebrate together. They could hold the party in the huge barn that sat in the meadows between Granny's cottage and the ocean. 'I'll have to start calling it Kat's cottage,' Ronan said as he surveyed the area where they could set everything up. 'At least in the barn everyone will keep warm. The band can set up at the front there and we'll get some indoor heaters to keep the cold away. I've talked to the neighbours and they've got those little crofts they rent out. The guests can stay there and Mum and Dad at your place. You won't have to do anything. I just need the space to have a good old-fashioned shindig. Plenty of music, dancing and beer.'

Lachie agreed it was a good idea, as long as Kat didn't have to do anything. 'She gets really tired and I'm trying to make her rest. She's not good at sitting still and she hasn't even looked at her art since she's been off work.'

'Restless she is,' Orla told him. 'It's normal. When the baby arrives, she'll settle down.'

Now as Kat stood next to him and they looked out over the ocean, he thought that she was glowing. Tired but glowing. 'It's a long way for everyone to walk,' Kat said to Ronan as she looked at the barn. 'I'm not sure how I'll get down there and back. Especially back. You can't get a vehicle down the hill. It'll get bogged.'

'The guests will park next door and then all they have to do is walk across the meadow when they're ready to go home. It's a bit of distance but no one will mind. I've already thought of how you'll get up and back. We've got Granny's walker. It's one that also works as a chair. You can sit on that and we'll push you up and back. Just like a wheelchair really. I'll mow a track so it's easier.'

Kat rolled her eyes, visualising herself on Granny's walker getting pushed up and down the hill. 'How can you push a walker up the hill, you idiot. I'll just walk slowly. I'll be okay.'

'It'll be apples,' Ronan said, playfully hugging her and planting a kiss on her cheek. 'Nothing will go wrong. It'll just be a quiet celebration of two very important birthdays.'

Chapter Forty-Seven

The sun shone all week, the ground was dry, and the weather glorious for the day of the party. Ronan and his girlfriend Peggie, along with some of his mates, spent the morning setting up. It was the first time Kat had met the new love of Ronan's life and she was impressed from the first moment they talked.

'I'm from Sydney originally,' Peggie said. 'But I've spent a couple of years travelling around Australia and Europe. I was going to keep moving, but,' she looked up at Ronan, 'I met your brother and it looks like this is as far as I'm going to get.'

Lachie laughed. 'We're both a long way from home. But it sounds as though you're also happy to stay here in Galway.'

'I am. I'm not sure about the winters, but we'll see. Maybe I'll get Ronan to come out to Australia.'

Kat watched as Ronan and Peggie made their way down the slope to the barn. Lachie gave her a quizzical look. 'And?'

'Yes, okay yes. I approve. She's lively, friendly and hopefully can keep him out of trouble. It's a tick from me.'

* * *

From where Kat sat—just outside the cottage—the party area looked fabulous. Some chairs and tables were scattered among the blankets and haybales set up in a circular area. A small stage had been fashioned on a flat stretch of grass, and she could hear the music as they tested out the speakers.

'Great place for a party,' her father said as he came to stand behind her. 'No one to bother with the noise.'

'I wasn't that interested before today, but I'm excited for the afternoon now,' she said. 'Lachie needs to let his hair down and relax. He's been fussing and doing everything around here. He won't let me lift a finger.'

'Him and your mother. She's the same. I keep trying to get her to slow down. Maybe tonight we'll all be able to relax and listen to some good music. That fiddler is the best in the county. There could be some grand dancing. Not from you, mind you.'

She laughed. 'I don't think I'll be doing any dancing. Walking around is enough for me.'

* * *

Hanging onto Lachie's arm, Kat walked slowly down the hill. 'I absolutely refuse to sit in that walker. I'm not an invalid, just pregnant, and I've been exercising as much as I can to keep fit. I'll just take it slow.'

It was a steady but relatively easy walk down the hill. 'See, I'm not even puffing,' she said to Lachie. 'You should see your face. You're going to kill yourself with worry. Stop it. Relax. Have a few drinks tonight. You don't have to drive anywhere.'

'I'm not going to drink too much. What if you go into labour?'

'Lachie. I only went to the doctor yesterday and he said the baby doesn't even look as though it will come on the due date. He's thinking I'll go over. I told you that. The baby is sitting up high. Mum's an expert on birthing and babies, and she said the same. It hasn't even dropped yet. Please, I want to see you have a good time.'

Eileen brought a chair over for Kat and sat down next to her. Everyone from her family was there. Mum, Dad, Grace, Eileen, Ronan and Peggie.

The band began to play a lively jig as everyone settled in and as more guests arrived, the party started to warm up. There must be about seventy people here, Kat thought. Large barn doors were left open on the side and although the cold air filtered in, the heaters kept the space warm.

Through the doors the guests could see the moon as it ascended over the ocean, casting its gentle glow across the surface. The night couldn't be more perfect. 'Wow,' Lachie exclaimed, gazing across the bay. 'It doesn't get any better than this.'

'I don't know,' Kat replied. 'The views at *Vivre* were

every bit as beautiful. It's just different when you have a fiddler playing Irish tunes and Guinness flowing. It's always about the people, isn't it? Look at the good times we had in front of Jasper's cabin.'

He wrapped his arm around her shoulders. 'We did. And plenty more to come.'

* * *

As the night wore on and the beer flowed, the crowd got rowdier. Most were up dancing and there was a lot of cheering and laughing when Ronan and Peggie did a beautiful Irish jig together. 'Peggie is a well-known dancer in Australia,' Kat told Lachie. 'She won a lot of competitions and dancing is how he met her. Not at a competition. At the pub, of course. He's usually just a spectator.' She gestured to where the couple were beating out a rhythm with their feet, their synchronised timing, perfect. 'Ronan has to be very drunk to do that. He'll have a sore head in the morning.'

More singing and dancing followed and Kat stood up when her mum and dad waltzed to an old Irish tune. Everyone clapped and Lachie held out his hand for Kat to join him. They held each other and swayed back and forth in what resembled a waltz. He looked into her eyes and kissed her gently, and she whispered that she loved him to the moon and back. Above the bay, stars flickered, and the moon rose higher. The rest of the world disappeared. Evie was right, nothing mattered as long as they were together.

* * *

Lachie was a bit unsteady on his feet as he led Kat to sit down. He didn't think he'd had that much to drink, but Ronan and Patrick kept the beer flowing and he had been caught up in the excitement and beauty of the night. 'I think I've had enough to drink,' he said to Kat. 'I don't want to be sick tomorrow. I'm supposed to be cooking breakfast in the morning for anyone who's up to it. It'll be a good old-fashioned Aussie barbeque. See, we've got it ready over there for the morning.' He pointed to a table with boxes on it, an old barbeque set up nearby.

Ronan yelled out from the dance floor and the band stopped playing. 'Grace, Eileen and Kat. Over here. I want you to sing *Galway Bay* for mine and Lachie's birthday.'

Kat struggled to get out of the chair, but Lachie held her arm and helped her up. He walked with her to join her sisters and then stood to the side nearby. Grace and Eileen both obviously had plenty to drink because they bowed and curtsied, making a big fuss over Kat as they stood ready to sing. It was the first time Lachie had seen Eileen really relax. Usually, she was quite conservative and didn't curse or shout out quite as much as the others. Grace, as usual, was playing up to some of the party guests and he saw Kat shake her head as she waited for them all to behave themselves and begin the singing.

As the band struck up a tune, a few lines rang out, and then the girls started to sing. The familiar song of *Galway Bay* drifted gently across the meadows. A hush fell over the audience, a collective silence that spoke of their shared sentiment for this timeless melody.

As the song reached its crescendo, Lachie's heart swelled with emotion as he watched Ronan and then his mum and dad join in with the girls, their voices blending seamlessly in harmony. It was a moment of pure magic, a family united in song under the canopy of stars.

The music swelled for the second time and Lachie knew there couldn't be a dry eye in the crowd. The beauty of the performance, combined with the tranquil ambience of the night and the gentle breeze that brushed across them, created an atmosphere that was nothing short of enchanting. It was a memory that would linger long after the final notes faded into the night.

The applause had been long and hearty and the girls bowed and went back to join the crowd. The band started up a lively tune and the night continued from where it had left off. Kat sat for a while on the chair next to Lachie, but she seemed uncomfortable and kept moving around trying to find the best position to sit. After a while she stood up, one of Ronan's friends still talking to her about his planned trip to Australia.

Lachie left the barn to relieve himself. A makeshift toilet area had been set up a fair way down the meadow for the men. Ronan had also managed to organise a porta loo for the ladies which had been positioned close to the barn.

When Lachie finished, he stood under the stars and looked across the bay for a long while, as usual, the sight of the ocean drawing his attention. Shouts and calls from further up the hill at the party alerted him that somebody was calling out.

He turned around to see Ronan wildly waving his arms and screeching out his name. 'Lachie. Lachie McIntosh. Can you get up here? There's a slight problem.'

The music was still playing and he wondered if Ronan had run out of beer. There was more alcohol stashed in a tiny shed over further, just in case extra was needed. Grace appeared next to Ronan. She waved her arms in the air and jumped up and down but he couldn't hear what she was calling out. He did however see what happened next, when she jumped around too much and slid down the bank in front of her.

By the time he got to where the two of them were, Grace was rolling around on the ground, cursing and holding her ankle. 'Jesus Christ, sweet mother Mary. Feckin hell. I've broken my ankle.'

She had probably just twisted it he thought, as he bent down to have a look. 'Holy shit,' he said. 'It does seem as though you've broken it. That looks like some serious damage. Don't move.'

Ronan knelt down beside his sister. 'Move, Lachie. Move. Get back up the hill. You need to get to Kat. She thinks she's in labour. That's what I was yelling out to you.'

Lachie felt the blood rush to his brain and he stared at Ronan trying to take in his words. 'Go, man, go,' Ronan said, pushing him towards the party. Lachie stumbled up the hillside, sprinting to where he had left Kat. By now there was a small group of people around her as she hung onto her sister, Eileen. 'Are you okay, Kat?' he asked, peering into her worried face.

Eileen was studying to be a nurse but it appeared with too many drinks in her blood she had forgotten any training she might have had in regards to pregnancy and childbirth. Her words were slurred. 'Does she look like she's alright? She's in pain. Do something. Fix it.'

Patrick appeared, his face red and his breathing ragged. 'Jesus, mother of God. I was just having a piss and I've run up the hill because everyone was yelling.' He put his hand on his chest. 'I feel just like I'm going to have a heart attack.'

Orla came behind him and steered him towards a chair. 'Sit down, you crazy man. You've had too many drinks. I told you your health would suffer if you drank too much.'

'How far apart do you think the contractions are?' Lachie asked, looking from Eileen to Kat.

'I don't have a feckin watch on me,' Eileen said. 'Here you hang onto her. I think I'm going to vomit.' With that, she disappeared down the hill.

Orla was trying to appear calm but her eyes told Lachie a different story. 'There's a doctor here. His name's Angus. I'll go and find him. The band will know where he is. He's one of their brothers.'

She came back not long after. 'Sorry, he's asleep behind the hay bales over in the corner. He passed out over an hour ago and no one can wake him properly. He keeps falling back asleep. No use whatsoever!'

'Right,' Lachie said, keeping an eye on Kat who was now leaning over the chair and holding her back.

'The pain, Lachie. The pain. It's bad and it's in my back. There's pressure.' She let out a low wail and Orla's eyes widened. She was also clearly drunk and her words were jumbled and slurred. 'Holy Jesus, we need a doctor. That sounds as though the baby's coming.'

Ronan appeared next to them, waving his phone around. 'We've called the local doctor and explained what is happening. He said he'll get here as quickly as he can. He didn't seem too worried about a baby coming, but he was concerned when I described Eileen's ankle to him. He said he can get an ambulance to the cottage, but he won't get one down here to the barn. His instructions are not to move Eileen but we have to take Kat up to the cottage. From there, the doc said someone can drive her to the hospital. He said she'll be fine, and that a mother's first baby doesn't come in a hurry in these parts.'

Kat stood up and rubbed her stomach. Her face was white and pinched and Lachie held onto her arm. 'Maybe you should sit down. It's too early for the baby to come.'

'What the hell does he mean, by these parts?' Kat said, her eyes narrowing. 'What bloody difference does it make where someone is? Does he think we're special here and we just tell the baby to wait?' She let out a moan. 'I can't sit down. My body won't let me because there's an object vertically positioned inside me that won't allow me to bend and as for the *early* bit, what would you like me to do? Ask the baby to hold on a sec? Tell it this isn't a good time?'

Her eyes flashed at Lachie, and Orla shot him a look of warning. He needed to be careful what he said. A woman in pain was not someone to be saying the wrong thing to.

Eileen came back and rubbed Kat's back as another round of contractions started. 'Where's Granny's walker?' Eileen asked.

'It's up at the house,' Lachie said. 'Kat wouldn't let me bring it down here.'

'Run and get it. Sprint,' Eileen yelled at him. Ronan was also shouting at someone as he tried to get a friend to go and help look after Grace.

Kat grabbed Lachie's arm as she stared at Eileen. 'He's not leaving me. He's not going anywhere. You go and get it, Eileen. You're a fast runner.'

Eileen glared at Lachie and then took off up the hill towards the cottage. By the time she got back Orla and Patrick were trying to make their way up the hill to the house. Patrick kept falling backwards and at one stage Orla fell down with him, both of them rolling around before sitting up in the middle of the meadow trying to get their breath back. Raucous laughter could be heard as they tried to help each other up.

'Sweet mother Mary and the baby Jesus!' Eileen exclaimed as she positioned the walker in front of where Kat was leaning over, hanging onto a chair. 'Look at the two of them. Did you ever see anything like it? What sort of parents have we got? They're no help. Grace is lying with a broken ankle down the hill somewhere, and Kat's baby is about to be born in the middle of the meadow and those two are rolling down the hill and laughing.'

When Kat swung her head around to face Eileen and Lachie, it was if there were flames coming out of her eyes.

She was angry. Lachie had seen that look before, and he and Eileen stood like soldiers who had been told to stand to attention. Her directions came out between clenched teeth. 'Get me on that walker! Get me on it and up that hill! Now!'

Eileen threw Lachie a look and they stood on both sides of Kat, helping her position her bottom on the seat provided on the walker. For a moment it appeared that had been an easy task, and Lachie exhaled audibly. Maybe it would perform as a wheelchair. But the walker was old and the fabric that Kat sat on quickly gave way underneath her. She sunk into the pouch beneath, her legs hanging over the edge and her feet no longer touching the ground. Her knuckles were white as she clenched the handles. 'Go. Just move. Get me up to the cottage at least.'

Pushing her up the hill was an impossibility. Ronan had run out of time to mow the path, and in some parts the grass was so thick, the walker's wheels wouldn't budge even when they tried to drag it up backwards. One tyre was also flat, which didn't help.

They stopped several times when contractions came, and Kat had suffered through them, unable to do much else. She squeezed Lachie's hand so tight he thought she had broken it, but he didn't dare say a word. Eileen had disappeared when the contraction started but quickly returned, running towards them with a wheelbarrow in front of her.

'This might work better,' she declared.

There was a tense silence between them as they manoeuvred Kat out of the walker and into the wheelbarrow. Lachie put his coat under her and scowled at Eileen until she also took hers off and positioned it behind Kat. He took hold of the handles and going as fast as he could without bumping Kat around too much, pushed her slowly up the hill.

* * *

Thankfully there was only one more contraction before they reached the cottage. Lachie could see car lights and he hoped it would be the doctor arriving. With any luck there was an ambulance also, although with only one in Clifden, he wasn't sure what the plan was with Grace also in trouble further down the hill.

As the doctor hobbled towards them, Lachie spotted Orla and Patrick resting on two chairs. 'Sure, we'd jump up and lend a hand,' Orla hollered. 'But Patrick's heart's racing like a hare on a hunt, and he's seeing stars, so we'd best stay put. I'm feeling a bit queer meself. Doctor Kelly's on hand now, so we'll all be grand. Good Lord, Kat. What are you thinking, riding in a wheelbarrow?'

While the doctor asked a run of questions, Eileen and Lachie manoeuvred Kat carefully out of the wheelbarrow. It took a bit of pushing and pulling, and in the end, Lachie put his hands under her arms and lifted her out while Eileen held the wheelbarrow so it didn't tip over. Kat's face was pinched and she grimaced with the pain of moving from her mode of transport to a standing position. Lachie propped her up, his own heart racing with the stress of everything happening.

Doctor Kelly, who moved slowly and appeared to be

riddled with arthritis, assessed the situation, annoying Kat even more when he continually tilted his head to the side and asked her to repeat her answers. He leaned on his walking stick and closed his eyes. Eventually he opened them and started to explained his solution to the dilemma. 'The ambulance should be on its way soon, however it could take longer than what we want. I'm going to leave it to deal with the one called Grace with the broken ankle. I'll get the boys to carry her up the hill and wait for the ambulance to arrive. They'll need to sort of make a chair with their hands and someone can support her leg. That should be easy enough. The trouble with this young lass here,' he checked his watch, timing another one of her contractions, 'although I feel she has plenty of time, the issue is that the hospital in Clifden has temporarily closed for a few days. Renovations. She'll need to go to Galway, and straight away. I'm not keen to wait until that ambulance arrives.'

Running his hand through his hair, Lachie started to panic. Everyone had been drinking a lot. There was no way anyone should be driving to the hospital, but with the baby coming early, that was exactly where Kat needed to be, and with Clifden being closed, there was no choice but to go the extra distance to Galway.

The doctor who was quite stooped over, straightened up slowly, holding one hand on his back. He was old and had tiny glasses that sat halfway down his nose. Lachie looked again. He must be in his eighties or nineties. Jesus, was that allowed?

'I don't drive any further than the streets of Clifden so I can't help you out. But you're all in luck because I have a plan. A grand plan,' the doctor said, holding his knobbly finger in the air. 'I came prepared. Your vehicle, or rather your carriage awaits you, Madam.'

Kat was taking long breaths and Lachie could see she was close to losing it. The last thing they needed was for her to abuse the doctor. He was the only one who had some idea of what needed to be done. And, apart from Kat, he was the only sober person in the vicinity.

Chapter Forty-Eight

Lachie helped Kat walk slowly to the other side of the cottage, where the driveway led out onto the road. 'We're parked at the front,' Doc Kelly said.

'Everyone always seems to have a plan,' Eileen muttered. 'It better be a good one.' She raised her voice so the doctor, who seemed to be a bit hard of hearing, could hear. 'You mean you're parked at the back, not the front?' Eileen bellowed as she followed close behind. 'We call that the back because the front faces the sea. So really, you're saying there's a vehicle that can transport Kat at the back of the cottage.'

'Well, it's the way I came in. So it's really the front. Where you brought the patient up from the meadows beyond is the back of the house. I know a front door when I see one and that was the first thing I saw when I drove in.' He stopped and leaned on his walking stick for a moment. 'I might only be able to see out of one eye but that's the front of the house.'

Kat squeezed her eyes shut and leaned heavily on Lachie's sturdy frame. 'Hold onto me,' she groaned. 'Let me catch my breath while this contraction rolls in, and for the love of all that's holy, tell that doctor and Eileen to shut up. I swear, Lachie, if I step out the back of the cottage and find a carriage and horse waiting, I'll go stark raving mad.'

'It's okay. I'm sure he won't let us down. He's a doctor.'

'He's as old as the hills and deaf as a doorknob,' she whispered. 'He can hardly walk and I'm not sure how he drove here. I'll not have him delivering our baby, Lachie. Promise me that won't happen.'

He helped her stand upright, the contraction dissipating for a moment. At the moment he wasn't sure if he could promise her what she wanted. Unless some form of suitable transport and a sober driver miraculously appeared at the front or back of the house, the sinking feeling in his stomach told him that the baby could be born right here at Granny's cottage. He stared at her stressed face. 'Of course, Kat. We'll get you to the hospital somehow.'

As they rounded the side of the house, the doctor's grand transportation plan came into view. The three of them stared at it with eyes wide as the doctor kept walking. He stopped and turned around. 'What have you all stopped for? There's no time to lose. I told you I had a plan. Did you not hear me say that? Are you all deaf?'

Lachie's voice came out like a squeak. 'It's a hearse. She's having a baby. She's not dead.'

'Not yet,' Kat muttered. 'I can't go in that. I don't

want to bring a new life into the world in the same place where someone dead has been lying.'

'There's not a body in there,' the doctor said, waving his hands in the air. 'Bodyless. See? The vehicle belongs to my brother-in-law. He's visiting me from Dublin and his other car wasn't working so he drove his business vehicle. I brought him along because I figured he might be handy. He followed me here. There he is in the front seat, waving at you all to hurry up. He's a non-drinker so thank the lord for that. It doesn't appear anyone else here fits that bill. Now get a move on the lot of you. The soccer's on in a couple of hours, so there's only a narrow window of time for him to drive you to Galway and get back to my place in time to watch it.'

Kat and Lachie stared at each other. 'There's no other option,' Lachie consoled her. 'If we wait for an ambulance from Galway, it'll be over an hour to get here and then another hour to get back. We could have you to the hospital in Galway in that time. I really don't want to drive, Kat. I'm over the limit and if anything happened, I'd never forgive myself. This fella is sober and the vehicle should be reliable.'

'It'll be alright,' Eileen reassured. 'The baby won't be born in the hearse. It'll wait until you get to the hospital. I know this for sure.' Eileen went to say more but Kat's glare stopped her.

Just then, Doc Kelly's mobile phone rang. It took him a while to locate it in his pocket and when he did, he dropped it twice and then picked it up before finally putting it to his ear. 'Hello, Doc Kelly here.'

The phone was the oldest flip phone Kat had laid

eyes on. Another contraction rippled across her stomach and her back felt as though it was going to snap in half. 'Lachie, help me in the back of that hearse. I'm starting to feel a lot of pressure, down you know where.'

The look of alarm on his face did nothing to calm her, as she listened to the doctor talking on the phone, and confirming that, yes, he understood, the Clifden ambulance that they were going to send for the girl with the broken ankle would not start. There was something wrong with the engine. The doctor was on his own.

Just then a group of fellas suddenly appeared from around the corner of the house. They had made a stretcher out of the plastic picnic table that had been down where the party was. On it lay Grace, who was moaning loudly and looked to be in as much in pain as Kat was.

Doc Kelly took control, waving his walking stick in the air to show who was to go where. 'Right lads, job well done. Push that stretcher straight in the back next to the other lady. That's it love, move over. The vehicle is big enough to carry the two of you. Grand. That's just grand. Now the husband of this lady who is pregnant needs to sit in the front with the driver who's from Dublin and has no idea how to get to the hospital. He'll need directions.'

The boys carefully placed Grace next to Kat and the two of them clutched each other's hand. For once they were both silent. Lachie jumped in the front, giving the driver a nod.

'Okay,' the Doc said. 'We can shut those back doors. We don't want those two flying out when you're driving over hill and dale. Eileen pushed forward and put her leg up on the back of the hearse, as if she was going to get in the back with them.

'There's no room for you,' the doc said. 'Get out.'

'I'm going with them. I'm a nurse. They might need me.'

With that, she swung herself in and crouched between them, peering through the front at the driver. 'Drive. Drive as fast as safely possible.'

As the doors closed, Kat had one final glimpse of the crowd, which had gathered and was now waving good-bye. Ronan, Peggie, Mum and Dad were there, as were all the friends who had gathered. 'Have a great night,' was the last thing she heard from Ronan as the doors clicked shut.

Chapter Forty-Nine

Waking up to the sun streaming in through the hospital window, Lachie rubbed his eyes and pulled himself upright in the recliner chair he had slept in the previous night. His throat was parched, and he could feel a headache coming on.

The room was quiet, and he sat up properly and looked around. His eyes fixed on Kat, who was asleep in the bed beside beside him. When he stood up, the recliner creaked, but she didn't wake, and he took the opportunity to gaze at her while she was sleeping. Her hair was spread out on the pillow underneath her, and although her face was pale, she looked rested and much better than she had the night before when they arrived at the hospital.

A faint smile touched her lips and she made a little snuffling noise, which she often did when she slept. He watched her for a bit longer before moving around to the other side of the bed. His newborn daughter was in a cradle beside the bed, wrapped in a white shawl. She had rosy pink lips and a tuft of dark hair on her head. Her eyes were closed and she slept just as soundly as Kat. He touched her hair and stroked her head. Bridget. Bridget Mae. She was the sweetest baby in the world and was born a good size, considering she had arrived a bit earlier than expected.

A nurse walked in behind him and he turned around to greet her. They whispered so as not to wake Kat. 'She's a bonnie wee lass,' the nurse said, her Scottish accent strong and with a beautiful musical lilt. 'Both are doing well and the baby's a good weight.'

'Thank you so much for last night. You must be tired. You're still on shift.'

'The nurse looked at her watch on the front of her uniform. 'Aye. It's eight am and I'm finished now, but I thought I'd check on your wife before heading home. Your sister-in-law dropped some clothes off for you. The bag's at the nurses' station. I'll be back late this afternoon. I'll talk to you both then and see how you're going. Both Kat and her sister are doing well. Have a good day and make sure to get some sleep yourself. You look like shit.'

While Kat was asleep, he took the opportunity to go and collect his clothes. There was a bathroom that husbands could use, so he had a shower and freshened up. Another visit to the canteen for some Panadol and coffee left him feeling much better. When he popped back into the room, she was still sleeping, so he went back out and rang Orla.

Orla sounded as bright as a button. 'Lordy be. Lordy be. What a fuss last night. It was a sad state of affairs that no one was sober to drive the poor girls, although the hearse worked great. We'll have to buy that driver some lotto tickets for his efforts. I'm not sure what would have happened otherwise. Patrick is still in bed. After you rang last night to say the baby had arrived, we sat up for another hour and toasted the new arrival. I feel great this morning but not him. I don't think he'll get out of bed all day. I'll rouse him later, though, and make him come up to the hospital for a visit and see Grace as well.'

'That'd be great. Kat's sleeping at the moment, and visiting hours are at four this afternoon.'

Orla laughed. 'Oh, we Irish don't worry about visiting hours. Those times are just because they have to put something official up on the wall. No one takes any notice of them. We can visit both Kat and Grace.'

'How is Grace? That's why I was ringing. She's in another section of the hospital and I know Kat will ask when she wakes.'

'She's grand. All good. They'll operate today and she'll be on the mend. She can give you more details when you see her. Eileen is back home and sleeping also. Get some sleep yourself, Lachie. You sound like shite.'

Chapter Fifty

This time when Lachie went back to the room, Kat was awake and he approached the bed in awe at how well she looked, considering what she had been through. He pushed the bassinet closer so that the baby lay next to her. Kat put her hand over the top and touched Bridget's hair. 'She's so little,' Kat said. 'So precious.'

'A baby girl. She's just beautiful and so are you. You did so well, Kat. Especially considering everything that was going on.'

'It was bound to happen. Granny would have loved all that chaos and kerfuffle, so much shouting and carrying on. Mum and Dad falling over in the meadow. Grace breaking her ankle. What a night. I'm glad it's all over, especially the labour.'

'You were amazing. Lucky we got here when we did though. How's the pain?'

'I feel a lot better now that I've slept. When I woke up and I could see you sleeping on one side of me and this little one on the other, I just went back to sleep. I knew everything was alright.'

'My mum and dad send their love. I rang them not long after the nurses brought you both back to the room here. Just a quick call, but they know you're both doing well. They'll let the others at home know. I've just rung your mum and dad, and everyone, apart from your mum, is sleeping off their hangovers.'

She smiled, that beautiful smile that had won his heart. 'Mum doesn't get a hangover. Cast iron stomach. How's Grace.'

'She's okay. Your mum said they're operating today. I'll go and check on her later but your mum said she'll be up this afternoon and will stay with her to make sure all is okay. Your parents wondered where the name Bridget came from. They thought you'd choose a family name.'

Kat pulled a face.

'I'm just repeating what they said to me,' he quickly added.

'And did you tell her I named her after the nurse who got me out of the hearse, put me in a wheelchair and took over the entire process? You and Eileen were running around like chooks with your heads cut off and couldn't even remember my birth date, or other details for the forms you were both trying to fill in. That nurse, Bridget, saved my life. For me, after the string of calamitous events at the party, when I got here and saw her comforting face and heard her calm reassuring words, I think I would have married her if I could.'

'Well, it was all very rushed and chaotic, and no one told me that when a woman's water broke, it'd be like a flood. I thought your insides were falling out. I think I was within my rights to panic a little.'

'We were in the hospital foyer, surrounded by doctors and nurses. I wasn't going to die.'

'Well, Eileen was no better. Yelling at the doctor and anyone else she could find to give you pain relief, trying to tell them what to do and screaming at them to make your pain stop. At least I didn't do that.'

'Seriously Lachie. What a night. I told you there'd never be a dull moment with my family. When it was just you and me, everything seemed a lot calmer. Apart from the water-breaking incident, you handled the rest quite well.'

He chuckled. 'Well, I didn't really have a choice. I couldn't run away. I take you and your family as part of the deal. It could be worse.'

She shook her head and propped herself up on the pillows. 'Could it? Really? I wish I had a video of you and Eileen pushing me up that hill in Granny's walker and then the wheelbarrow. My bum was stuck in that pouch thing. And then the hide of Mum asking me why I was riding in the wheelbarrow. Legs up in the air. Imagine if the baby had come then. Lordy be. I don't even want to think about it.'

'There'll be stories to tell for many years about that night.'

'And you haven't even had your birthday yet. Ronan has a pub night planned for you and now there'll have to be a celebration to wet the baby's head.'

'Not for me. That party was enough for my birthday. I'm done drinking. I've got too many other things to think about. He touched the baby's hair again. 'She's so soft and new. A beautiful little girl. It's love at first sight. I've got you and now we've got Bridget.'

Kat took his hand in hers. 'The three of us. Our family.'

* * *

The family all came to visit at three o'clock. From the sounds of other rooms down the corridor, it appeared Orla was correct that no one took any notice of visiting hours. Kat was sitting up in bed, nursing Bridget while Lachie hovered nearby, fetching a cloth and a drink of water when she asked.

Orla, Patrick, Ronan and Peggie arrived together. Eileen came in not much after and then another four friends, who Kat had known since she was little piled in also. Three of Grace's friends popped in, before they went to visit Grace. The room was only small and Lachie pushed a table and some chairs out of the way so there was enough room for everyone. He had been making sure to check on Grace and see how she was going. 'Grace is out of theatre,' he told the others, 'and the surgeon said everything went splendidly. She's still sleeping so I'll pop back to see her later on.'

'Poor Grace,' Ronan said. 'She just went down like a sack of potatoes. Her foot went down a rabbit hole. Snap! I heard it.'

They all fussed over the baby and Lachie was happy to stand and listen. He found it hard to draw his eyes away from Bridget's little face and Kat reassured him it was okay to pass her around to the visitors. Everyone wanted to cuddle the baby. He wanted to remind them though that this wasn't a pass-the-parcel game, and she was not even twenty-four hours old.

No one else seemed concerned except him, so he bit his tongue and just smiled. When Kat started to look tired, he hinted that maybe it was time for everyone to leave and that new mothers needed their rest. His attempts were to no avail and the talking and laughing became louder and more raucous as everyone started to go over the events of the previous night.

Suddenly a loud voice broke the revelry and the room went silent. 'Right. Where do you think you are? Down at the local pub? Away with the lot of you, except the father. Say your goodbyes, hurry up now.' It was Bridget, coming back on shift. In a matter of minutes, she had taken the baby from Ronan, ushered them all out of the room—including Eileen who had tried to linger—and shut the door firmly behind them.

Chapter Fifty-One

A nurse brought Grace down in a wheelchair to visit Kat two days later. The operation on her ankle had been successful and she would be able to go home in about seven days. 'Mum will have to look after me though,' she said. 'I'm going to be out of action for a while.'

Lachie was also there and with the room nice and quiet with only the three of them, he persuaded Grace to stay a bit longer when she said she should get going. It was good to see her recovering and a bit more like her old self. She had missed the excitement of the first few days so she and Kat had a lot to catch up on. He watched as Grace nursed Bridget, who seemed to just eat and then sleep. Hopefully that would keep up once they brought her home. He had been staying at the hospital every night, although the last few nights he had gone back to the cottage to sleep. It had been handy staying at Orla and Patrick's house, but it was noisy with visitors always coming and going. He was looking forward to getting his family back to the sanctuary of the cottage.

His parents had made a U-turn somewhere in Northern Ireland and driven back down to see the new baby. 'Orla and Patrick were amazed at how fast we got here,' Chris told them. 'They said, Lordy, such a long way. But it was only 534 kilometres. Just a hop skip and a jump. I don't think anyone really realises what our distances are like in Australia. Wait until they come and visit us one day.'

It was a special moment for everyone when they came to the hospital to meet their first grandchild. Evie nursed the baby as she sat on the bed next to Kat. 'She's just gorgeous. You two have done very well. She's blessed to have such wonderful parents.'

'We're keen to get her home and enjoy these first weeks together at the cottage,' Lachie said. 'I've got the baby seat ready and everything organised. Orla told us that back in her day they just put the cane bassinet on the back seat of the car. She said all her babies bounced around quite happily and all the bumps and holes in the roads put them to sleep.'

Kat rolled her eyes. 'I told her that I'll be able to say to my children, back in our day when we went to the hospital to have a baby, we went in a hearse because everyone was too drunk to drive.'

* * *

Family and friends all visited during Kat's hospital stay and she was keen to get back to the cottage and enjoy some peace and quiet. So was Lachie. He had the baby room ready, a large bunch of flowers in the middle of the table and even dinner prepared for their first night at home. His parents had resumed their travels, Kat's mother was busy fussy over Grace, and Eileen and Ronan were both busy studying for upcoming exams.

'Just the three of us,' Kat murmured as they sat drinking a cup of tea out the front of Granny's cottage. In front of them the sea shimmered and the piercing calls of gulls sounded overhead. Lachie cradled Bridget, snug in her warm wrap. A gentle breeze wafted from the east, causing Bridget to stir and gaze up at them with her blue eyes. Lachie fancied she smiled at him for a moment, but Kat swiftly dismissed the notion. 'It's just wind,' she reassured him, sensing his thoughts.

'She reminds me of you. Those eyes and those little lips. I can't take my eyes off her,' Lachie admitted.

'I'm the same,' Kat agreed, her gaze lingering on their newborn daughter. 'I feel as though Granny Mae is watching over her too. Maybe she's the one who arranged for the hearse the night of the party.'

Lachie chuckled. 'Someone was definitely looking out for you and Grace.'

Kat rested her head on his shoulder. 'I'm glad I've got you to look out for me and Bridget. You're our calm amidst the storm.'

Chapter Fifty-Two

The days were full of changing nappies, feeding and doing the washing. They both revelled in their new roles as parents and settled happily into life with a baby. Nonetheless, they were still planning to move back to Australia. Kat had already started sorting through everything to see what she would take back with her. As much as she loved the cottage and being near her family, she had decided not long after Lachie returned to her that their life together would be mainly based in Australia.

'We'll be able to come back to Galway for holidays whenever we want, and I can always bring the baby back and stay for a month or so to catch up with everyone. By the time we fly Mum and Dad out once or twice a year, there'll be plenty of seeing one another. I'm sure the others will make their way out for a holiday too.'

Lachie made sure she was definite about her decision. 'Are you sure, Kat? I'm happy for us to live in either place. I know I'll struggle with the winters here, but I'll get used to it.'

'You'll never get used to it, and besides, I want Bridget to grow up in Australia. There are more opportunities there and the weather is a big factor for me. I want our children to grow up surfing and fishing, being outside and playing sport. Galway's a beautiful place, but there's not as much freedom for outdoor time. I want to be in Australia.'

'Where?' he had asked. 'It's a big place. Where will we live.'

'You say first. Where do you choose?'

'No. I want to hear where you want to be.'

'I haven't been there yet, but I've seen the photos and heard so much about it. I'd love it if we could live on Stradbroke Island. Your mum and dad call it Saltwater Place. I think that would be a grand place to live and bring up children.'

* * *

Bridget was four months old when Lachie and Kat boarded the plane to fly back to Australia. There had been numerous parties and send-offs, as well as tearful farewells. There had also been a string of minor calamities within the family that had at least not involved a hospital visit.

It was a wise decision of Lachie's to drive themselves to the airport in Dublin without a multitude of people to see them off. It was bad enough waving to them through the window of the car as the three of them with luggage piled high on the roof racks, bid farewell to her family and Galway. Her mum and dad were going to use the cottage and even said if they liked the change, they might live there. Ronan, Grace, and Eileen were happy to live in the Galway house. As they all said, 'It was only another four months until the big wedding in Australia. We'll all be together again very soon.'

'See you all in the Whitsundays in October,' she had yelled out the window before pulling her head back in and turning to Lachie. 'What an adventure we're on, Lachie. Another couple of days and we'll be home.'

'I love that you're already calling it home.'

'It will be my home and Bridget's. And I can't wait to move into your family's little cottage. What's it called again?'

'*The Magic Fish*. Don't get too excited about it. It's only small and basic although it's situated in a quiet area. Wait until you see the beaches and try the fishing. Stradbroke Island is a magical place.'

'Sounds exactly what I like. It'll be grand.'

Chapter Fifty-Three

The flight home was long and tedious, and with a four-month-old baby, travelling took on another dimension. Something had upset Bridget's tummy and Lachie spent a long while nursing her and trying to keep her amused. Kat was so tired that she kept drifting off to sleep. But one of the only ways to calm Bridget was to feed her. 'I feel like she's been hanging off my boob from Heathrow to Brisbane,' she said as they landed in Brisbane. 'It's one of those times when I think I could kiss the ground on the tarmac.'

There's still a car ride and then the trip over on the ferry. At least Mum's organised the car to be here for us.'

Kat had not been able to keep her eyes open and as soon as the car pulled away from the airport with Bridget buckled firmly in the car seat in the back, she fell asleep. She slept as they waited in traffic and puttered along in lines of traffic, she slept as they waited in line for the ferry and she slept as the car noisily clattered over the metal ramp to board the ferry that would take them to Stradbroke Island.

Bridget slept also and when Kat finally woke, it was to the sound of an Australian voice asking for their tickets. Lachie handed them over and then turned the car engine off. 'You've had a good sleep,' he said, turning to her before looking in the back seat. 'And so has she. Look at her, she's still out to it.'

Kat rubbed her eyes and sat up. 'She's making up for all that sleep she didn't get on the plane. I feel as though I've been run over by a steamroller. It's been a long trip to get here.'

'I know, but here we are. Get out and breathe some of that fresh sea air. It's a beautiful calm day and you'll see Moreton Bay at its best. I'll sit in here with Bridget.'

'I will get out. I need to stretch.' The ferry had turned around and pointed its bow towards the water that stretched like a glassy surface around them. As they sailed further out, she took a deep breath and drew in the salty, fresh air.

A gentle breeze drifted across her face and she turned her eyes to the water that was as blue as blue could be. The ferry picked up speed and before long, Lachie joined her, Bridget in his arms. She smiled, and made beautiful little baby noises. Lachie jiggled her up and down in his arms and squeezed her when she pressed her face to his. Kat leaned over and gave her a kiss and she mushed Kat's face between her chubby hands.

'She loves the kisses. There's not too far to go now. See out there.' Lachie pointed to the east, and spoke to Bridget. 'There's your new home. Sand, sunshine and beach. The beautiful Stradbroke Island.' In the distance the island spread across the horizon. Even from afar Kat could see the sand dunes on the western side. 'It used to be one island,' Lachie explained, 'but it split in two and the one we're going to is called North Stradbroke Island. Second largest sand island in the world. There used to be a lot of sand mining here but that's all stopped now. You can still see the scars in some places, but the vegetation is slowing taking it over again. There are two lakes we can visit and beautiful beaches as well as the three townships. We'll land at Dunwich, but then Amity Point is near to where we'll be at Flinder's Beach. Mum and Dad are at Point Lookout. I hope you like it Kat.'

She pushed her face towards the breeze, inhaling deeply. 'I already love it.'

Lachie passed Bridget to Kat. 'She's after a feed. She keeps nuzzling into me.'

As she followed him back to the car she turned back and took one more look. 'It's your new home, Bridget. Our new home.'

* * *

The *Magic Fish* was just the same as when Lachie had been a kid. Over the years, different members of the family had lived in it and for a while, he and Jasper had stayed there when they first came back from travelling overseas. In preparation for Lachie and Kat coming, his parents had completed renovations and the cottage even had a new roof. Nothing much else had changed though, and when their car pulled into the driveway, he stopped and looked up at the huge weeping paperbarks that lined the footpath. The grass had been mowed and the gate was open for them.

A glistening tin roof adorned the old-world cottage perched on timber stumps, its welcoming veranda stretching along the front. Clad in timber with criss-crossed timber bracing, the exterior exuded a rustic charm that Kat was immediately drawn to. The front door was painted a cheerful yellow with vibrant green trims, and a few steps led down to a spacious front yard.

'It's beautiful. I love it. Just grand,' she exclaimed. 'It's like something out of a storybook. How lucky are we.'

Lachie peered out through the windscreen. 'And, look, there's all the family waiting on the veranda. I'm sorry Kat. You probably wanted a bit of peace and quiet after that long trip. I thought they might have given us some time to wind down. Sorry, but they'll be dying to see us and the baby. Look they've got streamers and a welcome sign hanging from the veranda.'

She chuckled as she opened the car door. 'Lachie McIntosh. Listen to yourself now. Don't ever apologise to me for your family. After all you've endured in Galway. I love your family. We're blessed on both sides of the ocean.'

With that, she hopped out and shut the car door behind her. He grinned, watching her stride, then break into a sprint towards the cottage's front steps, bound for his mum first. The others huddled around her and there was a chorus of squeals and laughter as embraces were exchanged and everyone started talking at once. When Lachie lifted Bridget from her car seat and into his arms, her gaze darted everywhere, taking in the vibrant sunshine, the clear blue sky, and the leaves on the trees nearby dancing in the breeze.

'Here we go Bridgie,' he quipped. 'You've plenty of family to look after you anywhere you go. Some of them mad and crazy, but they'll always be there for you. They're a grand lot!'

Chapter Fifty-Four

Kat's first few months in her new home flew past and before she knew it, along with Lachie and Bridget, she returned to the Whitsundays.

Vivre had never looked better. The foliage was lush, the gardens colourful and tidy, and some of the main buildings had been painted. The entire place had been booked out for the family and guests, and extra staff had been employed. Evie and Kat had worked endlessly to ensure everything was as they wanted. Kat's family had arrived in Brisbane and were now making their way up to North Queensland. Morag, who had flown over from Western Australia with her boyfriend Ricky, had come a bit earlier to help with the preparations.

'Lordy be. Please tell me you didn't book your entire family to come out on the same plane,' she exclaimed. 'What could possibly go wrong?'

'Jesus Christ, no, Morag. Do you think I'm daft? We

flew Mum and Dad out over a week ago and they've been staying with us at the *Magic Fish*. Dad's fallen in love with the place and says he wants to live there. Reckons he could spend his days fishing in the sun and never have to wear a jacket again.'

'Wait until they see here; the Whitsundays. He might want to live here instead.'

'I'm pleased it's not too hot yet. I don't think he'd cope with the summer up here. The others have all arrived as well. Eileen and Grace flew into Brisbane a couple of days ago and Ronan and Peggie yesterday. They're driving up in two separate cars. Possibly fewer mishaps that way. They should be here by this afternoon and then the rest of the guests will also arrive. Some are driving up from Brisbane and others are flying into Proserpine. There aren't too many coming from Ireland. Only a dozen or so close friends, and they'll be here tomorrow.'

'And Jock? I heard he's back.'

'He is. He only arrived back last month. His dad is doing well now and when we invited Jock to the wedding, he said he wouldn't miss it for the world. We'll all be together. Lachie's family are already here and everything is set to go.

'Do you want me to cross my fingers, legs and arms, that there are no Irish calamities, no broken legs or punch-ups at the reception?'

'I feel very confident that none of that will happen. Lachie's family are calmer than my lot, and I've given strict instructions to mine that they must behave.'

'You're spoiling the fun. What's an Irish wedding

without a run of commotions and family fights to go with it.'

Kat lowered her brows and scowled at Morag. 'None. There will be none. No calamities or mishaps!'

Chapter Fifty-Five

Everyone settled into their accommodation, and although there had been a few big nights and lots of dancing, music and laughter, nothing had got out of hand. Kat's family had jetlag and slept most of the first day after they arrived, so that took them out of the equation. Lachie's lot was getting into the fishing and snorkelling and she enjoyed some quiet time with just him and Bridget.

* * *

The long-awaited day finally arrived, and as her mother assisted her in slipping into her champagne-coloured dress, she let out a sigh of relief. The weather was flawless, a sign that their beach wedding could proceed as planned. 'It's elegant yet simple,' her mother remarked as Kat twirled before the mirror.

'I adore it,' Grace affirmed, admiring the way the

wedding dress hugged Kat's waist before cascading outward. 'The style is so flattering.'

'It's just perfect for a beach ceremony,' Eileen chimed in, as she bounced Bridget up and down on her lap. 'Not too formal. And look at little Bridgie here. She's too cute.'

Bridget's dress was made from Irish linen that was soft on her skin and held a special charm as it had been sewn by Evie, the material coming from one of Granny's tablecloths. It had tiny puffed sleeves and a round neckline adorned with fine lace. The front panel had embroidered flowers of different colours on it with one more flower on the skirt that gathered softly at the waist. Bridget squealed as Eileen threw her in the air and then caught her.

Kat adjusted the front of the dress, ensuring every detail was perfect as she watched Bridget flying in the air. 'Please. Not today, Eileen. I want her calm. I want you all calm and me also.'

She fiddled with the bodice of her dress, which was a delicate arrangement of intricate lace that gently contoured her figure. A sweetheart neckline accentuated her collarbones and the skirt flowed gracefully, with just a hint of fabric gently touching the ground. 'I'm really happy with the dress. It's exactly what I wanted. Not too much fuss. I hope everything else goes as planned.'

Eileen pulled a face and tilted her head to the side. 'Nervous, are we? Wondering if he will show up.'

Grace laughed. 'I don't think you have to worry about that. I can see them all waiting from here. The guests are already seated on the chairs. Look at the sky and the sea. It's a perfect day for a wedding.'

'Sweet God, Mother Mary. Look at the time,' Kat pointed out. 'I'm already half an hour late.'

Her mother repositioned a brooch that belonged to Evie on Kat's bodice. 'Come here. That's not quite straight. Never mind the time. He'll wait. Now, let's have one final look. Spin around. Grand. Just grand. Okay. Off we go.'

* * *

The ceremony went off without a hitch, although Kat had been so nervous she nearly forgot the vows that she and Lachie had written and practised for weeks. In the end she remembered, and when Lachie kissed her and they were declared husband and wife, she forgot what she was supposed to do and threw her bouquet back into the guests seated behind her.

Eileen who was sitting with the rest of the family, and had just handed Bridget over to Lachie because she was getting restless, instinctively put her hand up and caught the bunch of flowers. There was lots of laughter and Eileen turned red as she sat down, the bouquet on her lap. When the ceremony finished and Kat walked back through the guests, Eileen handed the flowers back to her. 'Jesus, Mother Mary. Don't you be doing that to me. What were you thinking?'

Kat winked, took the bouquet from her and continued down the makeshift aisle between the chairs. Evie's father, Carlo, leaned forward and kissed both sides of her cheeks. He held her hand and she looked into his wrinkled face and laughing eyes. 'Welcome to the family,' he said before letting go and wiping his eyes.

What she would have given to have her grandparents here today. At least Lachie still had all of his. Evie's mother, Maya and her husband, David, also leaned over and kissed her and Lachie, and everyone cheered as Bridget blew the guests kisses before nestling her head into Lachie's chest.

Everyone was here and when Kat got to the reception and hugged Jock, she felt the tears threaten. He passed her a tissue. 'Don't cry. Tears of happiness I know, but don't start me.'

* * *

The reception was lively with music playing and everyone chatting and catching up. As the drinks flowed, the noise in the room became louder, and it didn't take long for the band to start playing some lively Irish jigs. Soon, everyone was up on the dance floor, and when Kat looked around she felt her heart swell with love for Lachie and Bridget and everyone they held dear.

Jasper who had been kept busy the last week with preparations, was really letting his hair down and seemed to be in the middle of a circle made by Kat's family. To their delight he was displaying his best attempts at Irish dancing and when he fell flat on his backside, the laughter was loud. Ronan helped him up, and they staggered around arm in arm, as though they were brothers and had known each other forever.

Bridget had fallen asleep in her pram with Maya, David and Carlo sitting beside as they talked to Orla and Patrick. Carlo waved at his grandchildren—Lachie's three younger siblings, Millie, Rusty and Hazel—who were all up dancing and having a great time.

As the music slowed, everyone linked arms and formed a big circle around the bride and groom. Lachie held Kat in his arms, and they danced to the beautiful tones of Ronan Keating's *When You Say Nothing at All*.

Once the official waltz was over, the dance music started to play again and guests continued to dance or mingle and refill their glasses. 'It's been the best night,' she said to Lachie, 'and no calamities.'

'It must be the calming influence of my family,' he said, laughing as he pointed to Jasper who had hoisted Grace onto his shoulders and was now prancing around the dance floor. Grace clapped her hands above her head and swayed to the music, hanging onto Jasper's head when he decided to dance a bit more vigorously.

'Jesus. Mary. I spoke too soon. If she falls, she'll break that ankle again. It's only just mended.'

'Turn your back. Don't look.'

She looked away, staring instead at the drinks table where a few people were gathered. She noticed Eileen standing up close to Jock, the two of them seeming to hit it off. 'I noticed them chatting earlier,' Lachie observed. 'I thought she said she wasn't interested in men. She sure seems to be interested in Jock.'

Kat watched in dismay, her eyes narrowing slightly as Jock wound his finger around one of Eileen's curls and then tucked it behind her ear, his face leaning close to hers as they engaged in conversation. Eileen was positively beaming and if her body language was anything to go by, she was doing her best to impress the young Scotsman and draw his attention.

'No way, Lachie. No, that's not to happen. Jock's had too much to drink. I've never seen him go after a girl like that. Look at him, puffing his chest out, and oh my lord, and all the saints. He's taken his tartan tie off and wrapped it like a necklace around her neck. Do something. She's too regimented and bossy. Go and separate them. That won't work at all. Get him away from her. Quickly.'

At that moment, Jasper, with Grace on his shoulders, came to a sudden stop in front of them. She shook her head as Lachie helped Grace down. 'You never told me your brother was such a handsome lad,' Grace remarked, her eyes wide as she fluttered her eyelashes and pouted her lip towards Jasper.

Kat grabbed Grace's hand. 'You and I need to talk.'

Jasper took Grace's other hand in his, dragging her away from Kat. 'This beautiful girl and I need to talk. You should have brought her out to meet me a long time ago. I'm just going to show her the beach up further; the stars and the moon. See you both later.'

With that, the two of them, holding hands, started jogging along the sand away from the wedding and its guests.

Their laughter filtered back to where Kat and Lachie stood. Kat was aghast. 'Oh no, not those two,' she protested. 'That won't work at all. Can you imagine the troubles? They're both as wild as each other.' Suddenly she held her hand up in the air. 'There's the breeze. That magical emerald breeze that Granny Mae said will be her. Can you feel it?'

The breeze lifted Kat's hair a little and Lachie leaned over and pushed her hair back from her face as he took her into his arms. 'I do believe in a bit of magic now that I've met you. A little Emerald magic, where love and family come together.'

As she relaxed into his chest, the warmth from his body pressing against her, she looked up into the sky. The moon was not up yet, but the sky was full of stars.

His lips met hers and she closed her eyes, allowing a wave of memories of both those lost and present to wash over her like the gentle caress of the sea. At that moment, she felt a deep sense of belonging, knowing she wouldn't want to be anywhere else in the world, or with anyone else but Lachie.

When they parted, their gazes turned skyward, drawn by the natural beauty above. A shooting star streaked across the heavens, a fleeting moment of brilliance before it reached the ocean.

'Magic,' Lachie whispered in her ear, 'It's a beautiful night. We call it saltwater magic.'

Nestled against him, she spoke softly. 'The ocean that binds us together. It's a grand place to be.' She snuggled closer, feeling the comforting warmth of his embrace. 'It's timeless,' she murmured, her words mingling with the soft sound of waves lapping against the shore.

As they stood together, gazing out across the vast expanse of sea and sky, they knew that in each other's arms, they had found their home—a place where every moment was painted with the hues of saltwater magic and every dream was as grand as the ocean itself.

~~~
~~~

About the Author

Rhonda Forrest is an Australian author who juggles writing and publishing, alongside teaching high school students. She writes captivating contemporary fiction and historical romance about relationships, family life and social issues, set amidst beautiful and uniquely Australian landscapes.

After bringing up three daughters and traversing several careers, Rhonda went on to teach creative writing, English and history. Her passion for literacy, history and travelling around Australia fuels her novels. Along with her husband, she divides her time between Tamborine Mountain and a century-old cottage with a rambling garden overlooking the waters of the Whitsundays.

Recent novels bring to life the remarkable characters and settings that make up the unique Australian heritage and take the reader on a journey from bush to beach, with steamy romances, riveting history and eclectic characters.

Some books are available in audio and large print and you can also find some titles available in Portuguese, Publisher- Leabhar Books Brazil.

If you enjoyed this book or any of Rhonda's other books, you can make a big difference by writing a review, or leaving a star rating on Amazon, Goodreads or Bookbub. A personal recommendation to family, friends, libraries and book clubs is another great way to share the books with others. You can also follow Rhonda on Facebook, Instagram, Goodreads and Bookbub.

Author's favourite - for your enjoyment, sample chapters from *Elizabeth's Star* are in the back of this book.

Website - https://www.rhondaforrest.com/

Saltwater Romance Series

SALTWATER ROMANCE SERIES

From the wild freedom of 1970s Australia to the tangled emotions of the present day, the Saltwater Romance Series delivers three powerful love stories.

Set against the rainforests of North Queensland, the Whitsundays, and the golden shores of Stradbroke Island, these novels explore first love, rebellion, second chances and the journeys that lead us back to ourselves, and to the ones we can't forget.

Also by Rhonda Forrest

OUTBACK QUEENSLAND ROMANCE SERIES

With a cast of eclectic characters and set amidst the rugged outback of Australia, the **Outback Queensland Romance Series** will introduce you to stories of friendship, resilience, and loving relationships that come together to triumph over obstacles defined by the past.

Two Heartbeats (Book 1) is followed by the sequel, *Time Will Tell* (Book 2)

Turn Left (Book 3), *A New Start* (Book 4), *Outback Magic* (Book 5) and *Echoes of the Outback* (Book 6) are stand-alone books with some links to the other books in this series.

'A dingo howls, a star falls.
Don't worry for me, I'll be home soon.'

We'll Meet Again trilogy is an epic World War II saga that will take you from outback Queensland to the jungles of New Britain, then back to the peaceful hinterland regions of the Sunshine Coast and Tamborine Mountain. Based on actual events that include the invasion of Rabaul, and the tragic sinking of the Montevideo Maru, these are emotional stories of love, survival, and the resilience of the families who waited for their loved ones to return.

Growing up next door to each other in 1960s suburban Brisbane, Ruby and Bobby should have an idyllic childhood. However, Bobby's home life is vastly different from the loving security of Ruby's family, and not even the sanctuary of their shared treehouse set high in a mulberry tree can offer him the safety he needs. Emotional and layered, *Silkworm Secrets* is a moving story about the secrets children keep, the power of friendship, and a love that overcomes the hardships of the past. *Forever More*, continues the story of Bobby and Ruby and reminds us of the good and bad in people and that a loving family can come in many different forms.

Whitsunday Romance - You may never want to leave!

Love by the Jewel Sea - Book 1

Summer by the Jewel Sea - Book 2

The Lure of the Jewel Sea - Book 3

Bindarra Creek Romance

Bindarra Creek Romance

BEYOND THE GATE - Mystery Romance at Bindarra Creek

CHRISTMAS AT FORREST GLEN - A Bindarra Creek Romance

A MAGICAL SUMMER - A Bindarra Creek Small Town Christmas Romance

A WINTER'S PROMISE - A Bindarra Creek Christmas in July Romance

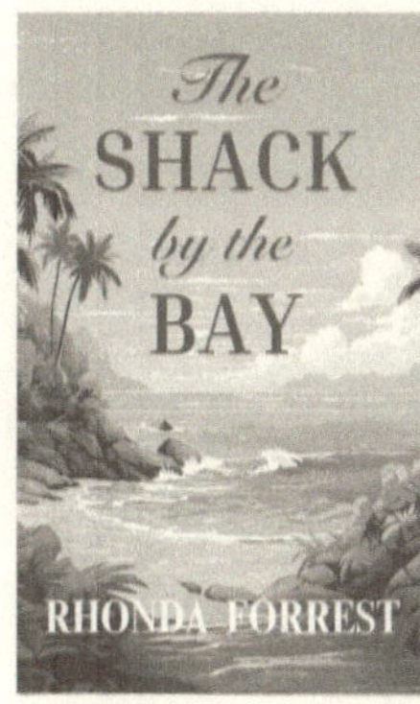

THE SHACK BY THE BAY - Whitsunday Historical Romance

Romantic and purely Australian, *The Shack by the Bay* captures the pristine beauty of the Whitsundays and the wartime memories of older Australians while introducing an eclectic blend of friends and family.

ALL MY HEART - A Tranquil Bay Romance

A small town and school - She only had to last six months.

KICK THE DUST - Contemporary Romance

'If I close my eyes, it's easier to hold onto a memory. When I open them, I think it might really be there in front of me.'

Sample Chapters - Kick the Dust

Chapter 1.

Liam Andrews held one hand over his eyes, shielding the brightness of the sun as he watched a brightly-coloured kite flutter and weave. He squinted anxiously, aware of the rising tension, the quickening of his heartbeat and a clammy sensation on his skin. It had been a long time since he had seen a kite fly and he stared transfixed as the twirling colours flashed above him.

Now that he was back in the safety of his home in Queensland, his morning swim routine, along with his art, were supposed to help him deal with his anxiety. He'd made the changes needed; a mowing and handyman business had taken some of the pressure away and the new property he had bought, which was only a short walk to the beach and lake, had provided a tranquil sea-change. Everything was in place for him to simplify his lifestyle and improve his well-being.

This morning however, familiar waves of fear rolled in and he wrestled with the conflicting notion of where he was. He took short sharp breaths, inhaling the salty air of the lake that lay behind the dunes of Cotter Beach, a tucked away coastal area south of Brisbane. He wanted the spinning in his head to stop, the blurry visions to focus.

A weight crushed his chest and waves of fear washed over him as he closed his eyes. Distorted sounds filled the air and the sand on which he stood moved and swayed, rising up to meet him.

He imagined the sand engulfing him, suffocating and covering his body. Under the sand there would be no pinholes to breathe through and the granules would eventually fill his nose and mouth, finding their way into his lungs that were throbbing with the imagined heaviness. It would be like drowning, except instead of water, a fine dust would cover him and infiltrate his body.

Feeling unbalanced and resisting the desire to run, to sprint over the dunes and escape as far away as possible, he forced himself to sit down. He ran his hands through his thick wavy hair, staring transfixed at the dark strands that stayed on his fingers when he placed them back on the sand. The thoughts he had been trained to put into place were blocked by the images in his mind and a sticky sweat tingled across his skin.

Take deep breaths, think about what you're really looking at. You're home safe in Queensland.

Liam sucked air in through his mouth and pushed it out steadily through his nose. He concentrated on controlling the choking feeling in his throat and clenched his hands together to stop the escalating panic.

Earlier he had enjoyed watching the family who were now flying the kite. A young woman and two small children had sat together and eaten their lunch, their chatter and laughter drifting across the water to where he was warming up for his swim. The young woman usually arrived at the lake alone, and like him, had a regular routine that saw them both swimming numerous laps of the lake around the same time each morning. Sometimes she had her children with her and on those days, she would not swim but instead play on the sand with the young boy and girl.

Liam was amused by her unusual style of swimming and in his mind had nicknamed her the 'butterfly girl'.

Today she was not swimming but had instead taken a kite from her backpack, helping the children assemble the pieces ready for its flight into the sky. The conversation between the woman and the children was inaudible, the wind taking their words in a different direction to where he was further around the shore of the lake. The two children jumped around excitedly, the smallest one, a young boy, indignantly placing his hands on his hips and stamping his foot when she placed the spool into the hands of the older child, a girl around seven, or eight-years-old. The woman bent down and talked to the small boy, who reluctantly clasped her hand, walking with her over to where the kite was being prepared for take-off.

The palpitations in Liam's chest had started then, as the young woman bent down and talked to the children. Her laughter and words lilted on the wind, a sweet sound mixed with the excited chatter of the children, transporting him back to another place, another time. He watched transfixed as she threw a handful of sand into the air, letting it go with the wind. His lips moved but no sound came out, instead the familiar words - *'kick the dust, kick the dust,'* resonated, echoed, bouncing around in his mind. A painful tightness overcame his body and he held his head with both hands.

The words did not come from those he watched, here today on the sands of Lake Cotter, but were instead echoes from an earlier life, one that no longer belonged to him, but would not let him go. A previous life that had left permanent scars, with repercussions that had to be contested on home ground; tussles in his mind, anxiety, dread, sleepless nights and the depression waiting around every corner for him.

***

It was seven years since Liam had returned to Australia and it was only recently—perhaps in the last twelve months—that he had truly turned a corner, regaining some of his former self.

He had come back looking stronger, more mature and seemingly full of bravado and confidence. However, below the surface of the tough exterior was a damaged, eroded shell of his former self.

His family had rallied around him and luckily been quick to jump on the warning signs that had presented not long after his return. They had stopped him from taking off and roaming the world by himself, removed the bottle from his hand and done everything they could think of to stop his spiral of self-destruction. Instead they formed a tight group around him, making sure he kept every medical appointment, picking him up and connecting him with the support groups nearby and even living with him when it was needed. They had taken turns to ensure he survived, watching over him as he clawed his way out of a deep hole of despair.

The year after his return was the lowest period in his life, but eventually he made progress. Step by step, one foot after the other, he moved through one day at a time, aiming for a distant light that he occasionally glimpsed. Life smoothed out a little, his mind balanced and he even managed to maintain a relationship with a woman he met after his return. After many years he reached the end of what had been a long, dark and twisted tunnel. Looking back now, he knew that his devoted family had saved his life, stopping him from going down a self-destructive path like so many others.

Today was the first relapse in a very long time and waves of nausea wracked his body as the familiar grip tightened around his heart, his ears aching with a pounding noise that reverberated in his head. He wanted to run; run as far away from reality as he could to get rid of the sights and sounds that punched in his head. He rubbed his eyes, looking down at the granules of sand against his feet, trying to control the moment, to kick the madness from his mind.

Chapter 2.

Some of the turmoil in Liam's mind that morning, was because the butterfly girl and her children were of Middle Eastern appearance. Although the children were dressed in western-style clothes, the girl and the woman both had their arms and legs covered, their head scarves revealing only a few fringe curls of dark hair. The boy wore a plain coloured T-shirt, and long trousers that the woman had rolled up for him when they first arrived at the beach. Later that day he tried to work out if the similarity in ethnic origin had accentuated the issues and flashbacks that he'd experienced when watching the family flying the kite.

The butterfly girl came to the lake around the same time as he did each day. Usually they were in the water at the same time, both intent on their swimming, but not too close to each other as they stayed in their designated areas of the lake. They had never had a long conversation with each other over the last two years, however they always greeted one another as they passed on the sandy track that led to the lake. A few words, a polite nod and a smile as they made their way to their individual spots to prepare for the morning swim.

'Good morning for a swim,' Liam would say with a smile.

'Yes, it's going to be a hot day,' the butterfly girl would reply.

'The water is warm,' Liam would add.

'The sun is heating it,' she'd say.

One day the butterfly girl had called out to Liam from a distance. 'Excuse me. Excuse me.' Her voice had reached him as he began to do his stretches.

A set of dark green eyes stared into his as she passed him his sunglasses. 'Thank you,' Liam said. 'I must have dropped them. I would have been lost without them later, when that sun gets up higher.'

'They were on the path. I hope you enjoy your swim.'

They stood staring at each other, an awkward silence between them.

The butterfly girl finally nodded her head before turning to make her way to her usual spot further up the beach. When she turned around to look back, Liam was still staring after her and she giggled, lifting her hand to wave to him.

A chuckle escaped his lips and he waved a couple of times before turning towards the water.

*

Sometimes the butterfly girl would arrive before Liam and he would watch her as she thrashed through the water. Her swimming left a lot to be desired, her arms slapping down on the water's surface, her legs kicking vigorously as she made her way to the other end of the lake. It was her habit to finish with a lap of attempted butterfly stroke. He stifled his laughter. Her arms lifted and flapped in an ungainly fashion around her head, before smashing down erratically into the water. After two years of practising each morning she had never improved, the style, the strokes, it had all remained the same from when he'd first observed her.

*

Liam had always loved swimming and it hadn't taken much persuasion from his counsellor to get him to return to the water on a daily basis. The stillness of the lake provided a perfect lap pool, although today he had to force himself to stand up and walk down to the water's edge. Still trying to control his breathing and shaking legs, he adjusted his goggles and strode into the lake. The water closed around him and he waded out further before diving across the surface, arms and legs moving automatically as he began the first of his laps.

Every part of his body felt rigid and he paced his strokes and kicks with the throbbing painful thoughts in his mind. All six foot of him powered through the water, his arms and legs pounding the water in a robotic manner. The words in his head blurred into a tiny voice, slowly disappearing as he concentrated. The sound of the water blocked everything out and his swimming style returned to a skilful gliding action, as he swam lap after lap across the lake.

By the time he left the water two hours later, his body ached, the pains in his legs and arms a result of the madness that had driven him at the start of the swim. His legs were like jelly; the number of laps he had swum today far more than what he normally completed. But the swimming had worked, the pain and throbbing in his mind, the flashbacks and panicky tension in his body had disappeared. In its place was a feeling of control, a tingling of the cool water on his skin and a calm sense of satisfaction.

He stood tall, looking up at the sun that was high in the sky. The warmth of its rays coated his skin and he enjoyed the prickly sensation of salt as it dried on his shoulders. The rest of the day beckoned, and he picked up his towel, walking back around the edge of the lake, past where the children and woman had been playing. A smattering of footprints on the sand and a tiny sliver of red string from the kite's tail, evidence of the family's activities that morning.

A blue headscarf similar to the one the woman had been

wearing was wrapped around a rock at the rear of the beach, the wind pushing it, trying to tear it from where it was snagged. He picked it up, the fabric, silky and smooth on his wrinkled palms, a faint whiff of perfume rising from it.

It was the one thing about the woman that confused him. On the days when she came by herself, she was dressed in typical attire for a woman swimming at the beach. Her one-piece swimmers were modest, and she made no attempt to cover the rest of her body or her head. Often, she would lie on her towel after her swim, sunning herself, her long legs stretched out on her bright towel. When the children were with her she wore long trousers or a skirt, arms covered and a scarf such as the one he now held in his hand, concealing most of her hair. She'd play with the children on the sand, usually throwing a ball or a Frisbee back and forth. Sometimes she took them over the dunes to sit and watch the ocean, or walk along the beach. He had passed her once when he was walking. She had been alone and had not seen him as she stood in the shallows, staring out to sea. Today had been the first time he had seen her with a kite, and now, able to think more rationally, he wondered if she had managed to get it up into the air.

A small dog that raced out from a narrow track behind the lake broke his thoughts. It spun around him in excited leaps, furry paws scratching at his legs as it tried to jump up. When Liam picked it up, a tiny pink tongue tried to lick his face and he laughed and gave the dog a welcoming pat before placing it back down on the sand.

Liam looked up and watched as his ex-girlfriend, Amanda, emerged from the bushes. Tall and blonde, she walked towards him, her hands trying to straighten her wind-blown hair. She stopped at the edge of the sand, frowning as the wind whipped the sand around her legs.

Liam stooped down and picked up the dog again before walking towards where Amanda stood, the look on her face bringing back memories of her often surly disposition.

'God, Liam, I don't know how you stand all the sand blowing around down here. I thought you'd be back up at the house by now. I really didn't want to walk down here. Shit, now I've got sand in my shoes, and—'

'It's nice to see you, Amanda. Did you just want to drop Casso off, or were you going to grace me with your presence for a visit?'

Amanda wrapped her hands around the fluffy dog, taking him from Liam. 'I would prefer it if Picasso doesn't come to the beach and he's definitely not to go in the water. I've paid a fortune over the last year to get his coat just the way I want it and,' she straightened a blue ribbon on the top of the dog's head, 'he's really a house dog now. You're just a cutesy, little city dog aren't you?' She nuzzled her face into the dog's white curly coat, Picasso responding by squirming in her arms.

Liam said nothing, knowing it was no use arguing. He had split from Amanda over a year ago, however they still occasionally spoke on the phone. Her new job often involved long stints overseas and Liam was the only person she trusted with the care of her beloved dog. He had, after all, been the one who had surprised her on her birthday a couple of years ago with the tiny bundle of fur. Even though Liam ignored many of her demands for the care of Picasso, she knew he would take care of him and make sure he was fed and warm at night.

Liam was doubtful if Amanda had ever actually been in love with him or if it had been more of a physical attraction. Often he had agreed with her, just to keep the peace. That was of course when he was thinking rationally. Throughout the two

years they were together there had been many times when
Liam had been stubborn, unreasonable and had put up a brick
wall. An impenetrable barrier that pushed them further apart.
Amanda liked things to go the way she wanted and although
Liam was sometimes compliant, at different times he
completely disagreed and then there was no budging him.
Before long, what had once been rational debates escalated
into infuriating heated discussions, culminating in huge
arguments, often resulting in Liam disappearing for days
on end.

Amanda was possessive and Liam had often thought she
stayed because she couldn't stand him being with anyone else.
Even though they were no longer together, her comments
verged on telling him how to live his life and reminding him
she was the best thing that had ever come his way. She wasn't
in love with him, but he could tell there was some connection
or control she liked to think she still had over him.

Liam had taken on a new purpose in life since they parted and
although she would still suggest different ideas or enquire into
any relationships he may be involved in, she trod warily. He
had grown stronger in mind and it wouldn't take much for him
to avoid any communication between the two of them.

Amanda remained connected, planning his art exhibitions and
ensuring there was no one else who might take her place. Once
she had been the central figure in his life. When she posed,
and he painted, his total attention focused on her and
whatever she wanted or needed at the time, she had received.

Liam's family had found Amanda to be aloof. They had,
however, kept their thoughts to themselves, relieved to see him
enjoying life and no longer struggling with so many conflicts of
the past. Amanda only just tolerated 'his interfering family',

and never made a connection with any of them. She showed jealousy to anyone else he was drawn to and went out of her way to avoid family gatherings or social events. She did acknowledge though, that they were more helpful than she was, when the darkness seeped in and wrapped around his mind.

For the first couple of years she ensured everything went the way she wanted. The relationship had been steady sometimes, however as Liam began to recover he started to focus on what he actually wanted in life. Their love of art had brought them together and Amanda had been the one who had pushed his painting career to where it was today. But the lifestyle she wanted was not what he was chasing, and slowly but surely, their lives began to take different paths.

After they separated, Liam purchased a run-down property not far from the beach. Amanda had tried to interfere in the decisions he was making, but Liam had taken on a new lease of life and stood firm on his choices. Eventually Amanda also moved on, although arrangements already made for an exhibition had kept them in contact. Liam looked at her now. No doubt it pleased her that he was still single, and she didn't have to vie with anyone for his attention when they were together.

Chapter 3.

The two of them walked along the path that led to the property, Amanda cuddling Casso as she walked ahead. She stopped when she got to the first small shed, passing the dog to Liam so she could hose the sand from her feet.

'God, I was only down there for a minute and I feel like half the beach is on my clothes and in my hair. Don't dare let Picasso get that sand in his coat. It'll make his skin itch. He has sensitive skin and my goodness,' her eyes widened, 'where did you get that exquisite scarf from?'

She pulled the scarf from between the fold of Liam's towel, the intricate patterns highlighted by the rays of sunlight behind as the breeze caught it, lifting it into the air.

'Oh, I forgot I had it. I found it on the beach, but I know who it belongs to. I'm going to return it when I see them next.'

'Is there something you're not telling me? Do you have a girlfriend? Perhaps you need someone to look after you.'

'No, I don't have a girlfriend. And I look after myself, you can't really say that you did.'

'I tried my best under the circumstances. You're not an easy person to live with.'

'What and you are? C'mon now.' Liam chose his words carefully, aware that Amanda's nonchalant attitude was just for show. During the time he had been with her, he had continually been frustrated and saddened by her jealous nature and prickly manner towards any other females he had been even remotely friendly with. Even after the breakup she had tried to interfere with his life and he was always careful not to let his guard down and offer her even an inkling of where his life or relationships were headed. A few times he had witnessed an extremely nasty streak in her and he knew much of what she said and did in public was just for show and not a true indication of her personality.

Amanda trounced off in front of him, turning around when she reached a small wooden cabin. She was a stunning woman, her bright red lipstick and large round sunglasses sitting perfectly on a face that was always made-up.

Theirs had been a steamy relationship while it lasted, and he had gone along with her whims, the payoff a pleasurable physical relationship that soured once he regained the ability to stand on his own two feet. It had been his decision to end it and even though she had tried to persuade him to give it another go, in the end she had agreed. Although there were some good memories, the only thing they now had in common or agreed on was his artwork. And this, Amanda concluded, was not enough to keep them together.

'Do you have any new work I could look at? I am after a piece for my new apartment. I realise that I would have to pay for it. Money's not a problem.'

Liam followed her along a rocky path through the cottage style garden, towards his studio. 'I don't think I have anything for sale that you wouldn't have already seen. At the moment all of my work is going towards the collection for the exhibition you're organising.'

'I hope you're getting quite a few together. I've promised them a good variety of your work.'

'I have quite a few pieces that I'll put in. They've been getting in some great life models at art classes, so I've had some good options.'

'Right,' she said, her voice taking on the efficient business tone that he knew so well. 'Let me have a look then.'

'I haven't done the final pieces.' His voice was cranky and he knew she would guess that he was stalling. Liam's studio had always been his own space and it was rare for him to let anyone else enter.

'For God's sake Liam. I need to be sure what's coming so I can work out hanging areas and what other pieces we can bring in to complement your work. I can't go any further in arranging anything until you let me see what's coming. Just a quick look.' As had so often been the case in the past, Liam conceded that it was easier to give in and let her have a look, rather than listen to her whining voice. Besides, he had made a commitment to the gallery and he would see the exhibition through. Therefore, she would need to see where everything was going to go. He had to admit she did have a good eye when it came to setting up displays and her forte was organising other people.

'Just quickly then.' He pushed opened the creaky wooden door, shafts of light from the windows that filled the opposite wall, greeting them as they entered.

'God, what a mess! When's the last time you cleaned up in here?'

'I've been too busy working, painting and going to classes. It's okay. Remember, it's a studio. I like it the way it is.'

A large wooden bench took up an entire wall, its top spilling over with paint palettes, brushes, jars, newspapers, rags and an assortment of oddities that one day may just come in handy. Its surface was a colourful kaleidoscope of artist's wares, to be picked up and flung back down again, chosen carefully during the flurries of work that took place in the sunlit room. An ancient velvet lounge chair covered in dark patterned cushions was positioned in the middle of the room. Casso took a flying leap before snuggling into the familiar soft cushions of the chair. Several easels with large boards propped up on them stood in a range of unfinished states, while finished works on canvas hung in no particular order on the walls. The room was awash with colour. Bright lightshades hung over chunky timber tables, joined by wooden chairs, painted in a variety of different colours. The furniture was complemented by the warm golden glow of the well-worn floorboards, splattered with drops of different coloured paint, unintentionally flicked there over the years.

'Can I look please?' Amanda asked, using her sweetest voice.

Liam pointed over to the far corner where the latest finished pieces were.

Stacks of framed works leaned against the wall, their colours hidden by cloth that draped across them. During their relationship Liam had asked Amanda not to enter his studio. He was guarded about his work, preferring not to share it with her before it was handed over for sale or hanging in an exhibition or gallery. His desire for privacy had caused many arguments between them, but thank goodness he had kept it that way, he thought, as he watched her pull away the cotton sheet from the canvases.

She stood for a long while in silence. When she spoke, her voice was loud. 'My God, they're amazing. The tones, the shapes—your work has gone from strength to strength.'

Liam had really come into his own with his art once he and Amanda separated. He had been able to focus, discovering and experimenting with new and creative styles. Without her pressure and clingy nature, he had attended as many classes as he wanted. Even though Amanda had been a suitable model for many of his earlier works, he had revelled in the freedom of painting a variety of women. His latest paintings were done at art class, the women who posed, sitting and standing in a variety of seductive and provocative poses.

Now she sounded sulky. 'Your work has changed. I can see a real difference from when you painted me.' She looked closely, appraising each one, peering closely and raising her eyebrows at some of the more risqué positions. 'You must have enjoyed painting these.' She pointed to the last two paintings, both of a voluptuous red-haired woman who posed with her legs spread slightly apart, her large breasts firm and upright, as she sat on a velvet chair in the corner of a room.

'They're just models to me, you know that.'

'They look like they're enjoying it.' She peered at the woman's face. 'After all, it's not every day a good-looking thirty-five-year-old artist wants to stare at your naked body for hours on end.'

'They don't just pose for me, there are other artists painting at those sittings as well. They are well paid, Amanda, and besides you never minded posing for me.'

'That was different, and I never sat for the entire class. You make it sound like I was just another model to you. At least you always hired a private room at the gallery where I could pose, so don't make out I was just one of a number for the classes.' She walked back and forth in front of the paintings. 'You've really captured the curves and shades in these. How many more do you have to do until the collection is complete?'

'I have another ten months, so whatever I get done in that time will go up. I am looking for something special to finish off the collection.'

'Was I once that something special?' she asked. 'I don't see any bodies here as perfect as mine. This one here,' she pointed to one of Liam's favourites, 'I can see lumps on her legs.' She peered closer. 'That is a vein! Honestly, don't you think it's better if those bits are left out?'

'As I've told you many times, it's not about what *you* perceive as the perfect body, it's about the emotion and story in the piece. That's what makes a painting really something.' His words were impatient and clipped; he was annoyed that she just didn't get it. She never really had. Thank goodness the choice of the paintings was his job and hers was the organisation, sales and exhibition part.

'Right then, don't forget to let me know when it's all ready to go. I'd love to see them all together under proper lighting.' She walked back over to the couch and picked up Picasso, her tone changing as she swung back into bossy mode. 'I have the dog dinners in the car. God knows, you probably wouldn't buy the right food. His bed and coat are there too and I have a list here of his other requirements.'

Liam covered the paintings before following Amanda through the door and up to the house. He silently counted to ten, holding on to his patience, waiting until she was finished nagging and telling him what he needed to do.

Holding Picasso high in the air, he breathed a sigh of relief, waving a little too excitedly as her red convertible drove slowly out of the driveway, rounded the bend and disappeared from sight.

'No, of course he wouldn't let the dog in the mud, or feed it scraps. No, he knew the dog wasn't allowed at the beach, or down in the bush and no, definitely there would be no paint splattered on him this time and he would stick to the routine and make him sleep with the dog-coat on, in his own designer doggy bed that had cost a fortune.

'Six months of freedom, Casso! Just you and me.' Liam threw the little dog into the air, catching him on the way back down, before setting him gently onto the ground. Casso twirled around chasing his tail before yapping loudly and then running back and forth through the muddy puddles lining the driveway. Leaping like a rabbit, he bounded through the long grass that flanked the edge of the lawn before rolling in the dirt that made up the newly-dug vegetable patch. Liam smiled and turned back along the path, the dog still running wildly around the yard, the blue ribbon left behind, floating in one of the puddles. He whistled once and Casso stopped in his tracks before jumping over a log and racing towards where Liam stood. He wagged his tail nonstop and faithfully trotted behind

Liam into the house. 'You and me are going to have a good six months,' Liam said as he shut the door firmly behind them.

~~~

KICK THE DUST - Contemporary Romance

'If I close my eyes, it's easier to hold onto a memory. When I open them, I think it might really be there in front of me.'
~~~

www.ingramcontent.com/pod-product-compliance
Lightning Source LLC
Chambersburg PA
CBHW020350220726
48290CB00014B/1452